THE SHACKLES OF CONSTANTINE

KELSEY ANNE YOUNG

ISBN: 0615688861

ISBN-13: 9780615688862

Library of Congress Control Number: 2012915774

CreateSpace Independent Publishing Platform

North Charleston, South Carolina

THE SHACKLES OF CONSTANTINE

PROLOGUE

J ade Orwell had been firmly assured of three things at Constantine Academy: first, that the Division was an enemy to be hunted down and killed with all the wrath of her own fierce magic; second, that Constantine Academy was a safe haven— her one and only refuge; and third, that the Academy was a place she would always be able to call home. Not one of these facts had ever rung true, and they certainly wouldn't help her now.

Christine had her claws outstretched before her. She lunged at Jade like a beast of prey, her eyes bright with rage. Jade let out a bloodcurdling scream she didn't recognize as her own. Christine fastened Jade in a viselike grip and clenched her throat, growling into Jade's ear. Something like a demonic smile played on the corner of

Christine's mouth before Jade felt herself go limp. She was plunged into darkness.

Even then, with her vision blinking in and out of focus, her limbs aching, and her breath hoarse, Jade flashed back to when it all started. She ruefully pondered a question that had been tormenting her for months. Why is it that the second before your life changes forever, there's no flashing red light? There's no small voice in the back of your head telling you to stop…to *think*. Jade had been alone. All she'd had was an aunt who loathed her, a hot, sticky breeze blowing through a half-closed window, and a burning, clawing desire to get away.

In truth, she'd always known it had been her own fault. She wouldn't have been here, with aches in her chest and Christine cutting at her flesh, if it hadn't been for herself. She'd been the one to drive herself away from her home. She'd been the one to open the door into Constantine Academy, and she alone had been the one to blindly trust a clan of paranormal strangers.

If you'd asked anyone when his journey to Constantine Academy began, he probably would have told you it was the door, or maybe the entrance exam, or the letter. For Jade, it was before that. She was destined to walk Constantine's arching halls several days before she knew of its existence.

Jade screamed as Christine's hold grew tighter, and she cringed at all she could have done to prevent it. Nine months ago she'd been expelled from a private school in the Division for reasons that, in comparison to her ribs burning under Christine's weight, seemed pointless now. Frivolous even. Her mind was tugging at the memory in her subconscious, which had been shoved away to be blissfully forgotten…until now.

CHAPTER 1

"**I**s your dad poor, or does he sell books because he *likes* it?" a voice mocked from behind Jade.

She didn't turn. She knew who it was and bit her tongue, her father's words ringing in her head. *One more fight, and I'll*...Usually that sentence finished with something only mildly parental, like grounding. As of late, though, he'd begun to think Jade needed time away, and his sentences were beginning to end with expensive anger management facilities such as Youth Temperance or Searching Within. Jade wanted to laugh whenever he brought it up, but couldn't because it made her sad to know he was worried, and then angry when she knew it was always the same person to blame for those conversations.

"If you could read, maybe you'd stop by and answer that question for yourself," Jade muttered, struggling to remain indifferent.

The girl laughed, her expression flooded with disdain. "Oh, was that code for, *Yes, we're broke. Please buy a book from him so I can eat tonight*?" She laughed again, inspiring an echo from the pathetic huddle behind her.

At last Jade faced her. She clenched her jaw, grabbed her tray, and shoved past the girl with such hatred coursing through her that even her restraint required energy.

"What, Jade? You can't take a joke?" The girl laughed sardonically, watching Jade leave the cafeteria. When Jade turned, taciturn, the girl smiled. "Just admit it and I'll be happy."

Jade pressed her tongue to the roof of her mouth before speaking. "Admit what?" she asked, only to meet a raised a brow in return.

"*That you've got no money to go to this school*!" the girl yelled. "That your dad is just too *lazy* to get a decent job—we all know, just say it!"

Jade closed the distance between them in only a few steps, and before she could stop herself, the girl was crying on the tiled floor of the cafeteria and Jade was in the principal's office.

"There's not really much to say about it," Jade mumbled, dumping her heavy bag onto the carpet. She'd been through this conversation a hundred times before.

"Have a seat." The principal sighed and took off his glasses, then ran both hands down his weary face. He repositioned his glasses carefully on the edge of his long nose, where they habitually perched. "It's not about what *you* have to say about this, it's about what everyone else has been saying. This is becoming a serious problem." He furrowed his brow and looked entreatingly at her, trying to elicit a sliver of remorse.

Jade gritted her teeth. "She had it coming," she returned, folding her arms across her chest. His office was always unnervingly cold. "And I don't remember there being a rule against self-defense."

"Defense!" he scoffed, his eyebrows raised in shock. He shook his head. "You're a smart girl. Punching someone until she's unconscious just because she said something you disliked is *not* self-defense! It's immature and *not* the standard of behavior we uphold at this institution. You know that."

Jade grimaced as his spit landed on the desk between them. She scooted back farther in her seat.

"It's not like she's in a coma. She's fine."

The headmaster sucked in a long breath. "Katherine, I think you're missing the point."

Jade gulped down a request for him to address her by something other than her first name and sank into her chair. *Katherine Jade Orwell*, she thought. She could still hear the head teacher talking, but it was as if from a distance. Her own name, Katherine, hung like a curtain around her thoughts. How could her parents have known when they named her so sensibly, she would bloom into the tyrannical child the headmaster seemed to think she was?

"Sorry," she murmured.

He checked the clock behind him, turning uncomfortably in his seat. "I invited your father in, Katherine."

Jade stiffened. All that usually happened was a call or a letter home, which Jade discarded before her father ever received it. "Maybe if we all sit and have a conversation, we can discuss the suitable punishment that I, in collaboration with the rest of the staff, have decided on."

"Detention?" she asked hopefully, leaning forward. "Or maybe you could just let this slide. I mean—" Unfortunately, Jade didn't get a chance to tell him what she meant. The phone screamed, and he picked it up on the first ring, watching Jade through two narrow eyes as he spoke.

"Mr. Davis speaking," he answered routinely.

Jade was grateful for the break in the interrogation. She let her head roll back against her chair and rubbed her hands down her face.

"Of course, let him in."

At this Jade shot up fast enough to feel the blood rushing to her head.

Mr. Davis pressed the phone back down on the hook. "Your father's here." He clasped his hands together and stared expectantly at the door.

They sat in silence like this until the door swung open and Jade's father trudged through, a worn book in one hand and a single, bulging pocket in which he kept his infamous deck of crimson and gold felt cards. His hair was combed back as neatly as ever. His eyes landed first on Jade and then on Mr. Davis.

"Mr. Orwell." The headmaster beamed, greeting her father with a benevolent smile.

Jade tried to remember if he'd ever greeted her that way in her entire life. Mr. Davis stood and shook her father's hand tightly.

"Call me James, please," her father responded, taking the seat beside Jade. He leaned toward her. "Long day?" he asked, with a hint of a smile on his face that didn't quite reach his eyes. Jade nodded and they both turned back to Mr. Davis. "So, to what do I owe the visit, Mr. Davis?"

"I think it will hardly come as a surprise to you, James, that your daughter injured one of our students during yet *another* fight this afternoon." He waited for James to say something, but received no response. "Now, this isn't the first time by any stretch of the imagination that she's done this, but I'm sure you understand what I mean when I say"—he paused again, and glanced at Jade as though he might find the right words written somewhere on her guilty face—"being one of the better schools around here, it leaves a somewhat negative impression on us to condone the kind of behavior Katherine regularly displays."

James had gone rigid in his seat. Jade didn't dare look at him, except from the corner of her eye. She could feel his stare glued to her, boring a hole straight through her head. He turned back to Mr. Davis. "I'm so sorry. We'll make sure it doesn't happen again."

"Well, that's just it, James." Mr. Davis stood, pulling his sleeves down by the cuffs and examining them. "We've said the same thing every time, and nothing seems to be changing." No one spoke for a moment. Jade felt something catch in her throat, thinking she knew exactly what was coming next. "We've decided that more drastic measures need to be taken, and so collaboratively, we've chosen…indefinite suspension."

Jade's mouth gaped. "Expulsion?"

"Not quite, but it could range anywhere from a few weeks to…several months. Possibly until the next school year." He yawned, scratching the top of his balding head. "I'm very sorry." He didn't look sorry at all as he went to the door and held it open for them. James was the first to get up and walk through it, his jaw clenched. He shook Mr. Davis's hand firmly. Jade followed him, her chin jutted out as she stormed through the door.

Under normal circumstances, the ride home would have been tedious at worst, but now it was torturous. James didn't breathe a word, but lost himself in thought, leaving Jade to bear the dreadful silence. At last, they pulled up to their decrepit house. He sighed and turned to face her. When Jade finally met his gaze, she could see the disappointment showing on his aged features. His eyes were calm, but his lips were pursed into a hard line.

"Kat." He paused, taking a deep breath. "I thought you were done with this. You promised me, remember?" His eyes twinkled with regret and a repressed anger Jade had become all too familiar with. "Not one more fight for the rest of the year. That was our condition. I thought we'd *finally* gotten past this."

Jade thought the only thing that stopped him from sending her away to an institution was the hope that she'd get better, that it was a phase…and the money, of course. Why couldn't he understand that nothing was wrong with her, that maybe it wasn't his concern how she dealt with things?

Jade stopped herself before she could come up with any more excuses. She *had* promised, but unlike him, she never regretted a single swing of her right fist, or one hateful word that came out of her mouth. If he'd been there, if he'd just *seen,* surely he wouldn't regret them either.

"Dad, I know. I just…I didn't mean to!"

James shook his head, his voice stern. "Kat, I'm sorry, but that's just not good enough. You're so much better than this."

Jade's breath was sharp and quick. Her head spun with anger. *Why didn't he understand?*

"Besides, Kat, you're stronger than these people. Just because you *can* hurt someone—"

"Doesn't mean I should, I *know!*" Jade interrupted impatiently.

"Then why do you do it, Kat? Why do you put me through this every time you get the chance? One day you'll be too strong, and you'll do something you'll really regret." He tapped his thumbs on the steering wheel and sat forward, speaking to the windowpane. "I don't want you to grow up and be scared of yourself."

"Dad, I'm not…if you'd been there—"

"Katherine, if you carry on like this, you'll do something that you *'can't help'* in the moment, and then end up regretting it for the rest of your life. I'm trying to protect you from that!" James yelled, his face red.

Jade had never seen him in such a fury, and it startled her. She pressed herself into the crevices of the seat.

"I'm not always going to be here to clean up after you. I'm going to speak to the school again, but… please *think* before you do things like this. I hope you've learned a lesson at least."

"Dad, I *was* thinking! I—"

"*Not hard enough!*" he yelled, his glare relentless.

Jade felt her eyes sting, and something wet welled over onto her cheek. She fought down the burning desire to race out of the car and slam the door hard in his face.

James let out an uneven breath. "I'm sorry, Kat. Don't cry," he muttered, wiping her cheek with his thumb. "I just don't know how this is going to work. Money is tight right now…It's not like we can just move to a better school." His voice trailed off, and he nudged open his car door after turning off the ignition. "Get your bags," he said as he disappeared into the house.

Jade flinched. Her mind held fast to the look on her father's face, laden with shame. She tried to cast it aside, but it was glued to her thoughts like ink on a blank page. Her steps were heavy and slow as she stumbled through the threshold and locked the door behind her.

James had taken position in the armchair, a book in one hand and a mug in the other. He set them down on the table beside him. Jade sat on the end of the long couch opposite him, sitting as far away as it allowed her.

"I *am* sorry, Dad." At last James looked up from his book. "She was talking about you and…money. She said you were too lazy to get yourself a proper job, and that—" Jade felt hot, thick tears rise in the back of her throat as she spoke. She choked them down. People always had too much to say. They didn't know when to stop, until they said just the thing that tipped her over the edge.

"You mean the one you knocked out?" James asked.

Jade nodded dumbly. She was relieved to look up and find her father smiling.

"Katherine Jade Orwell, since when do you care what other people think?" He smiled reproachfully, setting his book down beside him. Even then Jade could see the weariness in his brown eyes.

"I guess since people started thinking things about you," she answered under her breath.

James gestured for her to come toward him and pulled her into his lap. Jade knew she was much too old for it, but it seemed to pacify him, so she happily accepted the position on his knee. Up close, Jade could see the gray streaks in his black hair, and though his eyes twinkled with age, he flashed a childish grin and wrapped his arms around her by way of apology.

"Sometimes, Kat"—he rubbed his hands together and squinted his eyes as though he were thinking—"you have to play with the cards you've been dealt." He looked down toward the familiar deck of cards splayed between them in his hands. If Jade hadn't known any better, she would have thought they'd been there all along. James held the deck between his palms, and then pulled his hands apart: one palm down, the other supine. Like an accordion, the cards followed as if they weren't quite sure where they belonged. As James's concentration wavered toward Jade's bewildered face, the cards shook. He focused again.

"Choose one, Kat." He encouraged her with a nod of his head. Jade chose one, plucking it out of the air with her hand. Her father returned the remaining cards to his pocket and retrieved the last card from her to read. "Let's see," he muttered, his eyes narrowed.

Jade couldn't hide her own excitement. Her father had been pretending to read her cards for years, but she never tired of it.

"Hmm," he said. "Yes, I thought so." He considered the card a moment longer. "Certainly about the right time…"

Jade laughed. "So? What's the verdict?"

James showed her the card with the inscription—an illustration in dark ink and watercolor like all the others.

It meant nothing to her. "This one says you'll be going"—he flipped the card around to look at it again before he continued—"you'll be going on a very important trip soon."

Jade raised a brow. "Is that all?" she asked.

He shook his head. "And you'll meet lots of new people…" He paused again, treading carefully through his words. "And that soon you'll finally understand what I've been trying to tell you all these years."

Jade dropped her eyes to her lap. She did understand why he wanted the fighting to stop. She didn't need a card to tell her that.

"But, Kat," he insisted, meeting her eyes. "I'm *always* proud of you, regardless. You know that, right?"

Jade smiled, wishing he wasn't so forgiving so that she might feel a little less guilty.

"And as far as I'm concerned, selling books *is* a proper job."

"I know," Jade whispered, shuffling the deck of cards in her hands, hoping to imitate the celerity with which her father always seemed to handle them. "But no one else seems to."

James pulled at her chin. "Keep your head up, Kat. With patience, and maybe a little magic"—James grabbed the deck and turned it face up, shuffling through the cards—"you'll find exactly what you're looking for." He pulled a silver locket from the deck, hiding between two golden, felt-lined cards.

Jade gaped at him, and he tossed it to her. She inspected it with wide eyes, admiring its broad face and smooth, oval edge. The silver chain spilled over her fingers and shimmered under the lamplight. She wriggled a finger between the crease along its side and flipped open the latch to reveal a faded picture of her father. She beamed and snapped it shut again.

"Speaking of magic, you have to teach me that one day."

"Every great magician is entitled to his secrets." James chuckled. "Do you like it?"

Jade nodded thoughtfully, rubbing it against the flat of her thumb. "It's warm."

James nodded with a wink. "That way you know I'm safe." He grinned in a way that made Jade feel young and gullible again. He sidled back in his chair and prompted Jade off his lap. She sat back down on the couch, still scrutinizing the locket. At last she put it in her pocket and looked up to find her father taking another sip of his mug. "So, Kat," he began, returning to his book, although she could tell he wasn't really reading it.

"Yeah?"

"What would you think about spending some time with my sister?"

Jade shot up, furrowing her brow. "Aunt Cynthia?" James nodded, still not taking his eyes from the book. "Why? If this is about earlier today—"

"It's not," James interrupted hastily, meeting Jade's eyes briefly before he readjusted himself in the armchair. "I just think it would do us all some good for you to get away for a while."

Jade bit her lip. "So this *is* about earlier today." She moaned hopelessly, sulking into the cushions.

James shrugged. "Kat, you need this. I need this. I know it's hard for you around here, without a mother..." His voice was gentle, but he stopped as though he'd lost his train of thought. "Maybe there are things you can share with her, that you can't talk about with me."

"Dad, there is *nothing*—"

James held up a long finger. "It doesn't hurt my feelings. Your mother used to tell me this day would come. I think it will give you time to reflect on what's important to you." He looked up at her briefly. Jade wondered if he could see the thoughts of her mother playing across her face. It had been a long time since they'd spoken of Madeleine. All Jade remembered of her was long, dark hair like her own, and thin, slender hands. Jade supposed her mother had already been ill for some time by then. She couldn't remember. Either way, it was just the two of them now.

"It's only for a little while."

"A *while?* How long is that?" she asked, her words sharp with rising panic.

"I'm not sure. It could be a few days, or maybe a few weeks."

"But *why?* Just because of today?" she asked, aggravated.

James set down the book. "There are just a few things going on right now—"

"With what? The bookstore?"

"Yes," James blurted, before Jade could continue her inquiries. "I'll be busy…and besides, haven't you been wanting to see your aunt anyway?"

Jade would have laughed if he'd been asking her this under any other circumstance. She flashed back to the last time she'd seen her aunt and almost shuddered. James's sister was more than ten years older than he was, and her face seemed, to Jade, capable of only two emotions—embitterment and indifference. "What could *possibly* be going on with the bookstore?" Jade asked.

James sucked in a deep breath and yawned. *You're stalling*, Jade thought impatiently, folding her arms across her chest. She didn't like being lied to, and certainly not by her father.

"Dad, Aunt Cynthia hates me, and you know it as well as I do. She calls me *Katherine*," Jade said disgustedly, grimacing.

"That's your name, isn't it?" James offered, looking up with a smile on his face.

"But the way she says it, Dad—she knows I hate it. She does it deliberately. We won't stand an hour together." Jade gestured hysterically.

"Two things, Kat. First"—he began, customarily holding up a finger—"Aunt Cynthia doesn't hate you. And second"—James took a long gulp from his mug, and Jade wondered briefly how it was he hadn't finished it already—"when I asked you what you thought about it, I never said you had any *choice* in the matter. I've already booked a plane ticket, and called her to ask if she'd mind." Jade hoped vaguely that her aunt too had been thoroughly repulsed by the idea. "She said she'd love to, and she'll be picking you up at the airport tomorrow at noon."

"Dad, this is unbelievable!" Jade could feel the frustration boiling back up inside her.

"Kat, I'm sorry, but I don't want to take any risks." Before Jade could ask him what he meant by that, he continued. "Run upstairs and pack. I'll be waking you up tomorrow at eight." James set down his cup and hurried to find the right page in his book.

Jade blew out a long puff of air, but she knew there was no point in arguing. She picked up her bags from the floor and rolled her eyes once she'd turned her back to him. Parents could be so difficult.

Once she was in her room, she carelessly rummaged through her drawers and thrust a handful of clothes onto the floor. She grabbed the biggest duffel bag she could find from inside her closet and heaved the clothes in, wondering how she would possibly entertain herself in the weeks ahead. She zipped up the bag and set it beside her door. At last the lights were off, and Jade leaped onto her bed, dreading the upcoming, empty mornings and evenings spent under Cynthia's protective glare.

CHAPTER 2

"**K**at! Your plane leaves in two *hours*, and you're not even dressed!" James yelled.

Jade could hardly hear him over the hot, running water, and had to lean out of the shower to respond.

"Dad, I'm hurrying!" she called back. She could hear his footsteps as he anxiously paced in front of her bedroom door. She turned off the tap and ran to get dressed. She shrugged on a sweater and pulled boots over her jeans. At last she threw her duffel bag over her shoulder and opened the door.

"Jade, your hair is still wet." He seemed concerned as he hurried down the steps. "If you catch a cold, I'll be mortified. Is that sweater enough? Take my coat as well." He offered her his enormous leather jacket, which smelled of coffee and mint. She folded it over her arm.

"Relax, Dad, I'm not going to the Arctic." She chuckled wearily. James shoved a brown paper bag into her hands, looking anything but amused by her comment.

"That's breakfast. You can eat on the way there," he muttered, searching his pockets for the car keys. Jade picked them up off the dining-room table and handed them to him. He took them with trembling hands.

"Dad, you're shaking," Jade said, stopping before they could reach the door.

He turned and forced a laugh. "I'm just nervous," he mumbled, pulling her gently toward the door. He wrapped an arm around her and kissed her forehead.

Jade frowned and watched him fumble with the keys again as he shut the door behind them. "Why?"

"Why what?" he asked, opening the car door. Jade waited for him to scramble into his seat before she continued.

"Why are you nervous?" she asked.

"I'm just not used to sending my little girl away." He smiled awkwardly and hastily backed out of the driveway.

Jade laughed. It was true they hadn't separated in years, but she wasn't exactly his little girl anymore.

"But Cynthia's doing us a favor, so I can't be too upset."

"Sorry, where does the *favor* part come into all this?" Jade asked, watching the road slip beneath their tires.

"We've talked about this, Kat. I don't want you to be here for the next few weeks."

"Right, so you're shipping me off to Aunt Cynthia." Jade's words were lost in the roar of the engine. She rolled down her window and hoped the wind would dry her damp head.

"Did I lock the door?" James asked.

"Yes," Jade murmured. James turned to her.

"When you get there, it's important that you listen to Cynthia, okay?" Jade sighed, but didn't argue. "And if something happens and you can't find Cynthia or me, just stay in the house and you'll be safe. Unless—"

Jade's brow rose in alarm. "Unless what?"

"There might be another visitor."

"What's his name?" Jade asked cynically.

"It's a she, and she might be coming to take you on that important trip I told you about last night. Her name… well, that doesn't really matter too much as long as you got the first part." He winked at Jade, who couldn't take him seriously when he pretended so avidly to predict her future.

Neither of them said much the rest of the journey, but Jade let her thoughts fill with the familiar scenery rushing past them. Even that couldn't quell the uneasiness swelling in the pit of her stomach. She wondered how long it would be before she came back. Every time she turned to look at her dad, he was watching the road warily, as though it might spring to life and swallow them whole.

At last they pulled up to the right terminal. All too soon he was hurrying her toward security.

"You have everything?" James asked briskly, checking her bag with a cursory glance.

Jade nodded. She felt her throat grow dry and her breath quicken. It seemed as though time was hurtling past and only now was she beginning to realize how many questions she had. *Why did she have to go? How long would she stay?*

James crouched until he was a head shorter than her. He smoothed out the wrinkles in her sweater. "How are you feeling?"

"All right," she said. The words came out as more of a squeak than she'd intended.

James clasped her hands in his, which were rough and calloused, but gentle enough. He rubbed the back of her hand with his thumb and something in her palm pricked her. She opened her hand quickly and saw what was inside.

"You almost left it." James grinned. It was the oval locket he'd given her the night before. Jade smiled.

He pulled her into a tight hug, but held her longer than usual. She could hear the muffled sound of his heart beating beneath his shirt, and let its steady rhythm calm her nerves. "Now go, or you'll be late," James urged, letting her go and nudging her into the line. There was something grave behind his cordial wave as he watched her go through the gate, but he was turning on his heel before Jade could recognize it.

By the time Jade grabbed her bag again he was gone.

***

"Ticket?" the woman asked, exhaustion creeping into her artificially enthusiastic tone.

Jade, after some time, retrieved her boarding pass from her bag and pressed it into the woman's hand.

"Thank you. Next?" the woman called pleasantly.

Jade was lost in thought as she scrambled into her seat. As soon as she'd settled, Jade opened her palm to look at the locket her father had given her. Her hand was white where she'd been holding it. She unhooked the chain carefully and clipped it around her neck with some difficulty. Jade tucked it beneath her shirt. She was strangely relieved when the plane started moving.

***

Jade woke up a few hours later to find another smooth runway gliding toward them.

She scrambled to her feet and followed the crowd of people out into an austere opening, where she searched reluctantly for her aunt's familiar, bitter face.

And there it was.

Hiding between a young man and a tall woman stood Cynthia, looking as though she'd been plucked from another world and left on earth. She certainly *acted* as if that were the case sometimes. Cynthia stood straight and rigid, her hair slicked back into a neat, gray bun, and her beady brown eyes narrowed in scrutiny toward Jade. Her sweater was delicate lavender, and she wore a pleated, checkered skirt that reached an awkward position on her thick calves. As Jade sulked toward her aunt, she had the fleeting thought that Cynthia was in desperate need of a stylist.

"Katherine," Cynthia said when Jade was within earshot. Her voice was as shrill as ever; her disparaging tone dripped through every syllable. If Jade had been expecting a warm greeting, maybe even a handshake, she was royally disappointed. "You kept me waiting so long, I wondered if you'd bother to show up at all."

Jade nodded. "Sorry, our flight must have taken off late."

"I should think so," Cynthia muttered. She led Jade outside to the car—a silver Corvette with soft, worn, leather inside. The seats were plush and the windows were pristine and untouched.

"Do you drive this car a lot?" Jade asked.

Her aunt shrugged, toggling the shift before backing up. "Yes, why?"

Jade shrugged. "It looks pretty new." She didn't have to take one look at Cynthia before wanting to take back the compliment.

Her aunt steered out of their parking space. "Well, Katherine, when you're my age, and you've worked as long and as hard as I have, you'll be able to afford this kind of thing." They were pulling out of the garage now, and her aunt continued with the air of someone who had an audience. "Speaking as a *practical* woman, I can tell you, it's no easy road getting the kind of things I have." Jade turned toward the window and shut her eyes.

Already, Jade wondered how long she would be able to withstand her father's absence. He and his sister were unnervingly different, and it made her miss him all the more. Oblivious to Jade's remorse, Cynthia continued to speak in a loud, boisterous rant.

Jade peeked one eye open and saw rolling plains and hillsides encompassing them. Cynthia had always lived far out in the country. James lived in the suburbs, but they had always been within walking distance of civilization. Jade was already feeling homesick for the bustling city noises she was used to. She let her mind conjure theories as to why her aunt didn't like the city, but then thought it wasn't as if any part of the city would like *her*. Jade traced a lazy finger along the chain her locket dangled from and gulped down the tears in her throat.

"*Katherine Orwell!*" Cynthia bellowed. Jade turned, startled. "What did I just say?"

"Hard work pays off," Jade guessed, only slightly guilty that she hadn't been listening. She turned back to the window, and her heart sank when she realized they had almost reached Cynthia's house.

Her aunt scoffed. "Sometimes I feel as though I'm talking to a *wall*."

They were driving through an archway of trees, one that had become so overgrown that the branches intertwined, knitting a green canopy above them. Cynthia slowed the car as they pulled up to her enormous house.

"Well, don't just hang around—get your things. I'll show you to your room."

Jade dragged herself out of the car and wished that her father had had two friendly old parents, or a really nice younger brother instead. As she considered the idea, Jade remembered that her aunt had been the only relative of her father's she'd ever met. It wasn't as if she hadn't asked about the others. In fact, Jade had asked profusely, but whenever she did, her father would always either refuse the topic, or recline in a chair and mumble something vague or unintelligible about not wanting to discuss it.

From the outside, Cynthia's house looked like a derelict building more suited to the front cover of *Dracula* than a suburban home. The difference was that the only evil creature haunting this particularly decrepit dwelling was Cynthia herself. From the copper spires that jutted out of the dark, shingled roof, all the way to the ancient foundations that supported it, the house reeked of Cynthia's misery.

Cynthia led Jade in silence through an extravagant hall, where the arches were long and wide and tapestries hung on every surface. From the dark, faded color of the red carpet, to the firm, stone grooves in the walls, every nail that held the structure together seemed to cry for escape. Jade wondered despairingly if she might ever hear her own voice among those cries.

Once they had walked what seemed to be the length of the house, they reached a narrow, spiraling stairwell—or rather, a never-ending maze—which led into even darker corridors in the house. Jade felt her legs become heavy as she tried to muster the strength to lug herself up the stairwell, step by step. The stairwell was becoming narrower and narrower—she couldn't even spread both arms out on either side of her. The only light came from a small slit window that overlooked the rolling plains outside.

Jade could hear her aunt's shuffling footsteps still trudging up distant steps, but the more she thought about climbing farther, the dizzier she became. She sat with her back against the cool stone, across another identical wall. Jade's eyes rolled over it absently, exploring the grooves of stone and small crevices.

Opposite her, there wasn't a door—at least not as one might ordinarily describe a door. It wavered between an indentation in the wall and a slab of stone that looked as if it could be on a hinge. If she strained her eyes, she could imagine a brown tinge in the stone, maybe even a stain of old wood etched onto it. Jade stood, leaving her duffel bag on the steps. There was something odd about it, about the way she could almost—when she narrowed her eyes, or the light caught the wall at the right angle— envision a kind of waning arch.

Certainly if it were a door, there would be a knob near to where her hand hovered in the air. If she could just reach out and pull it, she could be sure—

"Katherine Orwell, what *are* you doing?" Cynthia demanded reproachfully, her piercing voice shattering Jade's thoughts.

"My legs were hurting—I just stopped to catch my breath," Jade started, but her voice soon trailed off as Cynthia's gaze drifted from Jade to the wall and back again. Jade slid her hand back into her pocket.

"Did you see something of *interest?*" Cynthia growled.

Jade met her glare with a raised brow. "No. I have yet to see *anything* of interest."

Her aunt smirked and turned on her heel, gesturing for Jade to follow. Jade cast one last glance at the wall, but the door—or whatever it had been—was nowhere to be seen.

Jade caught up to her aunt. Cynthia hadn't turned around once, and it struck Jade as rather presumptu- ous that Cynthia had expected her to follow. She could just as easily have turned her back and walked *down* the stairs instead.

"Why is my bedroom so high up?" Jade asked, her voice hoarse and tired.

They'd finally reached the end of the stairs. Cynthia stopped one step below an elegantly framed door with a curling handle and a plaque that read PRH.

"Aside from keeping you out of trouble," Cynthia answered, "the view from up here is pleasant, and there's plenty to keep you…occupied."

Cynthia held open the door and seemed sufficiently satisfied by Jade's reaction. Jade felt her eyes widen in wonder as she took in the room. The floor, unlike the rest of the house, was not flagstone or marble—it was a polished, honey-colored wood. A plush rug lay on the floor, glittering in the sunlight. It was the bed, though, that caught Jade's eye. She couldn't imagine anyone's need for anything of that size, let alone *her* need for it. The dressings were silk and had threads of silver woven into the seams. Jade certainly didn't remember this room from her last visit.

She rested her bag on the chest at the foot of the bed, and turned to her aunt, resigned. A bedroom of this ca-liber could only mean one thing. Jade was there to stay for a *long* time. "Thanks," she muttered. Most of her had meant it to be genuine, but she couldn't entirely conceal the melancholy in her tone.

"Of course, Katherine. If you're going to stay here, you might as well stay in a room you can stand," Cynthia said with a sweep of her hand.

Jade could more than stand it, and if any other elderly woman had offered it to her, she would have expressed this profound gratitude. Now, she felt content to simply nod in agreement.

Cynthia crossed the room and pointed to a long shelf of books. Some had leather bindings with golden scrawl written along the spine. Others were plain, or didn't have any writing at all. "James said you liked reading?" she asked, turning to Jade with a raised brow.

"Yeah." Jade nodded, reaching for one of the books.

Cynthia pulled Jade's wrist back firmly and let go. "Well, you can't have these, Katherine. Not one. These aren't even mine to give away. They're my son's."

So that's who PRH is. Jade thought.

"You can, however, indulge in my library. Most of my important books are kept near the top anyway, well out of danger from your dirty hands and carelessness—"

"Who says I'm careless?" Jade asked defensively. She could think of a thousand worse flaws in Cynthia.

"Katherine, it's clear enough from the way you dress. Your hair is frizzy, your posture is about the likes of an ape, and your pants are ten sizes too big. You're lucky I don't take them right now and throw them out the window." Cynthia set her jaw determinedly and clasped her hands together into one tight fist. "Dinner will be ready at six," she instructed, breaking the silence. "I expect you to be dressed and neat when you come down." With that, Jade's aunt scuttled away, shutting the door firmly behind her.

CHAPTER 3

Following the scent of spiced food, Jade wandered the halls until she stood before a vast archway through which she could see her aunt, looking as meticulous as ever, setting silver platters of food in the center of a long mahogany table.

Cynthia didn't seem to take any notice of Jade at all as she scurried to and fro, balancing silverware and glasses in her hand. Jade cleared her throat as Cynthia laid down the last steaming dish. The plates alone were as elaborate as the rest of the house. Floral patterns were gilded onto their delicate frames. The handles were adorned with colored stones and pebbles that glittered extravagantly under the light of the chandelier that hung overhead. Jade couldn't help but feel resentment toward her aunt—a woman with everything to give and no sliver of a conscience to bother. She'd never, in Jade's memory, extended a hand to James, and any interaction at all was ephemeral at best. Allowing Jade to stay at the house was likely the greatest sacrifice Cynthia would ever make.

"Katherine," Cynthia began, resting her long, spidery hands on her hips. "Your shoes."

Jade glanced at her bare feet. "Would you like me to go get them?" Jade asked, wriggling her toes on the tile.

Cynthia's face tightened. "It hardly matters now, but socks would suffice for tomorrow." Cynthia pointed Jade to a velveteen chair on one side of the table, and after settling into her own seat, she gestured for Jade to serve herself. Jade chose her food arbitrarily, and gathered it into a misshapen pile on her plate, trying to avoid Cynthia's critical gaze all the while.

Jade picked up her fork and began eating, having until now been oblivious to her hunger. The food was warm and soft, and the bread steamed as she tore it apart. She barely breathed between bites. The meat was rich and tender, with just enough grease that each bite fell off the bone and melted in her mouth.

"Well?" Cynthia asked, dabbing her mouth with a napkin.

"It's good, thank you," Jade answered, swallowing hard. Her aunt was pedantic about table manners.

"Better even than *James's* cooking, I expect," she scoffed. "I'm the one who taught James to cook in the first place."

Jade nodded in mock interest, and gulped her food down with a swig of water, before cutting up the rest of her food.

"Katherine, hold your fork properly...like this." Cynthia showed Jade carefully with her own fork. Jade mimicked her. "Good, now sit up straight and take your elbows off the table. It's rude." Jade did so, but fought down the urge to ignore the comment altogether.

They ate in silence for a few minutes, giving Jade a chance to rekindle a more congenial tone. "Aunt Cynthia?" she asked, looking up.

Cynthia glanced at Jade over thickly rimmed glasses. "Yes, Katherine?"

"Did my dad tell you how long I'd be here?"

Her aunt sat forward in her seat, looking at Jade thoughtfully. "*A while,* I think he said."

"Did he tell you why?" Jade asked, treading carefully for fear her aunt might erupt and condemn her questioning.

"He'll be busy with the bookstore," she answered, eyeing Jade suspiciously.

"Is that what he told you?" she asked with a raised brow.

"That's what he told *you,* Katherine." Cynthia took a deep breath and pushed her glasses farther up her nose. "And honestly, it's not my place to tell you the comings and goings of your father's affairs. All I can say is that he is a capable man who has everything he needs, should any harm come his way." She pursed her lips.

"And is that what you expect?" Jade asked, a hard lump in her throat. "Harm?" She'd known her father had been lying, but hadn't expected it to be about anything serious…much less anything dangerous. Jade wracked her brain for anything or anyone she could remember that had posed even the slightest threat. Nothing came to mind.

"Perhaps," Cynthia replied. She set down her fork then and looked at Jade squarely. "It hardly has anything to do with you, for now, though, so you can stop worrying and finish your meal without another word."

Jade pressed her lips into a hard line, letting her eyes linger on Cynthia a moment longer before turning back to her plate.

The rest of the meal passed in silence. Only the clashing of their silverware against the plates, and a soft breeze through the high arches of the roof, echoed around them.

Cynthia stood suddenly and smoothed her pleated skirt. She grabbed her own dish and covered the remaining platters with lids.

"Katherine, when you're done, I expect you to clear away your dishes." Jade nodded and watched Cynthia through the corner of her eye as she cleared away the half-empty pots and pans, and then hurried into the caterer's kitchen at the far end of the room.

Five minutes later, Cynthia reappeared and shuffled past Jade into the grand hallway. Jade threw her head back in exasperation and then stood. How many days and hours would it take for this stone to be something like a second home to her? She hoped her father would rescue her before she could find out.

Juggling her plate, silverware, and napkin in one hand, and her glass in the other, Jade kicked the chair back in with her foot and heaved open the door of the smaller kitchen, then set her dishes down on a low countertop. The room was about the size of her kitchen at home. Of course, beside Cynthia's dining table, the kitchen was dwarfed to the size of a coat closet. She brushed aside the thought and hurried out into the magnificent winding corridors that consumed the house. Passing the front entrance, Jade thought fleetingly of walking straight through it, but the thought was gone as soon as it had come, and Jade dragged herself along another wide staircase that led to the second floor. She wondered how her father was passing the evening. Probably he'd be closing the bookstore and shutting the blinds, or else eating alone at the table, or reading by the fire. Maybe he was contemplating ways to break Jade out of the house he'd sent her to. Jade thought the latter least likely, but held onto that thread of hope.

As she traced her hand along the rough edges of stone that lined the narrow stairwell to her room, she felt it catch on something sharp. She gasped and inspected her hand to see a thin red line well across her palm. Looking back at the wall, Jade realized this was where she'd been standing earlier, staring at a door that hadn't been there. Now, upon closer inspection, she saw nothing but a stone wall that protruded strangely at certain angles, forming a kind of arching pattern just a few inches above her. The dim light from the gas lamp cast shadows dark enough that Jade might almost have thought it was granite or wrought iron.

As she worked her hands along the rugged surface and pressed against it, the door became clearer, the stone turning to smooth brown wood in areas she hadn't noticed before. Stifling a gasp, Jade held her breath as her hands caught on a smooth, spherical projection just above her hip. She sucked in a quick breath of anticipation and looked around. Cynthia was nowhere to be seen or heard. Jade could feel a part of her drawing toward the door and another part recoiling. She watched apprehensively as her hand turned the knob and pushed open the door.

Inside the room, the walls were bare, but even in the dark, Jade could see the floor strewn with objects that looked long-forgotten. What remained was in ruin. Lamps were shattered, boxes had tumbled in on themselves, and curtains were dust-coated and choked with grime. Every part of the enclosure looked as though a careless hand had ransacked it, crushed it, and finding nothing, left it. Stacks had been toppled. Papers and clothes were left trodden and ripped on the floor. The air was damp and musty, and there was a sour smell left in the wake of years gone by. The silence too was almost unnatural and sent a shudder up Jade's spine.

The farther she moved into the space, the more she felt like an intruder, disturbing some dark ritual. Even the walls seemed to whisper hushed warnings. They had *seen* something. Even so, Jade moved farther, her heart beating in defiant protest as she forced herself through the darkness.

She drew the curtains back, letting the moonlight seep into the room. A kind of intangible connection fastened Jade to the room. She searched hungrily for an answer that seemed to linger in the air around her and reached out a hand to run her fingers along the velvet dresses that lay trampled on the floor, along with matching, strapped shoes. Behind the dresses, shoes, and mounds of boxes, the darkness hung around her like solid drapes. She let her eyes adjust briefly and saw two glistening pellets of light.

Jade thought at first they might be shards from a broken chandelier, but as she drew herself closer, there was a flash of blue, a spark flying between her outstretched fingers and the stacked silver rods she'd mistaken as glass. It was gone the moment her eyes caught it, and she was left with the agonizing uncertainty of whether or not she'd imagined it. Each rod lay inside a satin-lined wooden case. The one farthest on the right had "Cynthia Harrington" carved neatly into the wood. The next was empty, and "P.R. Harrington" had been written in sharp black ink. At the end was another empty box with "Arnold Harrington" scrawled into the wood. Jade wondered if this had been Cynthia's husband.

At last she withdrew one of the rods and let out a slight exclamation of shock. The object was made of silver—or at least something of that nature. She was certain now her eyes hadn't deceived her. The same flicker of blue light she'd seen before now encapsulated her hand and the rod, winding them together in a fluorescent web. Jade's heart rushed up into her throat. How could this be happening?

When she crept back from the shadows and into the light, she saw the rod was more crystalline than silver. It sat firmly in her palm, sliding easily into her grip. She scrutinized its smooth edges, which looked sharp and jagged in the light. There was something mystical and surreal about the way it balanced perfectly, even on her fingertips. She stared at it in awe—how regal, how beautiful a person would have to be to own such an object. If it had been Cynthia's, why wouldn't she flaunt it—hang it or frame it like all the other riches she'd never share?

The web of light disappeared, and she was left in darkness again except for the moon.

Jade felt her hand rise up, clutching the rod firmly until it was pointing at the window through which the moon winked at her. She imagined releasing whatever force lay trapped within that crystal frame. She willed something to happen, longing for the explosion she'd felt on the brink of uncovering.

The window breathed. No, it rocked; it bent so far inward that Jade could feel her muscles tensing as she pulled the invisible rope that seemed to connect the glass to her fingers. Her eyes were wide and her breath quick. Jade almost dropped the rod altogether. The window stopped rocking and remained still until Jade could calm her nerves again. She tried a second attempt, still surprised when the window yielded to her command, billowing like fabric. Suddenly Jade could feel the weight of it on the muscles in her arm and shoulder. The window moved in accordance to her thoughts, and the slow, slight movement of her wrist. When it was within arm's reach, she held it steady and stretched out a trembling hand—

"*Katherine Jade Orwell!*"

Jade tensed. Her heart skipped a beat. The glass frame was in free fall. Cynthia tore the rod from Jade before the glass could come shattering inward. She set it back in the flat pane it had been in and placed herself between Jade and the glass, the rod tucked under her arm. Cynthia's hands were curled into tight fists, her face contorted with rage. Jade had the urgent thought that if she ran now, Cynthia would be in no shape to stop her.

Cynthia pulled back a pale hand. In the darkness Jade could barely see anything but a faint silhouette, and then she felt a painful sting as something hard and flat smacked into her cheek. Jade staggered back, disoriented. She knew she could do much worse to her aunt, but her father's voice rattled around in her thoughts. *Just because you can doesn't mean you should.* She hated herself for being sensible.

Cynthia slammed the rod down on the desk behind her and whipped back around to face Jade. "You will *never* disobey me again," Cynthia hissed. Though her voice shook, her face was stony.

Jade clenched her jaw, but her anger was quickly fading because a more pressing matter was at hand. "What is this place?" Jade whispered.

"This is private, Katherine." Jade thought she could see Cynthia's bottom lip quiver. "I realize you and James have little respect for me and my rules unless you want something, but this—this has crossed the line, Katherine."

I'm sorry, Aunt Cynthia, I didn't realize, Jade wanted to say, but somehow the words were stuck in her head, and wouldn't materialize into sounds. "Who are you?" was all she could manage.

At last Cynthia blew out a gust of air and turned to look at the door. Her eyes were glistening. "Please go," she muttered, not looking at Jade.

"Aunt Cynthia—" Jade suddenly found her voice, but it was too late. The tears had vanished from Cynthia's eyes, and her face was red. Jade couldn't help but think that the pain she felt on her red cheek was nothing compared to that she'd inflicted on Cynthia.

"*Go!*" Cynthia roared. Jade staggered out of the room and ran up to her own bedroom, slamming the door behind her. She realized she'd been holding her breath. She exhaled now and felt numb all over from shock and then the bizarre sympathy she'd felt for her aunt—that had certainly been a first. She heard Cynthia shut the door carefully and descend the stairwell in her slippers.

A familiar melody began playing, and Jade launched onto the bed, scrambling to untangle the contents of her duffel bag. At length she found her cell phone and flipped it open. "Dad?"

"Hey, hon, I meant to call you when you landed, but—"

"Dad, please pick me up. It's miserable here. We're going to kill each other." There was a silence on her father's end, and then he chuckled.

"Give it time, Kat. She'll warm up to you the same way she warms up to everyone."

Jade groaned. "Dad, you wouldn't say that if you'd been here tonight."

An even longer pause than the first ensued, and she could tell he was scared to ask why. He forced the word out. "Why, Kat?" His voice was weary.

Jade expected he'd been busy at the shop all day. "Well, first, at dinner she mentioned you might be in some kind of...trouble." He didn't answer, but Jade heard him take a deep breath. "Are you?"

James hesitated. "Kat, you know Cynthia, she's always trying to stir things up." James listened for Jade's response. There was none. "Continue with the story."

"Well," Jade started reluctantly, "I found a room..."

"What kind of room?" James urged.

She relayed the rest of the story to him hesitantly, but he didn't say a word throughout. When she finished,

Jade held her breath for the verdict. It probably would have been smarter not to say anything at all, but the story would be better from her than from Cynthia.

James smacked his lips. "Kat, you've got to cut her some slack."

"*Me?*" she asked hysterically.

"Just listen," James interrupted firmly. "Cynthia is doing us a huge favor. She's been through a lot the past few years, so if she asks you to stay out of *one* room, for goodness' sake, please *do,*" he begged.

"Technically she didn't say to *stay* out."

"Katherine!" He paused briefly. "It was implied." The silence ran long and heavy between them, and Jade couldn't bring herself to break it. She thought she heard the television on in the background and wondered if he'd bothered to fix it. "Kat?" James asked, his voice softer now. Jade made a slight murmur in response. "Don't get upset with your aunt. She's only trying to protect you."

Jade could hardly suppress a scoff of incredulity. "From *what?*" Jade waited for a response, but there was none. "Oh, come *on,* Dad, you too? I'm not an idiot! I know when people are lying to me."

James sighed, and Jade suddenly wanted to take it back. She could tell her father had been hurt by her tone, and maybe he had good reason for not having told her in the first place. Jade tried desperately to soothe her anger, but why was he acting so indifferent? Why wasn't he telling Jade she was right to be curious, that she ought to know more about the woman she called her aunt? *Because it's not your business,* Jade thought bitterly, clutching the bed sheets in her hand as she sprawled out on the bed.

At last he spoke, but his voice was wary, as though each sound could plunge him under a thick layer of ice. "Kat, there are things you just *can't* know right now." Jade could hear him swallow hard. "I asked Cynthia to take care with what she told you, because I need to give you time to—" He choked on the next word, and then gave up on it altogether. "There are still things to explain about our family. For now, I don't want you to bear the same burdens I do, all right?"

Jade sat up and was pressing into the pillows, curling her locket around her finger and then unwinding it in a kind of rhythmic motion. "What kind of things? Things that made you send me here?" Again there was silence on her father's end of the phone.

"Yes, Kat. Please just trust me when I say now is *not* the right time for me to tell you. Listen to your aunt, and I know you hate it, but you really have to obey her…for your sake and mine."

"What does this have to do with you?" Jade could hear the fear in her own voice.

"Kat—" James stopped himself, searching frantically for the words. "Katherine." Again he stopped, smacking his lips and sighing. "That rod…"

Jade frowned, and then remembered he couldn't see her. "What about it?"

"It's called an ethereal rod," James said with a sharp edge to his voice.

"What's it do?" she asked slowly, trying only to scratch the surface of whatever barrier made him recoil from her curiosity.

"It doesn't *do* anything, Kat. It's a medium."

Jade sat forward now, her nerves ablaze with anxiety. She tried to phrase her next question carefully, fearing he might not permit another one. "For?"

There was another pause that seemed to drag out into eternity. "A certain kind of magic," he finally said.

Jade gaped. A small voice was telling her he was lying, but the rest of her begged to believe him and know more. She felt her breath catch in her throat, and wondered if she'd ever regain the capacity to breathe again. *Magic?* she thought.

"But how? Dad, what—so does that mean I'm a... Could I do other things too if I were really—" She stopped, partially because she couldn't believe the words flying out of her mouth, but also because James interrupted her, ceasing her thoughts altogether.

"Don't even *think* about it, Katherine," he hissed into the phone. "Every time you do something like that, you're putting yourself and Cynthia in grave danger. Do you understand?"

Jade nodded, forgetting again her father couldn't see her. She muttered a reluctant yes.

"Good. I can't have anything happen to you, Kat. I care about you too much." If he'd been sitting in front of her, Jade would have curled up into his arms and told him she cared about him too, but all she could do now was wrap her arms tight around her knees and press farther into the pillows.

"When will I be home?" Jade asked timidly.

"Soon, Kat, I promise." James heaved a sigh and didn't speak for a few moments. "At first I really did send you there because I thought it would do us both good for

you to get away…and with what happened at school—"
Jade blurted out an immediate defense, but it was no use.
James wasn't listening. "I would have had you back in
weeks, a month at the most, but now…I don't know."

"Why?" she asked hurriedly, panic bubbling in her
chest.

"I got news that—and this is nothing to worry about,
really—I'll be having some visitors soon, and I don't
want you here when they come."

"What kind of visitors?" Jade clenched her jaw.
"What do they want?"

James laughed dryly. "You're awfully curious tonight."

"Of course I am after all that's happened. Maybe it's
just another reason why I should be home—"

"Keep your head up, Kat." He chuckled. "I don't
want to run up the phone bill too much, but I'll try to call
every night, okay? Just don't call too much unless there's
an emergency."

"What time…will you call, I mean?"

James thought. "Nine o'clock, probably. I have to go,
honey. I'll talk to you tomorrow."

Jade choked a good-bye and winced. She felt a jolt
when the line cut dead.

CHAPTER 4

The rest of the next week passed silently—too silently. Dinners were silent. Mornings and evenings were silent. Cynthia spent most of the time locked in her room, and Jade felt unbearably responsible for the stoniness she saw in her aunt's face. She considered apologizing many times, but it always stuck in her throat, because maybe her words would just tear up whatever provisional mechanism of relief Cynthia had created.

Dreams, though, were glorious. She dreamed every night without fail of worlds where magic was real, and where things were simpler, easier. When she awoke one morning some days later to warm sunlight bathing the stone floor and the printed walls of her bedroom, Jade wanted desperately to fall back into those worlds, but they were gone, just like the cool air chasing away the warmth coming through her window. Jade reached over to her bedside table, struggling to read the flashing numbers on her watch. It was almost noon.

With a certain measure of urgency, Jade took a hurried shower and dressed. She returned her hair to a familiar style, having abandoned hopes to please Cynthia. She strung her father's locket around her neck and furrowed her brow, wishing she had more than a locket to hold onto. It was still as warm as the day she'd first received it and she smiled at the memory of her father's words, *so you know I'm safe.*

Though still weighted with exhaustion, Jade found it easier now to navigate the intertwining halls, and found the kitchen hastily. Cynthia was nowhere in sight.

"Aunt Cynthia?" Jade called, standing just outside the doorway. She waited, but there was no reply. Jade called again, louder, letting the sound of her voice echo in the empty room.

"I'm in the library, Katherine." Cynthia's voice finally sounded in the distance. Jade followed it until she found the library a few doors down the hall from the kitchen. Cynthia was sitting in an emerald-green chair, surrounded by equally brilliant upholstery, with a writing desk to one side of the room.

Jade had never seen so many books in her life. They were stacked on shelves up to the ceiling, each bound in tight leather—some old, some new, some big, some small—and each with elegant gold, silver, or black font printed up the spine. The carpet was soft and burgundy, with an intricate design stitched into it. A small, bright windowsill faced Cynthia's chair, and Jade couldn't help but wonder how many rainy days had been spent snuggled up beside that window, reading through book after book after book. *None*, Jade thought. Cynthia wasn't the kind of person Jade could imagine snuggling up to anything.

"You needed me?" Cynthia asked, putting down her book and taking off her glasses. Her voice was as strict and rigid as ever. No surprise there.

Jade shook her head. "I wanted to apologize," she blurted before she could second-guess her decision.

Jade's aunt seemed to see her for the first time. She looked at Jade musingly, and set down both her glasses and her book on the desk beside her. For just a passing second, Jade thought she saw a minor resemblance between Cynthia and James, in the way her nose came to a sharp point, and her cheeks were long and narrow.

"Sit," Cynthia commanded. Jade did. Cynthia cast a glance at the grandfather clock behind Jade and pursed her lips. "Since you only just bothered to wake up"—she started, raising her brows—"I've already started cooking lunch." She paused as though expecting a sudden interruption. "I was going to eat my lunch outside. Where would you prefer to eat?"

At first, Jade wondered if Cynthia had in fact been talking to her at all. It was rare that Cynthia asked Jade for her opinion on anything, and since their argument, Jade's lunch had been waiting on a plate in the kitchen and she'd eaten alone. Jade hoped this was some sign of truce. She looked past her aunt and out onto the windowsill. "Outside sounds good."

***

Cynthia hadn't said a word since they'd sat down. She was staring into the horizon and threading her feet between the blades of grass. On her lap she balanced a plate, though she didn't seem to take any notice of it as her eyes traced the skyline.

Of course, Jade didn't mind the silence. She'd taken position lying flat on her stomach, basking in the yellow warmth of the sun, and reveling in the way the light breeze tickled her skin. So long as Jade didn't turn her head, she could pretend Cynthia wasn't there at all. Instead, she could lose her thoughts in the quiet. Among this swarm of miscellaneous thoughts, one in particular prompted her to break the silence.

"Arnold?" Jade muttered, mostly to herself. She turned to find Cynthia sitting cross-legged and rigid. Something in her eyes evoked a kind of curiosity in Jade, and she didn't think before speaking. "Were you married?"

Cynthia's first response was a kind of rueful laugh. "Your apology must not have been sincere."

"It was. I shouldn't have asked…but now I might as well know…were you?"

Cynthia looked away again. "We should have been," she murmured, absently moving the food around on her plate. Jade wondered if the heat had transformed Cynthia. Her sharp features had dulled so that they were softer and rounder than they had been, trapped between those cold, gray walls. Cynthia cleared her throat with a slight hesitation. "He loved it here—he used to force Henry and me out with him to watch the sun go up and down."

"Your son?" Jade asked, sitting up now so she could face her aunt.

"Yes, my darling son."

"I thought his name started with a *P*." Jade watched in apprehension as Cynthia's lips pursed and her eyes narrowed.

"He didn't like that name," Cynthia answered curtly, drawing her sweater tightly around herself. "I named him after his birth father, Peter, thinking…" Cynthia sighed, looking past Jade now as she took a bite of food. "Well, I don't know what I was thinking, but…" She let her voice trail off into the empty air surrounding them.

"But what?" Jade couldn't stop the question from hurtling itself from her mouth, and was surprised when Cynthia answered.

"Henry was ashamed of his first father…but he *loathed* Arnold." Something caught in Cynthia's throat, and Jade felt a sudden urge to offer some sort of embrace, but she refrained. Her aunt recovered from the momentary lapse of silence and continued. "He would spend weeks in silence, avoiding Arnold, wanting me to get rid of him—" Cynthia clenched her jaw as if to trap the coming words in her mouth.

"So that's why you never married? Because Henry didn't want you to?"

Cynthia smiled bitterly. "You could say that." Again Cynthia paused as if searching Jade's face for judgment. During the silence Jade curled her arms around her knees, feeling like a child being read a bedtime story. Evidently Cynthia approved of what she saw, because she continued soon after. "The night before the wedding… Henry disappeared." Jade felt her eyes widen. "He was young, so I told Arnold we had to call it off, until we found him…"

Cynthia heaved a great breath. "When he finally did come back—months later—h-he gave Arnold exactly the punishment he thought Arnold deserved. Or maybe it was the punishment I deserved."

"What was it?" Jade's voice was a whisper.

"Death—in that room we stood in last night."

Jade gaped. The bedtime story had reached a twisted and gruesome end, and she suddenly wished she'd never heard it at all.

"But—" Jade blurted, not quite sure why she felt the urge to interrupt. "Why?" she spluttered, unable to conceive of it at all.

Cynthia scoffed. "You wouldn't understand if I told you, Katherine. From what I've heard, you've been kept under a neat little rock all these years—don't think I'll be the one to pull you out from under it." She slipped her shoes back on and her features hardened again.

"Try me," Jade answered, grudgingly forcing the glare out of her eyes.

Cynthia considered her for a long time and examined Jade with beady eyes. She wrinkled her nose haughtily. "Would you understand what's meant by the term *pure blood,* Katherine?" Jade shook her head begrudgingly. "Pure blood is the blood that runs through your veins," Cynthia explained, looking as if she'd already explained this to Jade many times before. "It's blood that—" She looked around, now, as if expecting someone else to be listening intently to her words, but they were alone. "It's blood that pulses with magic. It's the kind where every part of you is nothing but magic, and only that." She paused dramatically, pleased with the hold she seemed to obtain over Jade.

"Are you saying that…that I'm some kind of…" Jade looked for the right word. "Magician?"

Her aunt let out a long, croaky laugh, without humor. "That, my dear, would be a disgraceful insult to your forefathers." Jade showed every sign of interrupting, so Cynthia held up a long, pale hand. "And it's another story entirely," she said firmly.

Jade struggled to refrain from demanding a better answer, though it was with slight difficulty that she did so.

"Unlike you and your father," she began, a sharp edge in her words, "I am only a half-blood." She spat the word like venom and glared into the distance. "Your grandfather was pure, and yet stupid enough to have a child with a woman who was mostly…human." She sighed now, regret overpowering the anger she'd shown before. "When he realized what he'd done, he hurried to have James with a pure blood he barely knew, and James was the child he'd always wanted. James was *pure*."

Jade could hear the jealously cutting into her words, and wondered if this was why their relationship had always been so strained. *Pure blood?* She'd read of them in books, but had never imagined—never even conceived that something so improbable could in fact be possible.

"It was only right of me to marry Henry's first father, because we were so…alike. He was mostly pure, but he had something else in him too. When we had Henry, we were newly married, and in love…but he died of illness when Henry was only four."

The pain in her expression was fresh, like an open wound. "It took me *six* years to find Arnold. When we met, I'd finally found a father for a son who could hardly remember his. Every time I saw him was like—" Jade was alarmed to see Cynthia's eyes misting, and her bottom lip shaking against the rigid set of her jaw. "But he was just human, and Henry thought it was a sin to associate with them, let alone have one as a father." She met Jade's eyes briefly, but turned again.

"I was asking too much of him, I know. He would have had to hide his skills, his nature—that's why I made the room for him, but that wasn't enough." There was a momentary lapse of silence as Cynthia tried to align her thoughts. "He ran, and came back with training—better training than your father, even—it certainly wasn't anything I could have stopped. Arnold was dead before I could lift a finger, and when Henry left, he told me…"

Now her breath was quick and shallow, as though she couldn't get the words out fast enough. She had repressed the memories for so long, she didn't have any hope of impeding the flood of pain that came with them. She hadn't forgotten them, though. Not one word had been lost in all the years that had passed. "He said…*it only starts with the humans.*" Cynthia shook her head mournfully, barely regaining her stony composure.

"Then what?" Jade whispered, lying on one elbow and resting her head in her hand, warring between whether or not to believe such a magnificent, dark, tale.

"Well, I wasn't going to report my own son, if *that's* what you're thinking," Cynthia snapped, fury coursing through her.

"But sometimes you wonder if you made a mistake?" Jade asked.

"I don't question my decision, Katherine. Sit up straight. You aren't a Neanderthal," she said pointedly, the reproachful tone returning automatically to her voice.

If Jade hadn't known any better, she might have thought she'd dreamed their conversation altogether. The transformed Cynthia was nowhere to be found. She'd vanished between one second and the next, and in her place stood a resentful old woman brushing crumbs off her pleated gray skirt. "Go inside now, Katherine. I've already told you far more than I ought to have done."

Jade furrowed her brow, but followed her aunt's directions. She motored back up the hill and ran down it, thrusting open the back door when she reached it. Just before stepping over the threshold, Jade looked once more toward her aunt, but Cynthia had gone.

Jade's room was warm and bright, filled with the light of the dying afternoon sun. When the phone rang, Jade darted toward her bag.

She looked at the clock on the wall and her breath quickened. It was only four o'clock. Though she didn't know why, Jade could feel apprehension creeping up the hairs on her neck as she ran to pick up the phone on its last ring. With trembling hands, she answered the call.

"Dad?" Her voice came out as steady as she could manage, but she knew it was higher and shakier than usual.

"Katherine," James interrupted, hurrying to silence her. There was fierce urgency in the way he careened through the word, and Jade could hear his breath harsh and fast in her ear as if he'd been running. "Listen carefully." He paused, and Jade was too shocked to cut in. "I love you so much…you know that, right?" James asked, his voice softening minutely.

"Dad, of course—why—are you okay?"

James let out a trembling breath. "Kat, I haven't been entirely honest with you." *I know,* Jade wanted to say, but her father was already speaking again. "Those visitors I told you about, do you remember?"

"Yes—"

"They've come sooner than I expected. I need you to do something for me, all right?"

Jade nodded. "Y-yes, of course," she stuttered, panic shaking her hands and fingers. She leaped off the bed, pacing, her breath quivering.

"Take yourself and Cynthia to the farthest possible corners of the house and lock yourselves up in a tower until I come for you. When you hang up, one of two things will happen—are you listening?"

Jade nodded, but then said. "Yes—yes."

"Someone may get to the house before me."

Jade gulped. "Who?"

"Her name is Constantine."

"How will I know it's her?"

"You won't at first," James answered, his breath harsh now—he was definitely running. "If she doesn't come for you, do as I said, go to the room you found and find something, anything, to hold them off—don't leave the house. Stay exactly where you are. I'm coming—" He cut off, and his voice suddenly sounded from far away. "*Wait!*" he bellowed.

"*Dad!*" Jade roared, clutching the phone now in two hands. She yelled his name again. There was a pounding noise in the background and a quick, shuffled movement.

"*Stop!*" Jade heard her father shout. There was a high-pitched whine, unlike anything Jade had ever heard, and then a bang.

"Dad," Jade whimpered, tears welling in her eyes.

James grunted. "Don't be scared." He was talking too quickly and too anxiously for Jade to feel anything else. "Your aunt—" There was a kind of screeching, metallic ring—a thud.

Then silence. *Beep...beep...beep.* The line was flat.

Jade's heart skipped a beat, and she felt her every muscle stop. She was holding her breath.

She wasn't thinking when she tossed the phone to the bed and launched down the spiraling staircase, dizzy with panic and anxiety. She finally arrived downstairs in the enormous entry hall.

"Aunt Cynthia!" she screamed, listening to the echo of her own voice as she hurried up and down the soundless halls. "Aunt Cynthia!" she called again, wondering if it was too late.

Jade searched everywhere. She ran from the kitchen with its great arching ceilings to the drawing room with dark printed walls. She even checked the library, her eyes dashing from the books to the couch to the desk, but never to Cynthia. Jade was drained of energy by the time she reached an unfamiliar corridor. She checked every room and tried every knob, but most rooms were locked, if not empty.

"Aunt Cynthia!" Jade cried, her voice hoarse. The clock was ticking away madly. At last she reached the end of the hall, and thrust open the last door. Her aunt stood with her back to Jade, a finger placed lightly on one of the posts on her bed frame. Her silver hair dripped water onto the carpet. She wore a white slip and her customary floral printed sweater.

"Didn't you hear me calling you?" Jade panted furiously. "My dad—Something awful has happened.

Someone was after him and…they found him." Cynthia didn't turn.

A hot, sticky breeze came in through Cynthia's half-closed window, but the drapes were drawn, and Jade couldn't help but moan in frustration. "Cynthia! He's your brother! At least pretend to care!" Jade cut herself off. Even if she listened carefully enough to hear the crickets outside, she couldn't hear her aunt's familiar, impatient breath. The silence, she suddenly realized, was infinite. She wondered how she hadn't noticed before. The emptiness around her was dense enough to hang like drapes in the silent room.

"Aunt Cynthia?" Jade breathed, approaching her with an arm stretched out.

She rested a hand on her aunt's shoulder, which felt as smooth and rigid as marble, and didn't move. Her eyes, Jade noticed, were glazed over, but wide with trepidation. Her eyebrows were raised, and there was a firm tightness to her lips, almost as though she were preparing to scream. Jade shook Cynthia's pulsing, yet frozen wrist in vain.

She nearly cried out in shock when something loud and quick thudded down the hall. She heard doors opening and shutting one by one as heavy footsteps came closer and closer. At last they stopped just outside the door, and Jade couldn't stop the fearful shuddering of her hands and breath. She wanted more than anything to jump out the window and plummet to whatever lay below—anything would be better than this.

For a long moment, she stood motionless. She could feel her thoughts lagging as she watched the doorknob turn over and over like it would never stop—until it did. Jade looked hopefully back at Cynthia. She'd never wanted anything more than what she wanted now—help. Jade remained as silent as possible, though she could hear the drumming of her heart within the cages of her chest.

The door swung open abruptly, almost tearing from its hinges as if it too were anxious to escape the wrath of the creature that grasped it. Jumping back, Jade felt for something sharp on the desk behind her, anything, but there was nothing. She turned again to the doorway, and a harsh scream tore from her throat.

At first it seemed that a great shadow had engulfed the room, but she was horribly mistaken. Whatever it was sprouted wings with sharp claws like daggers on each end. The wings were laced with black feathers, like a vulture seeking prey—except that this wasn't *seeking* prey. It had found it. The creature's body resembled a man's, but his skin was pale and blue, cracking over his bare chest. His eyes were white like the wall behind him, but they were scorched and ringed with red, as though he were bleeding from the inside out.

Before she could do so much as duck, Jade saw him launch himself at her, his clawed wings aimed at her chest. Fear and adrenaline sent a spark throughout her body, and her trembling legs jolted into a runner's crouch just fast enough to avoid the piercing blow. The creature was stuck to the wall, and Cynthia's frozen body had been thrust to the floor. Jade took off, buying herself some time until the creature pulled free of the plaster, tearing half the wall with it.

Jade was already halfway down the long, wide corridor. Her thoughts were too fast and disjointed for her to focus on anything other than to keep moving. Her heart was beating like a time bomb in her chest, roaring out in protest as she ignored the pain in her muscles. A dry, hoarse screech sounded behind her, and she glanced around to find the creature hot on her heels, pushing itself forward with muddy-black wings.

Jade skidded around a corner into the kitchen—a dead end. She was unarmed, inexperienced, and alone. She kneeled over until her stomach jumped, and she was sure she'd be sick, but there was no time to be afraid. The creature's shadow nearly filled the length of the room, and he smiled—or at least he grimaced. It was a marred and gruesome expression he wore, but he wore it well.

He flung himself at her, his wings almost brushing each side of the dining hall. As his wings drew closer, Jade saw that the shining feathers she'd seen before were not feathers at all. Each was jagged, like a glass splinter, and she shuddered to imagine how easily they might pierce her skin.

With driving aim and precision, Jade slid past him, her face brushing sharply against the edge of his claw. She felt warm blood trickle down her face, and heard him let out a raspy, triumphant cry. Her eyes darted around for something that could be used as a weapon. A long mirror that reflected into the room hung just behind the table. Jade hurtled toward it, and slammed a fist into her reflection, looking to see if the beast had followed her.

He had.

The creature reached two hands out as if lunging for her face, but then bent and grabbed Jade's ankles. Tears were flooding down her face uncontrollably. Blood was rushing from the fresh punctures in her ankles, and her head was throbbing. With the rest of her energy, she pounded another fist into the mirror.

Her hand was bloodied and her fist marred with small, splintered glass pieces, but inside it she held one long shard that ran to the end of her forearm. Jade felt her head snap back against the edge of the drawer as the creature pulled her down and dragged her off her feet. She cried in agony, and within seconds, she was pinned beneath him—his yellow nails digging into her neck, and his wings batting violently as he nestled them into a striking position. Jade knew she only had a few seconds, and yet part of her feared it was already too late. From this position she could see the excitement of the kill in his eyes. He knew she was as good as dead, and with this certainty he threw caution to the wind. She ripped the blood-drenched shard of glass from at her side, and plunged the sharp end into his pallid blue and red veined chest with enough force to cut her own hand.

She watched in frightful disbelief as he staggered back, his white irises meeting Jade's stunned face. He seemed confused and disoriented as black blood spewed from his chest as though it were being sucked out of him. He crumpled, his hands clasping and slipping along the end of the long dining table. The plates came sliding down toward him, crashing against the tile as he squawked and sank to the floor—then *through* it. The creature cried hoarsely, drowning in the rubble and the floor into which he had fallen captive.

Jade scurried to her feet, stumbling away from him.

And then he was gone.

All Jade could hear were the dying echo of his ear-piercing screams and her own heart pounding in her chest. Jade's throat was dry and swollen. It hurt from the shouting and the adrenaline that still coursed through her. She was breathing as heavily as a tugboat moving through water, and was on the verge of fainting when she saw a small white envelope hanging idly in the air.

She looked around warily and reached for it, listening to the tinkling crack of the glass beneath her feet. Her quivering hands ruined the glossy white letter, but she unfolded it carefully and let the envelope drop to the floor. In vain Jade tried to slow her quickening breath as she let her eyes roam over the neatly scrawled message. It read:

Dear Katherine Jade Orwell,

You were assigned a dimensional demon as your first task. You have succeeded in this assignment. Having succeeded, you have completed and passed the entrance exam into the world-renowned school of training—Constantine Academy. Here at Constantine Academy, we admire courage and talent in an elite group of young Illysians like you. Courage and talent are two qualities you demonstrated with grace and perfection during this exam.

We hope you will consider our offer to train you and develop your skills and techniques. If you would like to accept our invitation, open the door before you. If you choose to decline, please make your way out of the room. I will extend this invitation only once.

Best wishes,
Constantine

Jade looked up to find an arched wooden door in front of her. She circled it once and then stared incredulously. Where had it come from? She took a hesitant step forward, setting the letter down with great care, hoping Cynthia might find it should Jade leave. She clutched her right hand tightly around the cool metal knob. This was Constantine—the woman who was to be her rescue. Her father wanted this. Jade stared at the door in a stupor. The curiosity was too great. This woman, Constantine, was the answer her father had never given her. Jade leaped on it.

Why is it that the second before your life changes forever, there's no flashing red light? There's no small voice in the back of your head telling you to stop...to *think*. The sound of Cynthia's footsteps started down the hall again, clicking lightly against the floor, and Jade knew she didn't have long. She blew out a heavy breath and turned the knob, glancing back only once at the explosion of rubble in the once-extravagant dining hall. Plumes of dust swirled up around her, and she faltered—then thrust open the door.

CHAPTER 5

When Matt stepped through the doorway, an enormous, dimly lit hall greeted him. He shut the door behind him and watched the fire dance like pixies in the wrought-iron hearth. He'd been anticipating this moment forever, and he was finally here. He had made it—at last—into Constantine Academy.

At a young age, Matt had sought after his right to *this* school, *these* halls, and *these* illustrious professors that seemed to every Illysian the greatest troves of knowledge. His breath was still shallow and hoarse from the fight, and his blood still pulsed in a fearful flutter. Despite this unease, a happy memory kindled and warmed Matt's almost frozen limbs. Nearly five years had passed since he'd first learned of Constantine Academy.

His mind urged him toward the memory.

***

Matt's parents were sitting at the dining table while he and his close friend, Tom, scarfed down a stale portion of bread. It would be enough to tide them over, but work in the field was always strenuous, and hunger was an ever-looming companion.

"You've had enough, boys, save some for later." Matt's mother laughed gently, and pulled away the plates.

"I'm not full!" Matt complained, his legs kicking under the table with angst. "How can we work with empty stomachs?"

His father came into the room from the single bedroom that branched off near the small window beside the kitchen. "Now, Matt, your stomach is hardly empty. If anything, I'd say it is quite more filled today than it was yesterday. Every day you eat more."

"And every day they work us harder!" Matt almost yelled. He rarely yelled at his parents. His mother was sweet and kind, but quickly becoming older, unable to work, and therefore useless in the eyes of any wealthy Illysian.

Matt's father gave him a warning glance, his face turning into a frown. "Speak nicely, son, or you'll have *none* tomorrow."

"It's true." Tom hesitated. His own parents were out of bread, much less enough food to feed a family of three. "The food disappears." Tom spoke quietly. There were men on the streets outside, waiting for them to say something of just that sort—reason enough to kill the lot of them.

Matt sighed, percolating the frustration that seemed tangible in the room. "When will it change?" Matt asked, dejectedly shoving his plate farther away. Surely, even in the guttering streets he knew, a change from the dark and heavy and furiously familiar *must* exist.

His father and mother looked closely at each boy and then sat down. "There are places where such things might be possible." Matt's mother paused, looking at her husband for support to go on. He encouraged her. "Change is possible…if you pursue it."

Matt was skeptical. "Just not in *this* world."

His father scratched his stubbly gray beard. "There's always Constantine." His wife looked up sharply, but didn't speak.

"Who?" Tom asked.

"Constantine Academy is an *institution*—among the greatest in any world. She's magical."

"What?" Matt had asked incredulously. "How do you mean, 'magical'? What does she do?"

His father searched for the right words in their dilapidated ceiling. "She finds you, and she gives you the key to a new world. No matter where you're from."

"But *how* does she find you?" Tom asked, enthused. Matt nodded. A new excitement brightened their sun-kissed faces.

"If you work hard and do everything with all your might, she will bring you into her institution and transform you into proud warriors—military men!" Matt's father said. He struck his fist against the table as if it might be a podium, and as if his audience of two were an audience of hundreds.

Matt scoffed. "Sounds like something the rich people say—*work harder and maybe one day we'll give you a decent dinner, a few good pillows.*"

Tom chuckled.

"Constantine's not like the others, dear," his mother offered. "You wait and see." She crossed the table and pressed a feeble hand against Matt's broad chest. "You have a *good* heart, and she will see that from miles away. Just you *both* wait." She winked.

In the evening, while Matt huddled under rough sheets on his makeshift mattress, his mind had been molded like clay and set in stone as he considered the possibilities.

From that moment onward, Constantine Academy became a beacon of liberty. She stood as a mighty flag of myth and wonder. Existent or not, the sense of righteousness and purpose he owed her was as real as his insatiable desire to leave behind this place, which seemed to be the darkest corner of the world.

Matt didn't know what he'd expected—maybe a room full of other Illysians, ready with ribbons and trophies to congratulate him. Perhaps he had expected the headmaster to visit him, and explain to him what he would be doing for the next few years here. Certainly, if Matt had expected anything at all, it wasn't the empty, half-lit room he faced now. Surely this couldn't be the Academy he'd always dreamed of. *Surely* there was more.

At first glance Matt appeared to be alone, but as he surveyed the room, his eyes landed on a face. She was about a half a head shorter than him. Her eyes were dark blue and shimmered slightly in the orange light the fire cast upon them. Matt wondered how long she'd been crying before he'd gotten there. Even with her cheeks glistening, Matt could discern a kind of darkness in her eyes—an artful danger in her stance. Dark, loose curls cascaded down her back. She was thin and frail, like most of the women Matt knew from home. She too was underfed. She swept him with a cursory glance, and her eyes were shining, masking a kind of uncertain hostility. Matt's eyes wandered over her, and then met her gaze again.

"Who are you?" she asked, her firm inquisition breaking the silence. Matt saw the door he'd come through disappear beside him.

"Matthew Ferguson," he answered, shoving his hands into his pockets. He would have extended a hand to her, but she was standing too far away. She sidestepped the furniture between them to reveal the rest of her mangled body. A red gash ran the length of her cheek. Her arms were cut, but healing, the skin still swollen. Her hands were bloody, and the shirt covering her slender waist was almost torn through and splattered with blood—splintered with glittering glass.

"Dimensional demon?" he asked as she finally stopped in front of him.

The girl remained icy at first, even fearful. Then she nodded. "So I've been told." She held out her hand between them, and Matt shook it gently. "Jade Orwell," she said.

"How long have you been here?"

Jade glanced at the clock. "Thirteen minutes," she answered, staring back hopelessly at the empty space where he assumed her door had been.

Matt furrowed his brow. There was something strange about the small being before him. She was so slight, so slim, and yet the glare in her eyes was strong, as was the set of her lips. She was unlike anyone he'd ever seen. She was too plain to be rich, but something in her posture made her too proud to be from his home in the Keeping. He fixated on her, trying to determine what she was and where she'd come from, only to find that he couldn't.

As Matt surveyed the room, Jade did the same to him. He was tall, with tousled, light hair that fell around his face. His hands were blackened with soot, and his skin was red from whatever sharp claw had grabbed his flesh. There was something rough and worn in his features, yet the expression of his honey-colored eyes was childish. They held Jade's gaze with faint curiosity. He smiled and slipped past her.

"Well, I guess they'll be coming to get us soon then, Jade," he muttered, diving into the deep cushion of the delicate upholstery.

"Who?" Jade asked, sitting opposite him on the rug in front of the fire.

"Whoever it is they send for new students."

Understanding illuminated her face. "What an awful mistake," she breathed, squeezing her eyes shut before another set of tears could consume her.

Here, again, she surprised Matt. Why was she sad to be at Constantine Academy? Why was she not honored, ecstatic, bubbling with excitement at her own glorious prospects?

"What was?" Matt asked, leaning forward from the couch. Jade sat cross-legged and leaned her back against the bottom of the sofa. She could see his inquiring face from the corner of her eye.

"Coming here. Opening the door." She shook her head. "I should be home, looking for my dad—" She broke off, wishing she hadn't said so much.

"So, you're an orphan too?"

"No," Jade snapped, turning to meet his eyes. "I have a father."

Matt sat back up, throwing an arm over the back of the sofa, and staring into the fire. "I had a father *and* a mother."

"I'm sorry," Jade whispered, noting the past tense.

Matt was grateful, but surprised yet again when she didn't broach the topic any further. "You're not going to ask me what happened?"

Jade didn't answer. She had enough problems of her own to preoccupy her mind.

Matt slid down to the floor so that his back rested against the sofa. He sat close beside her. He stared, wondering whether he should tell her after all. "I'm from Juleria," he began. "A few months before they were taken, my parents asked the Oculus for an emergency portal. They're expensive, obviously, but my parents were willing to pay."

Jade raised an eyebrow. He was mad. That was the only way he could be talking with a straight face. He'd really lost it. "Oculus?"

Matt's brow rose. "The Oculus? That huge government that tells everyone what to do?" He searched for some kind of realization on Jade's face. "My parents used to say it was totalitarianism," he dared to say, searching for her response. "They had some pretty crazy ideas," he admitted.

Jade shrugged. "I've never been to…Juleria."

Matt's jaw dropped, but he closed it immediately.

"I recognize the word *Oculus*, though. Isn't it Latin?"

Matt nodded, on the brink of laughter. "You *recognize* the word?" He sighed. "Yes, it's Latin, but seriously, you're not from Recasteria?" He grimaced, and stared expectantly. Jade shook her head uncertainly. "From the coast?"

"Where exactly are we right now?" she asked, a new horror dawning on her. Was it possible that in stepping over that threshold, she'd stepped into a completely different—she dared to consider—new world? As far as Jade could tell, the boy sitting in front of her was human. There was no tail sprouting from his back, or any scaly wings and claws biting through his flesh.

"Constantine Academy," he answered, furrowing his brow with suspicion. Her questions confounded him. "East of Utopia. I live north of Utopia, and Recasteria is in the south."

Jade swallowed hard. She knew better than to tell the truth. What would happen to her if he knew she wasn't one of them? Or was she? And where was Utopia? He couldn't be suggesting an actual Utopia existed…except he was. He wasn't only suggesting it, but he *believed* it. Jade's head spun until she finally managed to spit out, "What's in the west?"

"The only thing in the west is the Lost Kingdom, and that's unmarked territory…unless you're an elf or a centaur or something. Which I take it you aren't." Jade shook her head. Elves? Centaurs?

"I'm from Juleria," she answered as confidently as she could manage. She wasn't even sure if she'd gotten the name right, but she said it softly enough that he barely heard her anyway.

When Jade met his eyes, she expected a mocking gaze, but instead received one of sly amusement. He winked. "Sure. So, you'll know what the Keeping is like, and how much the Oculus hates us?"

Jade nodded, smiling, because trying to pretend she followed was becoming a hopeless cause.

She had the sudden urge to jump through a window and just keep running until she landed on her front porch. James would be waiting for her with a mug of tea and a book. A gnawing thought pressed its way to the front of her mind, and she struggled to restrain it. James wasn't home. James was probably severely injured, alone, and scared out of his mind that they'd taken her too. Her hand brushed against her locket, where it lay heavily on her chest.

"As I was saying, an emergency portal is like the one we came through, except faster and…farther. In Juleria they don't allow them because it gives criminals a chance to hide from the Oculus and never be found. Of course, my parents *weren't* criminals," Matt added hastily. "The Oculus just doesn't trust anyone from the Keeping, because we have to work for money." He scoffed. "They were just scared—terrified, actually. They spent weeks trying to negotiate with officials, but it was useless. When my parents finally confessed their reason for needing one, they were taken away."

"And the reason was?"

"They said they were being hunted." He looked up, waiting for a skeptical outburst, but Jade was silent. "So the Oculus diagnosed them with paranoia, and apparently sent them to a special branch—an asylum."

Jade bit her lip. "At least you know they're safe," she muttered.

"But that's just it," he protested anxiously. "I searched every asylum in the city, and not one had ever come across the name Ferguson." He searched her face for sympathy, and found it in the crease at her brow. "Besides, when was the last time you heard of two patients being taken in by a *special* branch of the Oculus?" He spat the question angrily. "That's what they have doctors for, Jade. My parents were taken somewhere else…and not for that reason either. I'm sure of it.

"When I found out about Constantine Academy, I wanted it—I wanted to get out of the Keeping. I've seen others take the exam before, only twice, and each time they outran whatever was sent, but this time, I knew better. You have to *kill* it to pass the test. That's how they differentiate between us and the others," he said, his chest swelling with pride.

"Who are the others?"

Matt shrugged. "Half-bloods, humans, faeries, and the like. Constantine is an elite group of pure bloods. Only pure magic can kill a dimensional demon."

"I didn't use magic—I used a broken mirror shard and my hands," Jade said, holding up her shredded hands as evidence.

Matt laughed. "Magic isn't just charms and potions, Jade. Your magic runs through here," Matt explained, tracing a vein that curved through his own bloodstained arm. "Whatever you have in your hand takes the magic in your blood so you can fight."

Jade turned over her hands to see the veins that traced into her wrists. Matt suddenly bolted straight up and stared at one corner of the room. There was a creaking noise, and the wall appeared to move, revealing a hall flooded with light and a silhouetted figure. His hair was black and cropped in a way that made him seem older, as if he were from a different time. There was something disarming in his marble features. As he marched toward them, Jade watched his emerald eyes narrow with scrutiny.

In the half-light of the glittering fire, Jade could see shadows beneath his dark brow. He studied them cautiously, and then extended a hand to Matt. "I'm Aaron Henderson, and you're Matthew?"

"Yep—call me Matt," he answered, shaking Aaron's hand firmly.

"And you must be Katherine," Aaron continued, turning to Jade.

"I prefer Jade," she corrected, trying to decipher Aaron's cool stare.

He raised a stern brow. "May I call you Kat? It's easier to remember," he insisted, looking as though he didn't really care for her answer.

"Is Jade any harder to remember?" she countered. *Kat* only dredged up sweet memories of her father, and daunting questions of why she'd left him in the first place.

Aaron rubbed his jaw. "Yes. Yes, Jade *is* difficult to remember when your first name is Katherine." Jade could hear the sarcasm in his tone, and just as she opened her mouth to say something, his lips turned up in an easy smirk. He dipped into a low bow. "Please, follow me," Aaron commanded, making his way out the room.

Matt followed suit, filling his chest and mimicking Aaron's long strides. He looked back to Jade, who chuckled. They hurried to catch up with Aaron, who was marching purposefully down the narrow hall.

"Where are you taking us?" Matt asked, jogging to keep pace.

"The headmistress hasn't returned from the city, so you won't be seeing her until the orientation meeting tomorrow. I'm supposed to give you a tour of the school before lessons start." Aaron turned into a large, arched hallway with ceiling beams that interlaced into an elegant cross work of detailed stone and murals.

"What's your headmistress doing in Utopia?" Matt asked.

"*Our* headmistress was called into court."

"What for?" Matt asked, a slight edge creeping into his tone.

"How many reasons could a headmistress possibly have for going to court?"

Matt merely shrugged. They'd all stopped walking and stood in front of a window. The moonlight spilled onto the stone around them, bathing their faces with a delicate pale blue. "Lady Eleanor is on the board. They wanted her to be on the new jury."

"New jury?" Matt asked with incredulity. "She's with the Oculus?" Aaron nodded and turned on his heel, glancing only once at Jade, who showed every sign of confusion. She thought she saw him smirk again as he turned back around. Jade looked quickly at Matt, who stood aghast.

"As I was saying," Aaron began, leading them into an even larger hallway, "this is the South Tower. On a clear day, you can see some of the coastal estates through that window." Aaron pointed to one of the ornate windows. "Or so I've been told. It doesn't matter."

"Why?" Jade asked, her eyes lingering on the slightly ajar window.

"You'll never come down here unless you do something illegal."

"So this is like—detention?"

Aaron shook his head. "That would be a royal understatement. I couldn't tell you what they did down here even if I knew." He seemed to wait a second for her to catch on, but when she didn't, he explained. "The Oculus keeps some of its worst criminals down here—not all, but some. And the people who come in don't come out... not the *same* anyway." Matt gulped. "I could tell you plenty of stories, but we're pressed for time."

They passed several dark hallways, and Jade could feel hear a harsh drumming beneath her feet, like rattling chains or fists beating against the walls—or maybe that was just her own heart, beating against her chest.

Aaron made a sharp turn again, and here the windows were stained as in the enormous, old cathedrals Jade had always read about. The tinted glass shrouded the pure moonlight that struck against the unyielding pane.

"This would be the East Tower," Aaron said, his pace slowing again. "The only lesson you have here is law. You're both fifteen, aren't you?"

Jade nodded, peering into the long dark hallways on either side of them.

Matt cleared his throat. "Actually, I just turned sixteen."

"Good, so you both might be in a few of my classes," he said nonchalantly.

"Wait, how old are *you?*" Matt asked. Aaron considered the question, but then answered.

"Seventeen," he said. Matt looked strangely indignant as Aaron led them into a narrow corridor. On one side, instead of a wall, a balcony jutted out over what appeared to be an elaborate courtroom.

In the darkness that now enveloped them, Jade could only barely make out the round dome cut into the roof, and a banner hanging above where the jury would sit. Aaron led them past that into another hall with open windows on either side that looked out over an enormous courtyard. The blue stars blinked down at her from the sky, and showered the yard with glittering dust. She might have thought she could reach out and grab a handful of them from the night. Jade tore her eyes from the moonlit archway and turned back to Aaron.

"This is the North Tower?"

Aaron smiled wearily. "You're catching on."

Jade rolled her eyes and saw at the end of the hall a brilliant chandelier, reflecting a mirage of colors onto the dull stone. There was not a sound in the hall, except the harsh thud of their feet, and a murmur coming from around the corner. When they reached the corner, they faced two doors. The door on the left was made of iron or steel, with bolts and locks drilled into the glimmering metal. The other door was made of chestnut wood, with sharp engravings of script that Jade didn't recognize laced up the edges. Perhaps it was the dim moonlight or the lack of sleep, but the curving patterns appeared to slither up the wood.

"These are the dormitories," Aaron said. "Gender-separated, of course."

Matt released an audible sigh of disappointment. "Through there, right?" Aaron nodded. Matt looked back at Jade once, and smiled before disappearing through the iron door.

"Do you know each other from the Keeping?" Aaron asked Jade, lingering near the door. His face was stern, almost accusing.

Jade frowned. "Er, no." It sounded more like a question than she intended.

Aaron nodded, looking away from her. "You'll be staying in there, Kat...Someone should be waiting for you on the other side."

Jade let out an irritated breath, and reached a tentative hand toward the knob. *You'd think I'd know better than to open magic doors by now,* she thought bitterly.

"And Kat?" Aaron pressed, holding the door shut.

She turned and let go of the knob, taking an unconscious step back from him.

"Welcome to the Academy." With that he bowed once more and disappeared after Matt into the shimmering, metal doorway.

CHAPTER 6

The music was loud and spirited when Jade stepped through the door to the girls' dorms. It was an elegant, and somehow staccato, hum that filled the room. The light was bright and warm, red velvet covered the furniture, and the scent of sweet pastries bombarded her from all around. A crowd of about fifty girls twirled and danced about the room, smiles across their beaming faces.

Jade smiled, though she didn't know why. It reminded her strangely of the familiar nights she'd once spent curled up in James's lap…except he'd merely been doing card tricks. All kinds of strange things floated in the air here: paper airplanes with minds of their own and books levitating toward tables. Jade even thought she saw a ball chasing a young girl with two long, blonde braids.

A hand tapped her from behind. Jade turned away from the scene and met dark-brown eyes and a pixie-like face. The girl had platinum-blonde hair. She was slim, with long, sharp features and a kind of regal glimmer in her eyes. She stood at least five inches taller than Jade and looked down at her with a practiced eye.

"You're Katherine?" she asked, yelling over the noise. Jade grunted as a young girl darted past her into the crowd.

"Jade," she corrected with a smile.

"Camilla Holt," she said, shoving out a hand. Jade shook it. "Well, Jade, you can follow me. I'll take you to our room." She grinned and gestured for Jade to come as she threaded a path through the crowd. Jade barely kept pace as Camilla dashed in between the various dancing children and floating objects. All Jade could see of her was a bobbing head of silver-blonde hair and a bright red bow.

At last they were out of the crowd, and Camilla drew back a narrow set of curtains to reveal a spiral, stone staircase.

"Sorry about the noise down there. We found music in the basement, and everyone wanted to celebrate before school started tomorrow…You can't really blame them." They were walking down a carpeted hallway now, and Camilla led Jade carefully down the row of doors. "I didn't expect any more students to come. You must be the last of them. Constantine doesn't normally recruit the week before we start. Did anyone come with you?" she asked, stopping in front of an unadorned wooden door.

"Just one other," Jade said distractedly.

When Camilla reached the fourth door on the right, she cleared her throat and looked around warily before murmuring something incoherent. Jade furrowed her brow, and Camilla tried the locked door. She growled when it wouldn't budge, and stepped back again, only to repeat, though louder and clearer, "Pegasus." The door swung open as though someone on the inside had drawn it back urgently.

Inside was only one other girl, who introduced herself as "Justine Griffin from the Keeping." She was tall, dark, and once introduced, she spoke boisterously, showering Jade with questions. "How was the entrance exam? Are you hungry?" She ran through her words incessantly, commanding Jade's attention. She was genuine, reserved only if the conversation demanded it, and she seemed to know exactly what to say to fill the silence. Jade wondered about her foreign appearance. Everyone in this world they called the Illysium was beautiful. Justine had rich, golden-brown skin and long, black lashes. Her hair was a tangle of loose curls that framed her small face. She was a month older than Jade, and had been an orphan for four years and counting.

Camilla was her opposite—a well-to-do duchess from a district called St. Drewicks in Recasteria. She was equally talkative, but unintentionally callous. She demanded their attention when it suited her and secluded herself otherwise. When the conversation lulled, she was cold. Her attention seemed to be always wandering, searching. Naturally, she and Justine spent a majority of their time arguing.

When the music from the floor below began to die down, and the three of them were tired enough to sleep,

Jade's head was left swimming with questions, drowned in a hazy sea of inquiries left unanswered. *What was this place—this Constantine? Who were the students harnessed in her stony arms?* At midnight a loud bell chimed twelve times. It was this, this insignificant moment, that aligned Jade's thoughts. If she were ever going to help her father, Constantine would be the *only* way. Here she would learn to fight, and soon, with patience, she would find the people who had taken him from her, and she would kill them. Yes, once that idea had planted roots in her mind, there was no uncertainty.

Tomorrow, Jade thought decidedly, *I will be one more student at Constantine Academy.*

***

"Welcome!" a stern voice blared.

From where she sat in the colossal hall, Jade could see a tall woman—much taller than normal—stooping over a podium. The woman's hair was cut short, but it was coarse and blonde. Her dark eyes scanned the room sharply.

The woman had a certain unsettling air about her. She had gaunt cheeks and hollow eyes. Her lips were pale, and she wore a long thick cloak that reached past her feet and splayed around her on the floor, held closed at the neck by a single drawstring.

"Please seat yourselves, children. Face this way." She waited for the hustling and bustling noises of shuffling feet to cease.

The assembly hall was like an opera theatre. It was situated somewhere, Jade realized, in the East Tower. It had an upper balcony, a lower balcony, and levitating balconies that hung precariously from the walls where the senior students sat—or at least that's what Justine had called them.

Jade sat in one of the middle rows in the first balcony, and she could see Camilla's back somewhere in the front, giggling about the people on stage. Seated behind the podium were teachers of every age, looking on with admiration.

"*Pssst,*" someone whispered behind her. Jade twirled in her seat and met a familiar face. "Jade, right?" Matt asked, pleased he'd gotten her attention. Jade nodded. "Sleep well?"

Jade shrugged. "Well enough. You?" she asked.

Matt looked over his shoulder suspiciously at Aaron, who sat beside him.

"Sure. My roommate's a bit of a bore, though…how are yours?" She chuckled, stealing a glance at Aaron.

He caught her eye and Jade returned her gaze to Matt as the noise in the hall began to dissipate. "There are three of us in my room."

Matt winced. "It's a hard life."

"Tell me about it." Jade laughed before turning around.

The woman was clearing her throat now, and the room had gone silent. "Welcome, students," she began again, her voice clear and strong. "Here at Constantine Academy, we have a common tradition—one that the older students will know," she said, gesturing to a small group in the audience. Jade heard someone shut the magnificent pair of doors on the right side of the hall. "It is important when we enter this hall—the Grand Assembly Hall—that we show Constantine the respect we feel for her and the institution. The service she paid her country was an act of valor *never* to be forgotten. Every day we must take a moment to recognize this, and celebrate in her name by singing her anthem."

An anthem? Jade thought.

"Ms. Tutts, if you will." She stepped out of the way so a stout, plump woman behind the desk could emerge wearing plum-pink shoes and an unflattering pink overcoat. Jade wondered if this was normal attire, but none of the other teachers looked nearly as silly as she did.

"Repeat after me," she squeaked, her sharp nose pointing as she looked down at the audience. Jade heard Matt and a few of his friends snickering behind her. When the woman opened her mouth, though, the chuckling stopped. Her mesmerizing voice projected into the far-reaching corners of the hall. It was mesmerizing. Jade found herself and others repeating the tune, one by one, until they filled the hall in a way that made her heart flutter with excitement. Their unified voices echoed deep into the wooden floor.

Constantine, I cry for you, tell me where to go.
I depend on you alone, to shine a ray of hope.
In times through which I falter and if ever I despair,
No matter what confronts me, I know that you are there.

I surrender my allegiance to the vision that you sought,
And give my heart to serve those for whom you fought.
As you served courageously those you left behind,
I offer you now and forever my humble peace of mind.

*Your walls share haunted stories and secrets yet
unknown,*
*But your school will be my guide, my eternal, tender
home.*
*We come to you together, with our minds and hearts
unopened.*
*We know that you will guide us; it is us that you have
chosen.*

Constantine, I cry for you, tell me where to go.
I depend on you alone, to shine a ray of hope.
In times through which I falter and if ever I despair
*I see clearly what confronts me, and I know that you
are here.*

The melody was solemn, and the notes a melancholy
echo of a tune, but the room warmed to the words, as
though Constantine had been woken from her sleep and
were rejoicing with them. When they finished, the plump
little woman with the mesmerizing voice cleared her
throat contentedly and returned to her seat.

"Thank you, Ms. Tutts." The stooping woman had
returned. "For those of you musically inclined, Ms. Tutts
will be the orchestra director as usual." She offered a
gentle smile to Ms. Tutts behind her.

"I am Eleanor, your headmistress. You will *all* address me as Lady Eleanor, and I expect you to have the
utmost respect for both myself and my staff." She quickly
introduced the staff. "Every student in this room will be
taking six mandatory courses at Constantine Academy,
six days every week. Saturday, however, you will only
take one two-hour class. Failure to attend lessons will

result in severe punishment. If you cannot make time for Constantine Academy, Constantine will not make time for you." She narrowed her eyes and traced the faces in the room.

"For new students, here are our rules. First, no students should be off school grounds without permission. Breaking this rule will result in immediate expulsion. Second, training will *not* be used to kill fellow students or teachers. Third, the South Tower is *entirely* off-limits. Wandering students there will be questioned critically and punished appropriately." Again she bore down on suspicious faces in the audience.

"Despite the rules we have in place here, we want students to understand that for the next four years, Constantine Academy will be your home, and your fellow boarders will be your family. You will eat, sleep, and learn together, and by the end of your education here, you will have had a prestigious education that is unparalleled anywhere in the Illysium. You will be fighters," she asserted. There was a stunned silence in return, and Lady Eleanor seemed pleased by that. Something white slid past Jade's neck and stopped in front of her.

"If you look before you, you should see a sheet with your name and class on the top. Beneath is your timetable, showing lessons that have been chosen for you based on age, experience, and performance during the entrance exam." Jade was too absorbed in the fact that her paper was levitating to listen to the headmistress. Instead, she tugged the paper out of the air and examined it.

"Looking for the strings?" a voice mocked from beside her. She hadn't realized it, but a pale, scrawny boy about her age with dark eyes and black, straggling hair sat next to her.

"Just enough to tie your mouth shout," Jade answered, turning back to her sheet.

The boy snickered and whispered something to a younger boy sitting next to him. "Mind what you say, or I'll have my father lock you up for life," the scrawny boy said. Jade rolled her eyes, thinking the threat was mostly empty. Then again, as she was rooming with the soon-to-be-duchess of St. Drewicks, she wasn't so sure.

"Students will start lessons an hour late this morning, since some members of staff have not yet arrived. In the meantime the older students will escort you to the dining hall. At ten o'clock you will be taken to your lessons, and promptly at eleven, you will begin your studies here at Constantine Academy." Lady Eleanor pursed her lips, and began giving directions to the older members of the school near the front of the audience. They complied swiftly, and before Jade knew it, she was being shuffled along through the arching halls.

Through the open windows, Jade could see the sunrise, and it reminded her of the afternoon she'd spent with Cynthia. She struggled to suppress the thought. If she were going to train at the Academy, the last burden she needed was to remember all that she'd left behind. She lingered at the open window, where she could feel a cool breeze drifting in. She hadn't been sitting there more than a few minutes when she realized the crowd of students had disappeared into the North Tower. Jade cast her eyes back to the sun, trying to fight back sudden, aching thoughts of how her father had screamed out to her over the phone, then of how he'd lied her all those years and hadn't trusted her with the truth.

She remembered one lie above all the others—the one he'd so passionately convinced her of about the sun. He'd told her it was a chariot that could pull her into the other planets in the solar system, because they all revolved around the same sun. He told her once that her mother lived on the sun, and that during sunrise and sunset, she could see them waving at her. Jade had stopped believing that story long ago, but it was comforting at least to hide behind the facade that her mother was still alive, looking down at her. Madeleine had been sick, though. Jade remembered thin wrists and gaunt cheeks, and hospital beds, but nothing more. She never asked her father for the cause, not because she wasn't curious, but because the truth scared her, and she knew it hurt him. So she held her tongue firmly in place when questions about her mother threatened to surface.

That's how she ended up at the Academy. She always ran from truths she didn't want to hear. She never pressed her father, and this was the price she paid for it.

"What are you?" a voice demanded from behind her. She spun around to find Aaron scrutinizing her.

Jade didn't answer, but watched him climb up onto the windowsill in one step. He leaned toward her and spoke quietly. "Did you live with the humans? In the Division?" Again no answer. He looked concerned and frustrated, searching desperately to elicit a response. "I can tell. You're too plain and your mannerisms are all wrong. If you're not careful to act the part, you'll get yourself in a lot of trouble." He turned from the window and then back to her to see if she was listening. "I don't mean to scare you," he said, his voice low, guarded. "I've just seen it happen before. You'll be here one minute and gone the next. The Oculus doesn't care how old you are."

Jade was motionless. Aaron hopped off the sill, and his eyes caught hers for a moment. She looked at him dumbly, unsure how to respond. He turned on his heel to leave.

"Wait!" Jade burst out, calling after him. He stopped and looked over his shoulder. "You won't...you won't tell?"

A shrewd smile touched his lips, but he shook his head. "Your secret's safe with me," he said, so that his voice barely echoed off the walls. He rounded the corner at the end of the hall and was gone again.

CHAPTER 7

Before Jade could find her way into the dining hall, Justine caught her by the arm. She looked relieved to have found Jade. "I grabbed you a plate," she said over the rumble of students now scurrying past them into the open courtyard. "Sit with us." She led Jade toward a spot in the shade and rushed to introduce her to unfamiliar faces, including Camilla's two tall, lanky friends, Isabelle and Katy. Jade wondered if she would ever be used to Justine's ease. There was something in her voice that was blithe and assertive, and somehow perfectly eloquent.

Starving, Jade hardly said a word herself after being introduced. By the time she had finally scarfed down enough food to quell her hunger, she found herself alone with Justine and the young blonde girl she'd been introduced to once before. She was the same girl who had run past Jade the night before in the common room, chased by a ball. The long braids, the big, watery, green eyes—definitely the same one. Staring at her now, it was hard to imagine that anything so small and slight could pass such a difficult entrance exam. Then Jade remembered that many of the students at Constantine Academy were probably far more talented than she was.

As the first class of students was escorted to lessons, Justine turned to Jade hastily and asked, "What do you have first, Jade?" She peeked over Jade's shoulder at the timetable.

"I don't know…history's secrets?" Jade said.

Justine grinned. "Oooh, I love history. I wish I were in that class. But don't worry, we have loads of others together." She beamed, scooping the rest of the food on her plate into her mouth. "We've got battle strategy next," she added, gesturing to herself and the girl next to her. "Camilla says it's really good. She's not in my class, though—Hey, Matt!" Justine said, her attention flashing toward the entrance of the courtyard.

"You gonna finish that?" Matt asked, hovering over Jade's plate and nodding at Justine. Jade recognized the boy behind him, but Aaron was nowhere to be seen.

She hesitated, shrugged, and handed him an apple. He seemed to stall only momentarily before taking a bite. "You're not trying to poison me, right?" Matt joked, sidling in beside her.

"I guess you'll find out in a couple minutes." Jade laughed.

Matt grinned and then his face became serious again. He lowered his voice as Justine resumed her conversation with the girl next to her. "You know that kid you were talking to this morning?" Jade nodded, remembering how he'd threatened to lock her away. "Apparently, he's Grady Emerson's *son,*" Matt said, arching his brows. The boy who'd been standing behind Matt sat down now. "Sorry, this is Tom Snyder," he said, by way of introduction. Tom was shorter and slightly bigger than Matt, and his hair was dull brown and cropped close against his head. "We grew up together," he added. Jade introduced herself and then turned back to Matt curiously.

"So, who's Brady?" Jade asked, abandoning her food.

"*Grady* Emerson runs the Oculus."

"Oh?" Jade mused.

Matt regarded her skeptically. "You wouldn't happen to have history now, would you?" he asked.

"Yeah, first lesson," she answered, gesturing to her timetable.

"Good. I'll explain it on the way." Jade opened her mouth to say something, but Matt was already pulling her hand. "Tom, you have battle strategy now, right?" Matt asked.

"Yeah...I'll see you in the dorm." He spluttered a farewell to Jade and let Justine coax him into the conversation.

Matt and Jade followed a group of students toward the same lesson. He let go of her hand and gestured for her to follow. "Since you must have been living in some kind of *cave* your whole life"—he laughed, flashing a lighthearted grin—"I'll try to make up for lost time. The Oculus is our government." They were passing unfamiliar hallways now, and Jade hoped Matt knew where they were going. "The Oculus sees everything that happens in the Illysium, because of slaves called Ocumen."

Jade nodded, trying to keep up.

Apparently it was evident on her face, because Matt laughed again. "There are three parts." He held up three fingers and counted them off. "The Division, the Underworld, and us...the Illysium." Jade cringed at the word 'us', as if she'd always been a part of the Illysium, as if she weren't from the Division. "The Ocumen are henchmen, spies, whatever. Whenever someone is in the wrong place, they know about it before anyone else." Matt looked around anxiously. "In the Keeping, the Ocumen can kill you for no reason...or some law that means the same thing."

He led her down a narrow staircase with stone walls on each side, leading to a bland wooden door.

"Let's just say," he said with his hand on the knob, "annoying the guy who might *own* that one day isn't such a great idea." He winked and gestured for her to follow him into the classroom.

Jade returned the smile, but inside she was cringing at the thought that not everything in the Illysium was as magical as she'd once dreamed.

The class was enormous. There were around sixty students in the room, some sitting on the old wooden desks, some levitating precariously in the air, and some with their chairs turned strangely so they could chat with whoever was behind them. Matt waved to someone across the room.

"Hey," he said hurriedly. "See you later?"

"Sure," Jade answered, searching the crowd for a familiar face. It didn't take her long to find one.

Camilla was sitting at the front of the class with Katy and Isabelle. In front of their desk was a small wooden stage and a podium, where Jade imagined the teacher would stand. She wanted mostly to turn to another seat, but she'd already made eye contact, and lumbered over to where Camilla was sitting.

"I wonder what we'll even learn," Katy was saying. "It's not like there's much to teach us that we don't already know. Do you think it'll be hard?" she wondered nervously, twiddling her fingers.

Camilla let out a deep breath. "All classes at Constantine are designed to be rigorous, Katy." Camilla rolled her eyes as though she'd explained it before.

A few seconds later, Jade heard a crack and the sudden shuffling of feet. She didn't turn her head as the teacher stormed down the aisle. All she could hear was the click of his shoes on the floor. There was a loud gasp, and then another one, and more until several heads had turned.

When he reached the podium and dropped open a massive book, Jade saw why. On his right cheek was a red gash tracing from the top of his forehead down to the bottom of his jaw. The fresh wound was healing, but his gray curls parted where the wound reached his hairline, and the shape of his dark eye was distorted.

He ignored the students' faces as he ordered them each to take a textbook and exercise book from the shelves around the room. When they'd settled back into their seats again, he inspected them with a harsh glare.

"How many of you are new to Constantine Academy?" he asked, his voice raspy. A majority put their hands up. "And how many of you know how the Academy got her name? Why is it that we call Constantine *her* and not *it*? And why is it we call her *Constantine* and not *School of Training?*" No one raised a hand. "I thought as much," he said, resting a gloved hand on the podium.

"You there," the teacher said, pointing to Katy. She gulped hard. "Can you guess?"

Katy flushed a deep red. "Er...um...she was named after the...founder?" Katy answered, sliding far down into her seat. Isabelle smirked at her, stifling a laugh.

"Ah!" the teacher proclaimed. "But who was the true founder?" On the chalkboard beside him, he wrote *founder*. Again, no one raised a hand. The teacher sighed. "Not a very imaginative group, are you? The *Oculus* was the original founder of Constantine Academy. Who else? Who founded the Illysium?" No response. He growled. "The *Oculus,* of course. Who founded Utopia after the war?" Again there was a nervous silence as his questions became more and more aggressive. "The *Oculus!* The Oculus built your homes. They built the glorious gates of Utopia, the very principles upon which we each govern ourselves today."

He stepped around the podium and wrote a name on the board in print. *Professor Jackson.* "Today, if you haven't already discovered, I will be teaching you about the history of Constantine Academy. Make yourselves comfortable. This is not a simple tale." He waited for the shuffling and fidgeting to stop.

"Once, there was a young woman named Constantine." He paced the stage, the click of his boots echoing in the silence. "At twenty-five years of age, Constantine became the first woman in the Illysium to join our army. She proved, with time, to be a critical asset to the military, and we often turned to her for strategy, judgment, and magic. It was once said that she alone could cast a charm worthy of a *hundred* men."

Jade watched as several brows shot up.

"The Illysium had been to war often, against the Divisional creatures, but"—he paused until the room was dead silent—"a year later, Gammadorn was seen passing through the Division, and in doing so, he provoked our army to confront him. When he returned to the Underworld, he was angrier than ever before. Two weeks later he declared war against our world."

The students sat riveted. Jade tried to imagine it. How could there exist an entire world, with such a rich history, that she'd never known before now? Had her father known this world? Had he tried to protect her from it? Jade pursed her lips. She was still bitter that James had never confided in her—never trusted her with such a beautiful secret.

"What you may all know is that this war was the only recorded time in history that the Illysium fought the Underworld. What you may *not* know is that while we fought valiantly, we lost millions, and in turn, so did the Underworld. Demons came out in rage against us—vile, rampant creatures that knew no purpose, no sense of conscience. They murdered us at the command of a jealous and spiteful commander: Gammadorn.

"When Constantine offered us a plan to strike out against them, we took it and said 'Godspeed!' as we sent brave men and women onto the battlefields. As a military commander herself, Constantine was a strategic phenomenon. She and a handful of her best soldiers marched into the Underworld and singlehandedly isolated Gammadorn and imprisoned his wife. Here, Constantine made a covenant that would send Gammadorn and his demons back to the Underworld, forever."

Professor Jackson rubbed his jaw, where the red scar still pulsed, and then continued thoughtfully. "What made Constantine brilliant was her understanding of a man no one dared to cross. Gammadorn was capable of emotions that most demons are not. He could walk in human form and speak our language with ease and fluency, and he had a heart—a mind of his own. Gammadorn had married many years before. The capture of his wife gave Constantine boundless manipulation over both him *and* his army. She offered him two options: Either he could keep his wife alive but with a binding curse, or he could accept his wife's death and continue the war. Gammadorn deliberated one year, leaving our world to hang in a balance of fear and hope. When he accepted, Constantine placed a curse that bound Gammadorn *forever* to his wife. But with that, Constantine designed a curse for his wife that was alien even to the most brilliant minds. If his wife ever left the Underworld, she would die in blood, fire, and anguish, thus trapping Gammadorn to the underworld."

Jade swallowed hard, fearful of the rasp in the professor's voice and the dark certainty with which he spoke.

"Gammadorn agreed reluctantly to the treaty. With the war over, and a legacy that would never die, Constantine started this Academy. Once upon a time, she walked these halls. However, five years later she did something that would end her life as she knew it." Professor Jackson paused dramatically, taking position behind the podium again.

"She was found in *alliance* with the Division." There were gasps, and Jade remembered what Aaron had said earlier. She cringed inwardly. "As you all know, the Division is an enemy forbidden and absolute. They're people like you and me...without magic running in their blood, stripped of the great powers of the gods, a world that fights among itself, where they have no common enemy and seek only to reap reward the reward of selfish endeavor. These are humans, invisible half-bloods and faeries. These were the people Constantine befriended. These were the savages she helped to sneak into our world. Some even say she transformed her students into Divisional creatures—using them for repugnant experiments. It's mad, of course, but the line between madness and genius is a thin one, as I've always said.

"Discovering this, the Oculus sentenced her to a lifetime in Quarantine—"

"But, sir!" There was a general unsettling and all eyes turned to Camilla, who had risen in outburst, looking as surprised by herself as the rest of the students. "Can they *do* that? I've never—I thought it was—"

"Impossible? No," he said, boring into her with his dark eyes. "But rare? Oh yes, very rare indeed. Constantine, though, could not be restrained. Before they could send her into that black pit, she escaped three times. The Oculus was left with no choice. They cut her cell out of Quarantine, and they brought it far away into the deserted hills of the Illysium, where she had founded *this* secret institution. Around it, they built a tower so strong that not even *she* could escape. They killed her there, and they smeared her blood across the walls, the doors, and the gates, so that every passerby would see the fate of those who disobeyed the Oculus.

"As time passed, we reopened the school and provided staff to teach. The immortals in the Oculus have kept this school running for millions of years. And yet the mystery of the door remains! How, grounded miles and miles beneath our feet, can Constantine continue to offer young children a door into her madhouse?" He looked around the room slowly.

"They say that Constantine's ghost still walks these halls, and sometimes in the middle of the night, if you listen closely..." He paused, and Jade could feel a cool breeze creeping up her spine. "You can hear her cries for help, and the scream of her murder still echoing against the walls of the South Tower. Her spirit lives on within these walls, though her body is buried far beneath it."

Jade could hear each beat of her heart crashing against her ribs, and the sound of blood gushing through her ears. When the bell rang, several students jumped so high that they toppled their chairs. Even Camilla fell off her seat with a resounding thud.

Professor Jackson raised his voice over the clamor. "I expect full reports next week on the history and role of the Oculus in our foundation! Until tomorrow," he said, saluting them. With a snap of his finger, he was gone, and the students were left to scatter out of the room and race out into the openly lit hallways, where they could only hear the laughter of other children, and not Professor Jackson's scraping voice.

When Jade reached the stairwell Matt had led her down, she looked back only once at the decrepit walls of the classroom. She shuddered and shut the door behind her.

CHAPTER 8

"It's not really Constantine you know." Justine said later, having muttered a quick good-bye to the blonde-haired girl she'd been speaking to earlier. "The Oculus actually controls the entrance exam. That's what I've heard anyway, and all the history books say so. Still, it's a shame I'm not in his class," she mused. "It sounds *incredible*." Jade shrugged as they made their way to the next class.

"So, what was your friend's name again?" Jade asked as she and Justine maneuvered through the halls.

"You mean the one I was just talking to?" Jade nodded. "Christine."

"Oh," Jade said. "She seems sweet."

Justine nodded. "She is. She's two years younger than us, though—thirteen, I think. I'm glad I wasn't recruited that early. It's sad, isn't it?"

Jade shrugged. "If you're good enough, why not?" Justine shrugged, and they stepped into a crowded room. Jade surveyed the scene with wandering eyes. This room was small, compared to the last. The walls and grand arches were made of a fading chestnut wood, and cluttered shelves lined the back wall. They took two seats next to each other and rested their books on the floor.

"Well, well, well. Look who it is," a terribly familiar voice crooned behind them. The boy she'd spoken to earlier in the assembly hall took a seat behind her, and Jade clenched her jaw to stop herself from saying something she'd regret. "I don't think you ever introduced yourself properly," he said, swinging a leg over his desk.

"Jade," she muttered.

"Who are you?" Justine asked, her eyes narrowing.

"Nathan Emerson."

"Oh," Justine said, cowering back to her books, pretending to read through whatever notes she'd made in her last lesson.

"Where exactly are you from, Jade?" he asked, leaning toward her. "Juleria? Recasteria?" Nathan's friends snickered, but Jade ignored him, instead staring blankly at the crowded room.

"Hey! I'm talking to you!" Nathan spat, hurling a wad of paper at the back of Jade's head. She stood now and thrust her chair back into place. He jumped up off the desk and crossed his arms. "What are you going to do?" he asked mockingly.

Jade could feel a familiar anger building up inside her clenched fists. She jutted out her chin.

"Cry?" He laughed, his lips raised into a half smile. The door swung open then, and students hurried to their seats. Nathan turned toward the open door.

"Watch your back, Emerson," she threatened.

"Do you know who I am?" he argued, his voice rising a pitch.

When Jade didn't respond, and sidled into her seat, he growled but did the same, shoving someone else out of the chair angrily.

As with the other classes, there was a small podium at the front, though the stool behind this one was much bigger. The charms teacher was a short, stout woman with enormous heels and red hair. She clambered up onto the stool and still barely surpassed the height of the podium.

"Morning!" she greeted them, flashing a set of crooked teeth too large for her small face. "I think this year's class is going to be one of the best—all so eager to learn," she said gently, clasping her hands together excitedly. She had a drawling, artificial accent that went up and down through too many pitches.

"Must be from Utopia," Justine whispered, leaning toward Jade's ear.

"Now, before you all is a charmed sheet of blank, white paper. This shouldn't really be too difficult, since we've all dealt with charms at some point in our prior educations. Of course, reverse charms are an entirely different species of charm that allows us to strip an object of magic. Obviously it would not work on people, but for all intents and purposes, we won't concern ourselves with that. Firstly, everyone make sure your paper is strong and flexible. Quickly, please." Jade checked it, flipping over the card in her hand and setting it back down. "Now, each sheet of paper is another object, disguised. You will work to undo this charm, to uncover what's *actually* on your desk." She let out a bubbly laugh. "Can anyone tell me the most important part of casting?" Justine threw her hand in the air and flailed it frantically. "Yes, Miss...?"

"Justine Griffin," she answered.

"Go ahead, Miss Griffin."

"Well, I don't know much about reverse spells, but generally you've got to *think* about what you're trying to do, before you complete the charm, and each spell has its own different cast, which depends on how you move your hands, and the direction changes the cast, and also the charm," she said, stopping when she was out of breath.

"Well explained, Miss Griffin." Justine beamed. "Now, this year you'll only have to learn about a hundred and three charms, which will be perfected and tuned over the course of the year. Obviously we have different types of spells—reverse spells, defense spells, offensive spells, elemental spells, and...curses. Of course, you will only be learning the first four this year; the last is for those much more advanced in their studies."

A disappointed groan rippled through the room.

"Now then, to reverse the charm, you should be using this cast." The teacher drew a strange pattern of arrows on the board, and then demonstrated with her own hands. She explained again the process of thinking first and exaggerating the cast, but Jade couldn't help but imagine what a nightmare the next hour would be.

"The first to succeed gets chocolate!" the teacher said. By way of encouragement, she held up a bar. Jade didn't even recognize the brand. There was an anxious shuffling and scooting of chairs, and she reluctantly stood. Jade had never heard about charms and spells until that morning, and she certainly hadn't ever spoken of them in her "prior education." She grimaced as she watched other students enthusiastically waving their hands like complete morons. She wasn't sure if she wanted to burst into tears or laughter. The last time she'd used magic at all was in Cynthia's basement, and that hadn't gone well by any means. Jade sighed, but flexed her hands as if that might help her to cast a charm.

She glanced over at the shape on the board, and tried to remember what the teacher had said. *Think about it first, then do it.* Jade thought it was vague advice, but she did the best she could manage. She tried desperately to imagine stripping the paper of its charm as she rehearsed the shape on the board. When she opened her eyes, it had been to no avail, and she was left to exchange a miserable glance with Justine.

Jade tried again, moving her hands more slowly. She breathed as evenly as possible over the racket people were making in shouts of excitement. As she reached the last stroke of her cast, she felt a shock as she imagined tearing the charm away. It came as a surprise, a volt of electricity running through her arms to her shoulders. Then, the sensation was stronger, clearer. She began to release it—

"I did it!" Justine cried over the noise. "Miss, Miss, I did it!" She pointed eagerly at a book that now lay where her paper had been. It was titled *Constantine's History*.

Jade stared on glumly, wondering if Justine would at least let her use it to write that history report.

"Very good, Miss Griffin. Would you like to explain how you did it…to help the others who are struggling?" Jade was sure the teacher was looking pointedly at her, and wanted to argue she'd been about to do something, but there was no use.

"Well, I did it just like you said," she explained, shrugging. She flicked through the pages of the book eagerly. "I was just saying how much I like history."

"Keep going, everyone, there are still forty minutes left!" the teacher encouraged, ushering them to keep working. Justine carefully unwrapped her bar of chocolate.

Not much more happened in the remainder of the lesson, and Jade was beginning to think she'd used up all the magic she'd had…or had simply imagined it in the first place. "Keep going," Justine would say at random intervals. "Just *feel* it." Between her random, though encouraging, spurts of advice, Justine offered Jade enough chocolate to keep her fed for an eternity. She wondered why the bar hadn't been finished yet, and realized she was talking about chocolate the charms teacher had given them. It reminded her strangely of her father's cups of tea, and she found herself wondering whether or not he'd used magic around her before, quietly hoping she would notice one day.

"Jade, focus," Justine said, sitting up. "You're losing your focus." She offered Jade more chocolate.

Jade groaned. "Justine, it's just not…happening," she said, dropping her limp arms. Most of the students had finished their reverse charms, including Nathan, who voiced his success grandly. As Jade looked around, she realized she was the last person left. The teacher had come over several times to offer help, but her advice was as vague as it had been the first time. *Think first, then do.*

"Two minutes," the teacher yelled, sitting by the podium, looking bored. Jade frowned resentfully.

"Don't get all worked up, bud," Justine said as gently as she could. "Think first, then do." Jade wanted to roll her eyes, but to avoid hurting Justine's feelings, she sighed instead, and returned to her hopeless task.

Jade swung her arms in the familiar motion she'd been doing all lesson and opened her eyes. Nothing. Resisting the urge to scream, she closed her eyes and tried to drown out the sound. *Think, then do. Think, then do. Think...and then do.*

She tried to feel the shock running through her arms and shoulders, and to imagine grabbing the paper and peeling the charm from it. She could feel her own rhythmic pulse, and waited, continuing the motion slowly, carefully, waiting all the while.

There it was.

She felt the sudden jolt of energy, spreading like ice through her veins. *Magic*, she thought. *I've got it!* Jade waited for it to build, knowing the slightest interruption in her thoughts could shatter it. She let it simmer in her hands, on the tips of her fingers. She wondered what would happen if she left it there to grow forever.

"Jade, let go, *now*," Justine whispered as though she were standing by Jade's ear. Jade did as Justine said and opened her eyes. She realized when she did so why Justine's whisper had been so clear. The room was silent.

"Whoa," Justine said, standing up.

Most of the class was gathered around their table. Jade looked down at her hands—red hot and flaming as though she were holding torches against her palm. The fire in them burned and then faded as Jade inspected them. She didn't know much about magic, but she knew enough to know that it was not normal.

"Class is over—you'll find lunch waiting for you in the hall," the teacher squeaked from the edge of the circle that had formed. She seemed as stricken as the rest of them, her eyes wide with a mixture of horror and stupefaction.

Jade swallowed the impulse to ask panicked questions. She grabbed the *Guide to Charms* that now lay on her desk. She didn't dare turn back and was grateful for her sneakers as she hurried away, realizing when it was too late that she didn't know her way. Jade found a bathroom and stopped.

She swung open the door, dropped her book down on the sink, and sighed, splashing her face with water. She turned off the tap and searched blindly for a towel. A cold hand grabbed at her wrist.

"Careful," a quiet voice urged. A towel was placed in her hands, and Jade hurried to dry her eyes so she could open them. "You were about to pull the alarm."

Jade exhaled a sigh of relief. "Hey, Christine." She smiled genuinely.

"Hi. You're Jade, right?" Jade nodded. "Justine says you're her roommate." Christine offered a pleasant farewell and then hurried out into the hallway.

By the time Jade finally found her way to the dining hall, most people were sitting outside in the courtyard. Under the bright afternoon sky, Jade saw that the courtyard was a vast, open space of grass in between the four towers of Constantine Academy. Where she was from, it could have held five houses easily, each with a pleasant backyard. There were outdoor pathways there, and benches, and a small thicket of trees in the corner where ivy curled up the old stone.

"Long time no see." Matt grinned, approaching Jade. "How was charms? I hear you had an *interesting* lesson." He shoveled the food on his tray into his mouth.

"Says who?"

Matt shrugged. "News travels fast around this place."

"Apparently," Jade muttered bitterly. "I don't know what happened...I guess I just went over the top a bit."

"How?"

Jade tried to explain to him as best as possible, though it was difficult to explain something she didn't understand herself. When she finished, they were sitting on a bench, and Matt was looking at her like she'd grown ten feet.

"Scary," he muttered.

"Why?" Jade asked, finishing her food.

"I mean...what do you do next time?"

Jade furrowed her brow, unsure of what exactly he was referring to.

"I mean, when Justine isn't there to tell you to stop? How do you know that when you release it, you're not going to blow something up...or kill someone?"

Jade hadn't thought of it that way. She tried to reassure herself that it didn't matter and that she would never have to use magic again.

"I can't be the only one who can't control it, Matt. There have to be loads of people here who aren't trained enough to control it."

Matt returned a dubious look. "Sure there are. The only difference is that they don't *need* to control it, because the worst they could do is knock a table over." He shook his head and leaned back on the bench. "Hey, everyone has a different level of magic in his blood, but if yours is strong enough for *that*..." He frowned, staring hard into the high sun. "It's weird that your dad never told you."

Jade looked at him for a minute until he met her eyes again. She said, "My dad never told me anything."

CHAPTER 9

J ade's first warcraft class was tedious at best. Matt had fallen asleep at the front of the class, and the only reason Camilla was still awake was because Mr. Reynolds was the youngest of all the teachers, and had dirt-blond hair, blue eyes, and a rough face that Camilla said looked "lovely." Mr. Reynolds had been explaining for the past hour what they would be doing the following year, and didn't seem to take any notice of the class as he continued his lecture to the walls. Jade yawned, and was immensely relieved when the bell rang. She sprang out of her seat before Mr. Reynolds could finish his sentence.

Unsure how she would survive the next three lessons, Jade allowed one of the older students to lead her, along with others, into law. As Aaron had promised, law was in the East Tower, where the assembly hall and Lady Eleanor's office was. The class was held in an enormous courtroom with row upon row of wooden benches. The students took up most of the room, and were told to wait quietly for Lady Eleanor to arrive.

More and more spectators filed obediently into the long rows of wooden benches, and Jade could feel an air of excitement around her. Students were staring in anticipation at the enormous chair in the center of the ornate room. On one side of Jade, Justine fidgeted madly with a mound of scattered notes.

Justine growled, annoyed as Matt shoved through the aisle toward them and squeezed himself between Jade and Camilla. "Aren't you excited?" he asked, spreading his arms behind them on the bench.

"Sure," Camilla yawned. She removed Matt's arm from the bench behind her and roughly placed it back on his lap.

"Sorry." He turned to Camilla. "Whoa, I barely even recognized you," he said, astonished.

Camilla nodded and smiled sarcastically.

"You guys know each other?" Justine asked, raising a brow.

Matt shrugged. "Not personally...but anyone would recognize the Duchess of St. Drewicks." He repressed a smile and raked the hair out of his face. "She's practically a celebrity."

Camilla narrowed her eyes and turned away from him to whisper something to Katy on her other side. Matt sighed.

"We're *together*, Justine," Camilla said, rolling her eyes. "*That's* how he knows me." Justine stuck a tongue out at her when she wasn't looking. Matt grinned.

"Cool. Since when?" Jade asked perkily to ease the tension. Something that looked like misunderstanding flickered across Matt's face, but it was gone before Jade could recognize it.

"Twenty-two hours now," Camilla said.

Matt leaned in close to Jade and whispered, "It's *literally* killing me."

Jade chuckled, but didn't comment, hoping not to get involved in their bizarre love-hate-hate situation.

"Is Lady Eleanor teaching us?" Jade asked Justine, who'd finally sorted through her crumpled sheets. She had a pen and paper out and was scribbling on a leather-bound notepad.

"Well, I wouldn't really call it *teaching*," she said. Jade frowned, and Justine pursed her lips into a line, wondering how she would explain. "I was reading through a book earlier, and apparently we don't formally *learn* anything in law...it's more of an observational class."

"So we watch people debate?"

"Well, Lady Eleanor is on the jury of the Oculus. For the past, let's see, five hundred years, I think—they're all very old," she explained. "Everyone on the jury in the Oculus can practice law independently, and sentence suspects to...punishment."

"Like jail?"

"Sure. The South Tower usually." Justine grimaced. "Sometimes, though rarely, they put people in Quarantine."

"Quarantine? Like they did to Constantine?"

"Yeah...Quarantine is where they put treasonous criminals, escapees from the Underworld, and"—Justine lowered her voice—"people from the Division."

Jade felt her face turn hot. "What do they do to them?"

Justine shrugged. "Who knows? From what I've seen of them in the Keeping, it can't be anything good."

Before Jade could ask another question, Justine gestured for her to be quiet as the hall of students stood. Lady Eleanor clambered up onto the podium and drew her cloak tighter around her bony shoulders. She made a slight gesture with one of her black-gloved hands, and the rest of the hall slipped into the familiar chorus of Constantine's anthem.

Lady Eleanor gestured for them to sit down again, and the hall quieted immediately. Jade noticed a tall woman standing in the corner of the room. She had a vibrant face and dark blue eyes full of stormy seas. Her lips were pursed into a hard line, and she was facing Lady Eleanor. On her back she carried a weapon—a long ivory tusk with a pointed tip and a leather case. The exposed end of the tusk was embedded with something stark and blue that shimmered on its hilt.

Her hair enveloped her face in a fiery red mane, and her pale hands were placed resolutely on her hips. With such striking hair and a slender frame, she reminded Jade of the scarlet red that leaps from rosebushes in spring. Her jaw was soft and snow white. Light freckles danced around her face. Jade couldn't pull her eyes away from the woman. There was something alien about the accusing eye she cast toward Lady Eleanor. Jade wondered what subject she taught.

"Case One, please step up to the stands," Lady Eleanor said, stroking the heavy hammer on her desk. Jade heard the rough rattling of chains and turned back to the center of the room. Only then did she see the men in black trench coats encompassing the main floor. They were each tall and thin, all skin and bones. Their cheeks were gaunt, their skin white like gossamer stretched over their pointed skulls. They were ghostly, with blue veins traversing their translucent skin.

"Disgusting, aren't they?" Matt whispered, looking on resentfully.

"What are they?" Jade asked. Justine nudged her to be quiet, but Matt continued anyway.

"The Ocumen—genetically engineered robots."

"Seriously?" Jade asked, trying to decide whether Matt was being genuine or not.

He shrugged. "That's what they say in the Keeping—who knows where they come from. I used to think they were"—he looked around anxiously to make sure no one was listening—"humans."

Jade pressed her lips together. "What do they do?" she whispered, keeping a close eye on Lady Eleanor.

"Whatever the Oculus asks. They capture prisoners and live underground with them in the Quarantine... or down in the South Tower. They're everywhere," he growled. "They're the ones who took my parents." Matt made a gesture as if to spit at them and sank down into his seat, clenching his fists.

Jade sighed, but understood the feeling. "You'll get your chance," she muttered.

Matt shook his head. "Not soon enough."

"Quiet!" Lady Eleanor boomed over her podium, dropping the hammer three times. Matt and Jade received a scornful glance from Camilla and Justine. In the center of the room, a chained man stood, making a miserable jingling sound as he adjusted the torn clothes hanging loosely around him. His eyes were glazed over as he scanned the anticipating audience mournfully. "Case One, are you aware of why you were called into court today?"

Case One nodded glumly as Lady Eleanor peered down at a long scroll. "In December of last year, you were fined for your alleged relationship with a woman who, to your knowledge, had an immediate half-blood relative. Is that correct?" The man nodded again, his eyes drifting toward the crack of light shining in between the doors. The redhead was still standing there, sympathy etched into the set of her eyebrows. Case One looked straight through her.

"Later the following year, in July, you reportedly were found to have exploited your teaching decree to corrupt the minds of Illysian children through inadequate education of half-blood behavior. Is that so?" she asked, her pale fingers drumming the podium.

Again the man nodded, taking one last look at the door before meeting her eyes.

"Case One, for violation of the fifty-seventh decree, you will be sentenced to seven years in the South Tower of Constantine Academy." Lady Eleanor raised the hammer easily and let it slam down on the wood with a definite clatter.

As the hammer went down, an Ocuman grabbed the prisoner harshly by the arm. The prisoner's rusted chains burned and fell into a shower of ashes as they twisted away into the air and then disappeared altogether. Jade gasped. No lawyer. No jury. No last words. Where was the justice in that? The woman who'd been standing by the door clenched her teeth hard and stormed out, taking long, furious strides. She wrenched open the door. She was gone just as Case Two came up to the podium.

"Case Two, do you have any inquiry regarding your presence here today?" The woman bit her lip, worry creasing her brow. She eyed the Ocumen around her fearfully, seeming to contemplate which would be the one to drag her away. "Case Two, do you have any inquiry regarding your presence here today?" Lady Eleanor repeated more harshly, peering at the prisoner.

Case Two gulped and shook her head. As before, Lady Eleanor turned to her scroll sheet and cleared her throat. "In the summer of this year, you were reported to have *publicly* spoken ill of the Oculus, and even"—Eleanor paused to cast a disdainful look toward the squirming woman—"*conspire* against it by trespassing Chief Court."

"No!" she blurted, her eyes welling with tears. "No, Milady, I—I didn't—I was framed, and I would never, *could* never—"

"*Silence*," Lady Eleanor ordered. The Ocuman standing beside her opened a kind of pocket watch and inspected it carefully, looking from the woman to the watch and back. The entire courtroom was silent as he came to a conclusion.

"What is that?" Jade asked Justine, who was hunched over her notes.

"A telling compass…they scout out the liars."

Lady Eleanor bent over to allow the Ocuman to whisper into her ear. "Do you dare to lie to me?" Lady Eleanor asked, her eyes boring into Case Two.

The prisoner's lips quivered and she shook her head vigorously. "Please, listen to me! I've done bad things, but never have I spoken ill of the Oculus. My family is a respectable one, my father was a duke," she blurted, the words rushing out of her mouth as if she were racing toward the end of the sentence. "We were raised properly, I assure you. Lady Eleanor, you must understand, I never said anything. The Oculus has given me all—it's the air I breathe! I couldn't have known—"

"Case Two, for violation of the ninety-second decree—"

"I have children! Lady Eleanor, I have children, please don't—"

"You are sentenced to—"

"Please! You're a woman, you must understand!" Her voice was hoarse, and she choked through tears smearing her face.

"Seven months in Quarantine." Again the hammer went down with a definite thud that echoed throughout the silent hall. Every mouth in the room dropped open. Even Justine looked up from her notes.

"B-But—Quarantine?" the prisoner whimpered. An Ocuman wrapped an iron-tight fist around her thin arm. She pulled away fiercely, lashing out at him as her face turned red with tears and fright. "I won't survive the first week! You must know that! Oh God, no! Oh, please!"

Jade stood, trying to see over the students in the front row, who were also standing.

"Please." Lady Eleanor gestured to the Ocuman, but Case Two was sprinting away toward the door, her eyes wild with adrenaline and her lips trembling with anticipation. With just a few feet left to the door, she caught her foot on a step and plummeted onto her face. Jade felt her lips harden with rage as the Ocuman laughed.

The Ocuman clambered onto her back, and a knife shimmered in his grip. He threw it down through her chest and silenced the audience as he and his dead prisoner twisted into the air and disappeared.

The students were told to sit down immediately, and Case Three was brought up to the stand. Not one other prisoner was sentenced to Quarantine. Jade was relieved when the students were given permission to leave the courtroom. Lady Eleanor and the Ocumen stayed behind. Something in Eleanor's face had darkened since the first time Jade had seen her; and with the onset of those shadows, the image of this magical world in Jade's dreams had been nightmarishly and now irreversibly plagued by what was nothing short of murder. Jade couldn't help but wonder again if her father had known this cruelty, and if he had, why had he sent her straight into the lion's den?

When the students were finally able to talk again, Jade caught up with Matt. "Do they normally kill prisoners like that?" Jade asked as they approached the North Tower to return to their dorms.

Matt furrowed his brow. "What do you mean?"

"Case Two," Jade reminded him as they turned into the dimly lit lounge in front of the two doors.

"Oh." Matt shrugged. "She's one of the lucky ones," he said. "I'd say that was better than whatever they'd have done to her in Quarantine."

"I guess." Jade shuddered.

"I'll see you at dinner?" Matt said, backing away. Jade nodded and watched him hurry through the door. All Jade could think about was what he'd said. Case Two was *one of the lucky ones*.

She wondered if James had been too.

***

At the Academy, dinner was the most extravagant event of the day. Lady Eleanor took her seat on a brilliant golden throne placed upon a low platform that surveyed the body of students swarming around the hall. The unadorned wooden tables had been draped with white cloth and candles. On either side of Eleanor sat the other teachers, waiting impatiently for her to settle before they could eat.

How transformed the school was at night! The light from the candles warmed every stony surface, and the delight in the faces around Jade trickled onto her own.

The dinner was a loud and jovial one. The conversation never seemed to drift—it was a wire bright with life. The more she spoke to the other students, the more she felt she had no right to be there. They'd all lived in the Illysium their entire lives, and they were all brilliant. They were smart, friendly, and charismatic—a superhuman race that seemed devoid of the imperfection and faults she was so used to in herself.

As Jade watched, Aaron's words resonated in her mind. *You're too plain, and your mannerisms are all wrong.* The people at the table were nothing like her. Their gestures and manners were histrionic, meant for the stage rather than the dinner table. She admired the way they spoke of Constantine, and the stories of their entrance exams. What Matt had said earlier about these students was becoming irrefutably apparent. This school was for the best of the best. Every one of them had gone through the entrance exam, each had made it out alive, and each had been chosen by the best school in their world to represent the Illysium.

"I'll go first then." Camilla giggled, sprinkling a pinch of pepper onto her potatoes. "I opened the door because my parents always encouraged me to come to the Academy. They came here themselves when they were my age, and since I was little, they trained me. Anyway, I'm from Recasteria, so it's only natural I have a place at Constantine Academy." She looked between the faces that stared on at her, and Matt punctured the silence with laughter. Camilla rolled her eyes. "Well, why did *you* open the door?"

Matt spoke through a mouth full of food. "Please, Camilla, I'm from the Keeping." Camilla shrugged, and the others nodded in understanding as if he'd explained it all. "Anyway, this guy got in," he added, gesturing to Tom. "I wasn't going to let him come here without me. He'd never have survived." Tom nudged Matt with his elbow.

"Cut it out, I'm only a year younger," he complained in mock anger.

"Like a baby brother." Matt laughed, bracing against another punch. Jade grinned. There was an ease about Matt that made his laughter contagious.

Justine set her silverware down. "Hey, I'm on Tom's side. From what I remember of the Keeping, you were in my mother's office a hundred times more often than Tom."

Matt erupted from a hold under Tom's arm. "I only had so many injuries trying to protect this nut," he joked. He stopped laughing as Lady Eleanor descended the long passage behind his bench and headed toward the podium. His faced hardened as Tom let go of him, his own eyes trailing Lady Eleanor's gown.

"Why the look?" Camilla said accusingly, once Lady Eleanor had passed them.

Matt shook his head. "Don't you find it weird she's on the jury?" he asked, his eyes fluttering toward Jade as he spoke.

"Why?" Justine asked, when no one answered him.

Matt shrugged indifferently. "I thought the Academy was supposed to be separate from the government. Isn't sovereignty the whole basis of this school?"

He looked to Jade, who was staring at Eleanor curiously. "Or secrecy," she muttered. Aaron leaned forward, his voice low but sharp enough for them all to hear.

"Don't," he warned, "there aren't any secrets here worth the punishment of asking."

Justine nodded in agreement, her eyes lingering on Aaron's stern expression. "Matt, have you already forgotten what the Keeping was like? Let the Oculus do what they want. It's none of our business."

He exchanged a concerned glance with Jade, but before either of them could say anything more, Lady Eleanor stood, her long, black cloak trailing behind her as she moved to the front of the platform. She tapped a glass three times with her silverware, and the clanging echoed in the hall.

The students silenced, and every head turned to her as she rested her glass and silverware back on the table.

"Good evening." Lady Eleanor smiled, her face luminous and pale. "After just one day of education at Constantine Academy, how do you feel?" The students clapped their approval. Lady Eleanor held up a weary hand. "In the day that has passed, teachers have formed impressions, I hope—as have you. There are students in the room who will go on to do brilliant things one day." Matt nudged Tom with his elbow, but then just laughed. "Whether they become soldiers or the next Constantine"—Lady Eleanor gestured to the room—"they live among you as friends, roommates, classmates, and fellow Illysians. Here you can embrace the man or woman you will become. You can understand the strength of your powers and the limitless bounds of your capabilities.

"Having the ability to fight ruthlessly, strategically, and with powerful insight is a quality you will acquire here. With many students already having shown the full capabilities of their magic, we have decided..." She paused, and the room held its breath. Jade thought for a moment that Lady Eleanor was staring at her. "That every new student will be given his or her weapon within the *first* semester."

Justine and Camilla exchanged a look of disbelief.

"And on that note, I will leave you all to return to your respective common rooms as soon as you are done." In a flash, she was gone.

By the time Jade had finally finished eating, she was nearly the last one left in the hall, aside from a scarce few—including Nathan and his two bizarre companions. Jade was anxious to leave. The halls were dimly lit, and when she reached the familiarly engraved wooden door, she saw a figure move in the shadows behind her. She recognized it, but jumped all the same.

"Aaron?" Jade asked, narrowing her eyes. He stepped into the light and ducked his head, bowing curtly.

"Katherine." His voice was gruff and more hoarse than Jade remembered.

"I meant to ask you, is something wrong?" she asked, stepping toward him. Aaron shook his head.

"No, but it's late."

"I didn't see you in law today," she insisted, certain he was lying. Aside from dinner she'd barely seen him at all.

"I was there," he said apathetically. He looked toward the door and then back to her, his eyes unseeing. "I have to go, Kat." He bowed again and before she could ask him another question, he hurried away into the light flooding out of the boys' common room.

The door slammed shut behind him.

CHAPTER 10

The next few days at the Academy passed in the same fashion. First assembly, then breakfast, followed by history with Professor Jackson, who told them stories that seemed more in keeping with adventure novels than history. Then again, Jade supposed that in the Illysium, they were one and the same. This was followed by charms, warcraft, and rather than law, battle strategy and mythology. Somehow, even though she hadn't known Case Two in her first class of law, the woman still reached out to her in all her dreams, choking, gurgling blood, saying, *"You could have helped me! You stood there like a coward! You're not worthy of this school!"*

Lady Eleanor walked the halls all day, and even when she wasn't there, her presence was looming. Jade felt under constant surveillance. The classes were tireless, and charms was a daily struggle. The only prospect that inspired any perseverance in that lesson was that one day she could turn the men who'd taken her father into toadstools…or something.

On her fourth day at Constantine Academy, Jade learned what Mr. Reynolds called a *backhanded rift*. They stood in the courtyard, waiting in wild anticipation to try the maneuver themselves.

"For this exercise, students, watch how you must bend your knees first." He showed them, bending into a steep crouch. "Look straight ahead, back straight." He demonstrated this too. "And flip. Make sure to extend your arm as you come down." He executed an extraordinary flip, hammering down on the unfortunate cardboard box that stood as his victim. The result was a perfect turn in the air, followed by a fist into his opponent's head.

"Now I will let you try, but"—he hastened before they could start—"you must be careful, and if you have questions, ask myself or your peers. You must each get into pairs and help your partner to master this. Understood?" There was general agreement. "Also remember that this grass is charmed. If you fall, you will not be hurt—so don't hold back!" He gestured for them to continue.

What followed was utter chaos. Some succeeded at crouching and maintaining a straight back, but as far as the flip was concerned, most landed on their faces, blubbering like maniacs. Matt was among these few.

"I just…don't know what I'm doing *wrong*." He growled, crouched again, and dusted the grass off his clothes.

Jade laughed. She'd been having a lovely time watching Matt attempt the backhanded rift multiple times. At first she tried to give constructive criticism, such as "don't move so much in the air," or "extend your arm more," but they both agreed she wasn't helpful, so she was removed from her position as coach. When Jade stopped laughing, Matt was back on the ground, his hair madly askew, and he was spitting grass out of his mouth. Jade stifled another bout of laughter.

"Stop, Matt, look around you," she offered. "See what other people are doing and try to imitate them." Matt shook his head. He could see Mr. Reynolds across the courtyard surveying the failure with what looked like either disappointment or pity.

"I've tried that." He sulked, and then with a grin he said, "Besides, you're having way too much fun watching me. Why don't *you* try?"

Jade was afraid he would say this, but he refused her any more time to "supervise." They swapped places and he sat on the bench, apparently exhausted by the lesson.

"C'mon, Jade. Chop, chop," he said, in an attempt to mimic her. "Look at the others, see what they're doing."

Jade laughed, but then stood with her feet shoulder-width apart as Mr. Reynolds had instructed and crouched with a straight back. She counted down in her head and then propelled herself off the grass, which felt like a trampoline when she jumped on it. For a moment she was suspended in the air, but by the time it was necessary to get her feet on the ground, she was still upside down and the greenery came up to meet her face rather than her feet.

There came a quiet chuckle beside her. She seethed.

"I'm sorry. That's really good, just do the same thing *faster*," he encouraged.

Jade sighed. Her wrist was throbbing. She stood again and practiced crouching, then jumping and crouching and jumping. Matt yawned teasingly. "Jade, if I had to do it, so do you—now, *don't hold back!*" he urged, imitating Mr. Reynolds's voice.

Jade laughed. The impersonation was deplorable.

She tried again, preparing herself for humiliation. Out of the corner of her eye, she could see Mr. Reynolds surveying the two of them, who admittedly looked like they weren't sticking to the task. She blamed Matt for making her laugh too much, and told him to stop immediately.

Mr. Reynolds walked over. "How are you two coming along?" he asked.

"Fine," Jade answered, hoping he wouldn't stay long enough to watch her plummet back into the ground.

"Excellent. I saw you practicing earlier. Your technique is superb." He looked at Matt. "Anything you think she could improve on?"

Matt stared back. "Uh," he started. "No. Like you said, her technique is really good." Jade knew this was code for *I have no idea.*

"Well, why don't you try again, and I'll see," Mr. Reynolds said, turning back to Jade. She grimaced.

She stood again, her feet shoulder-width apart, her back straight, and crouched in the position he'd instructed. She looked in front of her at the target—a crushed brown box Matt had landed on several times in his string of attempts. Trying to ignore the eyes on her, she pressed up into the air and imagined she was in water. The floating sensation lasted only a brief minute, and when she opened her eyes, she was miraculously standing with her feet shoulder-width apart on the box.

Mr. Reynolds considered her momentarily. "Well done," he finally decided. "Katherine, right?" he asked, peering down at his roster of students.

"I prefer Jade," she answered.

"Mmm. Well done, Jade. You're doing very well." He noted something on his clipboard and walked away to help the other struggling students. Jade turned to find Matt wide-eyed.

"Okay…now how do *I* do that?"

As the week passed, Jade became sure this was by far her strongest subject. It was simple enough. She mastered most of what he taught them in the lesson. Once she'd learned the first flip, the others were easier, and she found a passion for jumping and turning, and—though she would never have admitted it to her father—fighting. Progress in other lessons was slow, and in the case of charms—nonexistent. The teacher was continually frustrated with her, either for not putting in enough effort, or for putting in too much and destroying what the teacher referred to as "valuable and historical furniture." Really, it was the same desk over and over again. After the second time, it wasn't *that* valuable.

The winter that came was a bitter one, and the warm, cradling winds of fall quickly spiraled into the gales that come and go with the cold. Inside the Academy, the halls were charmed, and the weather seemed to have little effect on Constantine's ever-nurturing hold on them. No matter the weather, nothing could dampen their spirits— everyone knew why they were there, and that thought elated them. *We are the best of the best—warriors of the*

Illysium, they would say at dinner. In fact, if it suited them, they would say it anytime of the day, and nobody could deny them the right to shout it right into the heavens, because as far as anyone in the Illysium was concerned, it was true. Constantine had declared it so.

Nevertheless, as time drew on, Jade found herself lying more and more often to deter people from associating her with the Division. Aaron's words hovered in her thoughts. *You'll be here one minute and gone the next.* She imitated their actions and gestures, sneaking into the library to read more about the place she pretended to come from—this place called Juleria in the northern region of the Illysium, otherwise known as the Keeping. Her roommates were valuable resources.

From what Camilla and Justine had described to her, Jade had sculpted a detailed view in her mind. The Illysium, according to Camilla, was like a perfect bubble. The Oculus had held everything in exact balance since the Illysium's battle against the Underworld. With the help of Ocumen, no one without magic blood came in or out of the Illysium. Ever. That left them with a pure society—no half-bloods, no lying, no demons, and absolutely *none* of the Division.

They were born to be perfectionists. Everyone had a place in the society. There were only two classes: the upper class, which was made up of the Coastal Estate families, and the working class, or the Keeping. The Keeping, from what Jade understood of it, was everyone else. Camilla had explained vehemently, looking snidely at Justine, that the two classes hardly ever mixed, and for good reason. Justine didn't seem to take the comment lightly, and retaliated by casting a charm that taped Camilla's mouth shut for the rest of the evening. Jade made Justine teach her that one.

According to Justine, there was a darker side of the Illysium that you wouldn't see unless you were part of it. She was. The Keeping was a laboring class that worked morning until night to do whatever was needed to support the Illysium. Usually that meant that any man over the age of twelve began in the construction industry, joined the military, or otherwise worked for the Oculus. Women were sent to do everything else, and only those who were chosen could join the military. Justine had followed her mother into the nursing business until her parents disappeared.

They weren't paid for their work with money, but at morning and evening, the Oculus delivered meals to their houses in white packages, and offered books to those who could afford time to study—which were few.

Throughout her days, Jade had to force herself to remember her purpose there. She gave her absolute best to every task, knowing that one day she would seek revenge, and when the time came, she would be absolutely, undeniably ready. She would be a true *warrior of the Illysium.*

One night, after Camilla had fallen asleep listening to Justine, Jade remained awake, riveted.

"…My mother was just the same," Justine was saying, leaning on an elbow so she could see Jade's face in the light of the lamp. "She worked as a nurse her entire life, and she was the *best.* There wasn't anyone else in the Keeping who could fix a person up like she could."

"So…what happened?" Jade whispered.

"Well, that afternoon there was a boy in the Keeping who had stolen the food from the Oculus's quarters. It was three streets down from where my mother and I worked. It was a field with a chain fence around it, and it was filled with food—all kinds of meats and pastries and little packets for the rest of the Keeping. He took a packet to eat that night—"

"Did they catch him?"

Justine nodded solemnly. "He was halfway home when he got caught. They took him to his parents and killed the lot of them on the spot."

Jade gasped. It was like something out of a nightmare. "With what?"

"A pillager. Took the life right out of them, but they fought to the death. That's what people are like in the Keeping, huh? Especially if they've got nothing else to lose." Her eyes simmered for a moment and then she lay on her back again. "That Ocuman came up to my mother's door, and we thought we were in for it. Then we saw he was bleeding through his uniform, and he told her to fix his wound so he could get on."

Justine paused dramatically. "My mom looked him dead in the eye and said, 'I'll help you when you stop killing these people.' And by God, she meant it. She bolted the door. I think he must have died there. I don't remember."

"And that's why they took your parents?" Jade asked, awed.

"That's what I think," Justine whispered so darkly that it almost sent shivers through Jade's spine. She went to sleep that night with terrible visions of the Keeping.

Never had she imagined such a black world. Even in her sleep, her mind could never conjure the horror of lifeless faces, of hunger by evening and death by the morning sun.

***

It was the last week of winter, and Jade woke up to an earsplitting screech.

"Wake up, wake up!" Justine shook Camilla and Jade eagerly. "We're getting our weapons today!"

At that reminder Camilla sprang out of bed. Jade, however, rolled over, burying her head deeper into her pillow.

"I'm probably going to get one of those diamond swords with a golden hilt," Camilla said.

Justine scoffed. "You wish. There's no way to predict your weapon, Camilla. Professor Jackson said Constantine chooses."

Camilla rolled her eyes. "Stop with that nonsense. I've heard his stories. I'm in his class. The *Oculus* chooses. The Oculus controls who gets in here, and they choose your weapons. The story about Constantine is just that—a story to make us feel more special than we already are. Constantine doesn't *exist,* Justine. Anyway, most of the Upper Estate owners have swords or shields. My mother had a dagger."

"Good for her," Justine muttered, shutting the bathroom door.

"She wouldn't know anything about that, you know," Camilla said to Jade. "Between you and me, Justine may be smart, but she's still from the *Keeping.*"

Jade abandoned her attempt to sleep and sat up, rubbing the exhaustion from her weary eyes. "So am I," she lied, slipping out of bed and grabbing a bundle of clothes from her bag.

"Oh." Camilla laughed. "But you're so much *smarter*, Jade—sometimes I forget," she answered, perfecting her hair in the mirror. Camilla flipped it melodramatically and tied it in a complex bun. "Here, this sweater will do that outfit some good."

Jade eyed it suspiciously and then smiled halfheartedly. "Thanks."

"Sure."

When Justine erupted out of the bathroom, Camilla hurried in.

"Good company, isn't she?" Justine chuckled.

Jade shrugged. "I guess you have to get used to it."

When the three of them were finally dressed, they hurried downstairs into the common room.

"Justine, Jade!" Jade recognized Christine's timid voice through the crowded room. Together the three of them scurried away into the assembly hall.

"I'd better get something good," Tom said to Matt, who had fallen into step with Jade and Camilla. They all threaded through the crowd toward a row of seats. Before long, the gathering of students was singing the school anthem with more excitement than they ever had before.

"Good morning!" Lady Eleanor greeted them, spreading her arms wide under her cloak in a gesture of welcome.

Jade caught a glimpse of Aaron in the front row, slumped down in his seat, looking bored. As if by some instinctive compulsion, he turned as if feeling the weight of her stare on the back of his head. He caught her eyes and she offered a guilty smile. She thought he returned it, but before she could be sure, he'd turned away again.

"As promised," Lady Eleanor began, "we have arranged the necessary schedule to help the Academy deliver to you the most appropriate weapons. Understand that these will be your training weapons for the next year at Constantine Academy. Many advanced students will go on to not need their weapons. Every weapon that is delivered will be in keeping with your skill. By skill, I mean your *natural* ability. Do you understand?" There was general consent throughout the room. "Within the next few weeks, you will be expected to practice using your weapon in *and* out of lessons. It will not be part of the curriculum at Constantine Academy, though all graduates are called upon to use these weapons at some point in their later lives. You will carry your weapon with you *everywhere*. Without your weapon, you're naked."

Jade heard Matt snickering. "Put some clothes on, man," he whispered to Tom. Jade felt a smile pass her lips, but it died with the anxiety she felt.

"You are vulnerable to every attack imaginable without the weapon you receive today. Again, think of your weapon as your armor, and the school grounds as a battlefield. Without your weapon, you die."

One of the teachers brought a stool to center stage and bowed to Lady Eleanor, scurrying back to his seat again behind the enormous table. In front of the stool, another teacher procured a short desk draped with white cloth.

"Will Amelia Argot please come up?" A short young girl with ginger hair and thick freckles walked up to the stage, an expression of petrifaction on her face. "Sit, child," Lady Eleanor ordered, pointing her finger toward the stool. The young girl sat hesitantly. "Place your hands on the table." She did so obediently. The table began shaking slowly, and then more and more violently, until it was jumping sporadically off the floor.

As if the weapon were hatching, it popped out of the fabric. The table shivered once, only to remain still again. On the table stood an enormous pocket watch with thick numbers around the side and a silver face. "And so you have your weapon." Amelia Argot beamed and scampered off the stage, clutching it gingerly in her small hands.

"I've seen those before. You can do all sorts of things with them—" Matt started.

"Shut up," Camilla urged, digging her elbow into his ribs. He laughed and returned his focus to the stage. Ten minutes later Jade recognized a name.

"Aaron Henderson, please step up to the stage." He stood and shoved his hands into his pockets. As with the other students, Lady Eleanor repeated the instructions. Aaron's face was unreadable. The table shook slightly, and as calmly as if he'd simply plucked it from within the fabric, a long, double-edged sword in a thick, black leather sheath and a dazzling stone resembling sapphire in the hilt materialized before him. Aaron grinned, holding the sword so as to inspect the thin blade before his face. He slung the sheath into the belt at his hip.

"I told you." Camilla sneered at Justine, joining in the applause. Jade smiled and clapped, still dreading the moment she knew would come for her soon. The next name Jade recognized was Camilla Holt, who flashed a brilliant smile and stood, walking pompously up to the stage, where Lady Eleanor waited for her. Camilla blew out a deep breath. She waited a few seconds before placing her hands on the cloth. The table jittered and then bumped up off the floor. At last, a black whip of braided leather shot up from the fabric and dropped, coiling perfectly before her. Camilla's face fell with disappointment.

"You cannot always have what you want," Lady Eleanor whispered to her as she stood and walked with as much dignity as she could manage back to her seat. Jade offered a sympathetic smile as Camilla slapped the whip down between them and turned back to the stage in disgust. Justine was called up soon after to receive what appeared to Jade to be a small wooden flute about the size of her forearm. It was unadorned, plain, dark wood, with a ribbon of red and gold tied onto the end.

"Do you play the flute?" Matt asked when she returned from the stage. Justine shook her head, nonplussed. Matt's face turned to stone when Lady Eleanor called his name. Jade gave him a thumbs-up, and he took a deep breath.

There was only silence as he stumbled up to the stage and dropped his hands on the table. The fabric fluttered excitedly, and Matt held his breath. When the table finally stopped shaking, there was nothing there. Matt clenched his jaw, his face turning a shade of red. He jumped back as the table hopped once more and presented a bow and a quiver of a dozen arrows. He heaved a sigh of relief and received thunderous applause from the audience.

"Why do they clap for some and not others?" Jade asked Justine over the ovation.

She shrugged. "I guess some gifts are just better... like Aaron's weapon." Inexplicably, the comment irritated Jade.

Jade was one of the last to be called up. She'd remained as placid as she could throughout the assembly, but as she walked up to the stage, she felt her heart thrashing in her chest.

She walked slowly up to the table, pressing her hands smoothly to the cotton covering. She waited for the table to move, and noticed how close Lady Eleanor stood— close enough for Jade to feel cold breath down her neck.

The hall of students waited for so long that Jade wanted to crawl up into a corner and cry. She didn't dare meet Aaron's eyes, though he was near enough to the front that it was difficult for her to avoid it. At the back of the room, Matt cleared his throat. The silence was infinite and overwhelming. Jade willed the table to move, to stir or tremble. The table would not budge. She considered knocking it over herself and pretending to procure something from it, but Lady Eleanor was already tugging her away.

"Perhaps another time," Lady Eleanor said gently, resting a gloved hand on Jade's shoulder. Jade thought her cheeks might have flamed red if she hadn't been so stunned. Wasn't she as magic as the rest of them? Didn't she deserve a weapon as much as any of the others?

Just as Jade was preparing to walk back to her seat, bitter and empty-handed, the table quivered in front of her, and the fabric billowed slightly. *Maybe it was wind,* Jade thought hopelessly. Lady Eleanor stepped back. The table continued to shake, more and more, until Jade was sure it would never stop. The more it shook, the more violent it became. Just as she'd seen earlier, the table began skipping up off the floor excitedly.

"Jade, step back," Lady Eleanor demanded. Jade scooted her chair back, and the table began darting wildly in the air, until it fell still again. The fabric was soiled, and the legs were cracked from the fall. The table had toppled over on its side, and sitting just in front of it was a small box. Jade looked quickly into Aaron's stoic gaze before she rounded the table. She crouched to pick it up. The hall of students waited, peering forward in their seats to catch a glimpse. The box was metallic and fit comfortably in Jade's palm. There was a latch on the side, and she opened it excitedly, her breath quick with apprehension.

Jade pulled out a match. One, then two, and three and four—there was nothing but steel matches in the box. Now she could feel her face turn hot, and someone in the audience laughed. It sounded like Nathan, and it rippled through the hall until every face in the front row but one was lit with mockery. Jade clenched her jaw and furiously walked back to her seat.

"Don't be upset, Jade," Matt urged, leaning behind Camilla to speak. "The weapon doesn't make the warrior."

Jade's first instinct was a sardonic reply, but she smiled meagerly instead, wanting desperately to disappear.

A thought occurred to Jade then, that her father had probably gone through the same thing if he'd been to the Academy. Of course, he most likely didn't have to endure the sneering that Jade had so dolefully suffered.

He'd surely gotten an elaborate sword like Aaron had, or a bow and arrows like Matt. Maybe he'd even received a telling compass like Tom had. Either way, Jade didn't want to imagine the devastated look on James's face if he ever laid eyes on her weapon. She placed the box in her pocket and felt something cold and wet slide down her cheek.

CHAPTER 11

att looked up from his page. Jade's face was flat as stone, her brow furrowed as her pen scratched over the paper. She had an elegant manner that entranced Matt. His jacket was draped over her knees, and her head was bowed under the dim light so all he could see of her was black hair as smooth as silk, and the shine of her locket swinging back and forth at her neck. She propped her sheet up against her knees, which were drawn to her chest. Since they'd received their weapons, she'd hardly spoken.

Determined to remedy this, Matt sat up. "Pass it here," he said. He'd been leaning on two legs of his chair and now lurched forward. He set down the book in his hand—*The Old War: How the Oculus Came to Be.*

He and Jade had gone down to the library to complete Professor Jackson's endless reel of homework, but as yet they'd only finished the first essay.

Jade looked up gloomily from the sheets of paper scattered around her and tossed him her matchbox. He swept the hair from his eyes and inspected it, twisting it around in his hands as if to catch it at every angle. "You're upset because you don't think it does anything special." Matt said plainly, looking toward her.

"I never said that."

"You don't have to." He pursed his lips and dragged his chair next to Jade's. If he leaned forward, he could see the color violet glimmering in her eyes. He looked back down to the matchbox and whispered teasingly.

"You want me to tell you a secret?"

Jade couldn't help but to roll her eyes, even though a smile was playing at her lips.

"It's not funny, Matt," she moaned, taking it back from him when he started laughing.

"Wait!" he protested. "I wasn't finished!" Matt snatched the box back out of her hands and grinned sheepishly. Jade tilted her head and waited. Matt pointed to the edge. "You see this?" he asked, tracing his rough finger around the lid. The metal box was made of little engravings that twisted like vine and left fine holes so that you could almost see through it. Jade nodded.

"Put your hand on top like this." He grabbed her fingers. After a moment of silence, he shook her hand and the box violently, and a striking white light shone from under his hand, and then disappeared. "Voilà. Now it's magic." Jade raised a brow.

"We learned that charm last week," she said with a kind of exasperation. She made the same light in her own fist, but admittedly, it was much dimmer.

"Oh, c'mon, Jade." He held up the box between them. "You can't be so down about it. Look." He paused for a minute. "It just has to know what you want it to do. Ms. Tutts told Tom that the weapon starts to work well once it *feels* needed." He put on a kind of pitiful face. "You just have to nurture it."

Jade laughed, but only at the absurdity of his ideas. "Really?"

Matt nodded firmly, but then he was serious again. "Just give it time." He shrugged, and handed it back to her. She didn't really believe him, but gave him a smile anyway. It was strange how he could always coax one out of her.

Slowly, Jade found herself melding into the student body despite her horrific weapon. If there was one thing she loved about the Academy, it was consistency. Every morning they had breakfast, then assembly, then two more lessons and lunch. Usually it was around this time that she saw Matt and Justine, and, on occasion, Tom.

It wasn't difficult for Jade to imagine Matt working on the fields in the Keeping, cultivating what he called jodnobbers. Jodnobbers were small, modified animals that grew underground. In the summer and spring, they would uproot themselves one at a time, like eggs hatching, only to be reared, hunted, and sold to important places in Utopia.

Unlike Tom, who was long and gangly, Matt was tall, and he had an athletic build that he claimed once to be the only good thing the Oculus ever gave him. He never made such comments in public, and when Jade asked why, he clenched his jaw.

"That's why they took my parents," he would say. Ever since, Jade let him talk to his heart's content. It was dull, admittedly, but she'd rather him tell her than be dragged away for telling anyone else.

He was partway through one of these long-winded complaints when the clock in the dining hall struck for dinner to be served. Justine came rushing over from somewhere in the courtyard and sat down in front of them. "Where were you?" Jade asked.

"Choir." Justine shrugged. "Ms. Tutts seems to think I've got a real knack for music."

"Do you?" Matt asked, staring impatiently at his still empty plate.

Justine chuckled. "It might explain this." She withdrew her flute from within her bag.

"Play us a tune then," he said more enthusiastically now that the food had arrived.

"I can't indoors. It's too loud."

"Will you after dinner?" Jade asked.

Justine nodded, her mouth full. "If you want."

The dinner was among the best so far. Matt must have said so at least seven times. The meat was grilled tenderly, and its rich scent filled the hall. When they'd finished, they walked around the Academy's enormous courtyard. When it emptied later in the evening, and the sun had gone down, they took a seat on a bench beside the trees.

"I'm surprised you didn't eat the napkin too." Jade laughed, having watched Matt devour a whole serving of meat and then three servings of chocolate truffles.

He grinned, patting his stomach as if to console it. "I've gotta make up for lost time." His eyes darted warily toward Justine, but she was nodding.

"Tell me about it. You know in the Keeping, nurses only get four bars and a basket of wheat?"

"Even your mother?" Matt asked, relaxing a little. He could vaguely remember Justine's mother from a long time ago. "Didn't she work twenty-one hours?"

Justine nodded. "Twenty-eight, if you include double shifts."

Matt heaved a long breath. "That's rough." Then he remembered. "Hey, weren't you going to show us your flute?"

Justine winced, but took it out. "It doesn't really do anything."

She waited for Jade and Matt to sit down on the bench facing her. Jade took a seat and scooted over for Matt. He pretended not to see her and sat down right on top of her.

"Hey!" Jade laughed, shoving him off her lap.

He straightened up again and feigned a Utopian accent. "Ignore her, Justine, she's incredibly rude—"

Jade elbowed him in the side and hushed him as Justine raised the flute to her lips.

The music was beautiful. It started at one note. It was quiet, timid, touching Jade's ear and cradling it, holding it, then it vanished as Justine took a breath. Before Jade could notice the pause, another note had returned and then another as if the first note had invited millions of others, even more beautiful, to take its place and dance in its stead. Jade's ear fed on it, craved it until the passing notes came and went and flourished into music.

The feeling was magical. It soaked into her ears and seemed to quench a thirst Jade had never felt before now. She followed the music up and down into the night with angst. She watched in a kind of silent stupor as Justine's hands glided over the instrument. It beckoned to Jade. *Here*, it said. *I'll take you somewhere*. The music resonated in the courtyard. It commanded the attention of every nerve in Jade's body. She could feel herself tense for the crushing end. It was a jarring, staggering melody that seemed too intricate and too beautiful to come from a single instrument. It might have brought the sky to its feet as all the stars in the turned to find the source of this mystic tune.

It took Jade into a warm place, where there was a lit hearth and a nutcracker and a family sitting around a dinner table and snow falling through the window. The music came clearly, but softly, like padded footsteps on a woolen carpet, James sitting in an armchair. The swift notes pattered in the air like snowflakes on the eve of winter. And then they melted away and gathered like ribbon falling on the floor, sweeping through the air—

It was gone just as it had come. Jade was at a loss for words. Where the night had once danced against the music, there was nothing but dull silence, a blunt, hideous echo of something magnificent.

"Whoa," Matt muttered. His smile from moments ago had vanished.

For Jade it had been so vivid, not just the music, but also the image, the people, the warm carpet underneath her. Her father.

"Justine, you're…" Jade paused. There was no way to describe it. It had been a trance out of a half-remembered dream. "You're *incredible.* Have you ever played it around anyone else before?" Justine shook her head, stuffing it back into her bag unceremoniously. "That's why you don't know what it does," Jade said, exasperated. "It's…it must hypnotize or something, I've never—"

"It's a spangler," Matt corrected.

"A what?" Jade asked.

"You know, it makes you see things, coloring the real world with things that aren't there."

"Do you think?" Justine asked excitedly, pulling it out again. They went on like that for the rest of the night, wondering what it had done to them and what they had seen. Jade couldn't help but feel a pang of envy. The pathetic box of matches in her pocket seemed to weigh a ton on her way back to the dorm.

Usually, having hurtled into the evening, Jade would return to her room, study, and then hurry to dinner, which had slowly become the epitome of her weekdays. Sundays were what the staff at the Academy called "catch-up day," and what everyone else called "extra school."

Although Constantine Academy was unlike any school Jade had ever dreamed of, it was still a boarding school, and as such, the teachers were always there. During the weekends seminars were held, which Justine adamantly dragged Jade along to. Both Justine and Christine had ardent passions for their education, a quality Jade would much rather have admired from a distance. Nevertheless, she was comforted at least that the tedious hours rarely went to waste, and her performance had risen to a level that, at the very least, was not profoundly humiliating.

When the snowfields of winter melted away, and spring grasses took their place, Jade had almost come to a level of competency in charms and had mastered four flips and the backhanded rift in battle strategy. Mr. Reynolds had expressed the ultimate commendation.

Week after week it was the balance beam, then the rope, then flips. Jade had conquered most, and at the height of it all, she marveled at how far she could go, how her body seemed to soar of its own brilliant accord. The room would spiral past her in a blur, and then she would land again on her feet with a kind of invincible pride, because no one, not even at this magnificent school, could match her.

On Sundays they were given leave to relax. Other than mealtimes, students were free to roam the Academy's endlessly winding hallways—except the South Tower, which was irrefutably and undeniably off-limits.

Consequentially, with nothing rebellious to do *inside* the Academy, most gathered in the courtyard, mingled in the abandoned classrooms or practiced their craft in the garden surrounding the North Tower. Eventually, Jade came to know everyone by face, and her roommates— or at the very least, Justine—had proven not only good company, but also good friends. Jade had doubted at first the ability of two such different characters to meet on a common ground, but they had at least established an ever-increasing tolerance for each other.

Having thus far had a reasonably uninterrupted few semesters at Constantine Academy, Jade hadn't expected in the least the events that took place next. It was a Monday afternoon in spring when the rumors first began to circulate.

"Have you heard?" Camilla asked, rushing into the dorm. Jade didn't answer, she was poring over a book she'd rented from the library, *Why the Oculus Was Established: World Peace and the Eternal Illysium.*

"What about?" Justine asked, her head hanging upside down from the bed as she popped the last of the dessert she'd salvaged from dinner into her mouth.

Camilla rolled her eyes. "Only what the whole *school* is talking about—Constantine might be back!"

Both Jade and Justine sat bolt upright. Constantine was dead. Declared by the Oculus as long ago defeated, caged for her experimental works on students she'd once taught. She was a martyr now and nothing more.

"How can you say that?" Jade asked, shuffling to the front of her mattress. "She's been dead for *millions* of years!"

"Who says?" asked Justine, equally incredulous.

Camilla smacked her lips after applying a thick layer of gloss. "*I* heard from Katy, who'd heard from Isabelle, who *saw* that somebody wrote it on the wall in the courtyard…in *red,*" she added dramatically.

"Is it still there?" Jade asked as the clock struck eight.

Camilla nodded. "I can show it to you." She hurried to lead them back down the steps of the common room. They walked out into the night in their bare feet and pajamas. "There," she said, pointing. Through the darkness Jade saw a growing swarm of students crowding around the farthest wall of the courtyard. Written next to the South Tower in blood red was, "I'm back. Welcome to my madhouse."

Admittedly, Jade felt goose bumps on her arms and legs when she read it, but she blamed it on the wind. She jumped a foot in the air when Matt poked her shoulder from behind.

"Can you believe that?" he asked, addressing the three of them.

For the first time in a few weeks, Jade saw Aaron standing close beside him. He was staring at the wall darkly, his hands shoved into his pockets, concern etched into the weary lines of his face. He turned to Jade for her response.

"It *seems* unlikely…but it wouldn't be the first time Constantine has taken someone by surprise."

Camilla scoffed. "*I* would mind very much—she was a madwoman driven insane by her own practices. If she tried to turn me into a human, or some other gross Divisional creature, I would be *mortified*."

Jade nodded in mock agreement. She could lie now without even flinching.

"Maybe it's a prank," Matt said as the body of students began to disperse.

Within a few minutes, Ms. Tutts hurried them back into their separate common grounds, ordering them to go quickly before Lady Eleanor reprimanded them. However, even Jade couldn't help but linger and watch the fresh dye drip down the wall.

Prank or not, the words evoked an eerie atmosphere, and at noon the next day, it was silently agreed that everyone would eat in the hall instead of the courtyard. Oddly, for some time after, the words remained— deep scarlet. The staff washed and scrubbed the walls feverishly, yet the writing remained, dripping, as though it were bleeding from Constantine's wall. The harder they scrubbed, the faster it ran—the deeper the wound. The writing disappeared arbitrarily a week later, and it seemed that the entire student body had seen it twice first-hand.

"Silence!" Lady Eleanor commanded some mornings later. She ordered them to follow Ms. Tutts in a brief singing of the anthem, but the noise resumed as soon as the song had run its course.

"Students!" Lady Eleanor yelled again, her eyes scanning the room angrily. "In light of recent events, I understand there is concern among you," she began. "I respect your fear, but I also ask that until we discover the root of events, please do not speak of this among yourselves, and even more importantly, among those who do not attend Constantine Academy. I will *not* repeat this!" she said firmly. The hall was quiet enough that she could have whispered it. "The Oculus was alerted of these events last night, and will have the utmost involvement in this investigation. Until I can shed some more light on it, students who choose to discuss it will be *heavily* punished." With those last words, she dismissed them all and hurried away.

Since Professor Jackson had been called away into Lady Eleanor's office for an expert opinion on the matters at hand, the first lesson passed in tedium. When it was finally time for battle strategy, Mr. Reynolds warned them all that they would be engaging in a new type of strategy today. He pointed first at Nathan. "Would you like to start off? I'm sure your father has given you plenty of training in the area of black magic, yes?"

Nathan smirked. "Only the best for the best." He clambered up onto the long, shallow platform, now bathed in the red-pink sun of the afternoon.

"I thought so. Choose your opponent wisely." He let the class form a tangled ring around Nathan.

"If he chooses me, I'll be so angry," Justine muttered to Jade, who chuckled, but couldn't agree more.

Nathan scanned the room, smacking his lips. "I choose…" He closed his eyes and let his finger guide him. It landed dead on Jade's face. "Jade."

"Your eyes were open," she growled accusingly.

Mr. Reynolds grinned. "Now, now, Nathan. Why don't you choose someone different…like this young man?" he suggested, patting Matt's shoulder. Matt looked up, alarmed.

"It's fine," Jade insisted, judging how Matt would fare against Nathan.

"As you wish." Mr. Reynolds waited for her to stand before Nathan on the stone platform. "Rules first, though." He stood between them. "There will be *no* weapon use, *no* maiming, and absolutely *no* killing." Mr. Reynolds looked between them suspiciously and then stepped back into the ring around them. "Three, two, one."

Nathan fired something at Jade too fast for her to acknowledge the flick of his hand.

She ducked swiftly, rolling out of the way as another small, stinging, incandescent orb shot at her. "Jade, fire something!" Justine yelled, her face tight with dread. This was beginning to feel like a charms lesson.

Like what? Jade wanted to yell back, she could feel adrenaline drumming through her veins and wished she could walk up to him and give him a good punch in the gut like she'd done with others far heavier than Nathan.

Jade found herself dodging a red bolt this time. She scrambled to her feet. Finally, when her breath was fast from running, and Nathan's face was red from laughter, Jade stopped dead in her tracks. She knew she could fire something at him, the only question was *how*...and *what*? She pursed her lips into a hard line.

"This is fun, Jade, don't stop. Really," Nathan said through his laughter.

Something hot burned in Jade's fingers and she tried to will it through, her hands trembling with the heat. She didn't dare look at them, because she knew the sight of them would stop her. Nathan backed away, letting a silvery sphere grow in his hands until it covered his face. Jade didn't move, desperate not to descend back into her magical void.

As the warmth flared in her shaking hands, Nathan withdrew farther, until his heels had reached the end of the platform. His hands jerked, and he released the mounting charm, striking Jade squarely in the chest. He knocked the breath and the heat from her. She fell to the floor, and her vision blurred through tears.

"Out of line!" Matt roared. Mr. Reynolds didn't move, his eyes flashing between Jade on the floor and Nathan. Jade pushed herself up onto all fours, holding her breath to stop her head from spinning.

"Stand up!" Nathan bellowed, approaching again. Jade glowered. She stood, swaying on her feet, resentful. She gathered her strength again and let a boiling, fiery sensation build in her hands. There was something shining in the corner of her eyes—were those her fingers? Jade waited and waited as patiently as she dared.

Whatever was happening silenced Nathan, and his spinning refulgent orb flickered and died. Jade could feel the tension in her hands stretched like a rubber band.

"That's enough," Mr. Reynolds said smoothly. Except it wasn't. Jade let it build more, waited, and approached Nathan, whose eyes were full of terror as her hands drifted through the motions of her cast.

"Jade, he's right, *stop,*" Justine said behind her. The room was silent, and Jade's mind flickered back to what Matt had said. *How do you know that when you release it, you're not going to blow something up...or kill someone?* With those words echoing in her head, Jade drew back her right hand, flaming red and quivering. The energy snapped like a whip and released itself furiously upon Nathan's body. He fell to the floor. Jade staggered back, the weight of the charm heavy in her muscles, and the unpracticed tendons running along her forearm.

Nathan was looking at Jade's hands in wonderment, and she couldn't resist the urge to follow his gaze to the burn marks that traced up her wrists. Nathan stumbled up. "You'll wish you hadn't done that." He pressed his lips into a thin line, his nostrils flaring and his hands stirring.

Ms. Tutts had often said that the movement of the cast reflects its purpose. If true, Nathan was about to kill someone. His hands swirled in a wrath of impassioned anger, and between one palm and the other, something vicious swelled and swelled. Jade swallowed hard. The look in his eyes was thirsty for revenge, and she was in no position to counter him.

"Nathan…" She put up her hands. "Don't. Let's stop," she said calmly, her eyes darting toward Mr. Reynolds. She could see students edging away from Nathan through the corner of her eye and wished she could do the same.

"No!" he bellowed, his hands still stirring. "*I* get the last word!"

Jade could tell that what had begun as an exercise was quickly spiraling into a full-fledged battle. She moved her hands through the only defensive cast she knew, and again the heat coiled around her and bathed her arms and the tips of her fingers. Nathan fired. His charm struck Jade once more, but there was enough magic in her veins that she only staggered back a step. She fired something back, hoping only to throw him far enough off balance that he might stop. He didn't. He fired again, and she sidestepped him. He drew back his arm, and the magic bubbled easily to the surface of his fingers as though it had been lying beneath in wait for Jade. With every shot, Jade could outmaneuver his by a fraction of a second, but to win, she needed to be better than that. With every step Nathan only grew angrier, his face turning red, his raging hands storming through the motions of a cast Jade had never seen before.

"Now, Nathan, let's not—" Mr. Reynolds began to speak, but it was far too late. Nathan thrust his hands in front of him, and a white-hot charm exploded from his palms. Jade felt something strong like iron strike the back of her head just as she was dangled in the air midway through a flip. Her locket ripped away from her neck. She reached out a hand, but it hit the wall lining the court. She could feel her eyes rolling back as blistering rods bit through her flesh. She wondered for a second what he had done to her, and she felt her spine aching as though he had sliced her down the middle, her heart still beating in a final sprint to save her. Camilla and Justine rushed to her side, panting.

"Nathan, what were you thinking?" Matt yelled.

Jade shoved off the groping hands angrily, her eyes darkening as she approached Nathan, and regained motion in her arms. She'd never felt the burn under her flesh as she did now—a sharp sting bulleted into the electrified tips of her hands.

"Finally decided to put up a fight?" Nathan crooned.

Jade clenched her fists, and the same powerful gust of energy she'd felt before returned to her hands, full of vengeance. She dared herself to look at them, and they were alight with anger. A voice of reason was begging her to stop, but every fiber of her being wanted to fight him. Her legs bolted forward, and she drove her two burning hands onto his chest before he could raise a finger. In a flash, Jade's entire body pulsed with an electrified glow, and Nathan careened away from her into the air—his body lit with the furious red charm.

He flailed his arms, and stared down at her, the conviction in his face giving way to petrification. He screamed. The ground rushed away from him, and he crashed against the stone wall, and then slid down, scraping his face against the jagged stone. When he stopped sliding and the air settled around him, Jade stared at his bloody face, then at her quaking hands. She didn't dare meet another eye as she grabbed her locket from the floor and sprinted away through the gaping arches that led back into the Academy.

Tears welled in her eyes. All she could imagine was James shaking his head. *You're so much better than this*, he would say. With her locket safely cupped in her hands, she ran into the nearest bathroom she could find.

She sat against the wall, pulling her knees into her chest, thinking all the while of what her father would have said if he'd seen her. *You're not trying, Kat.* Nathan was the kind of person who did that just because he could, so why shouldn't she…just because *she* could?

You're better than him. Conscience came to her in James's gentle voice. She wondered how it had happened. She hadn't meant it to. She hadn't meant to hurt him so badly. She was afraid of the unknown power hidden in her palms. It had consumed her. James's face wormed through her thoughts. *I don't want you to be scared of yourself,* he'd said.

The thought suddenly occurred to Jade that maybe her father had warned her. Could he have known she was different than the others? Was he afraid of her too? Jade dipped her hands into the sink and splashed water onto her face. When she looked up, her eyes were glittering in the mirror. She was startled by what she saw there. There was a hardness in her eyes that she was unused to that turned the gentle blue sharp like violet. She wondered if the girl she'd left behind in the Division, sitting in James's lap, would ever come back. Then she remembered, the Illysium was no place for the gentle hearted. In her effort to be a part of the Illysium, the Illysium had become an integral part of her. She was afraid of it.

Jade wiped away the tears guiltily and heard the bell ring. She grabbed her locket and fingered its smooth surface. It was still hot, pulsing, and Jade remembered sitting on James's lap when he'd jokingly said, *so that you know I'm safe*. She wondered now if he'd meant it. Having crashed against the stone, it now lay face up in her palm, wounded. Inside the spherical brass locket was a picture of her father, his eyes twinkling, with four-year-old Jade slung over his shoulder, giggling. On the other side of the locket, she noticed something that hadn't been there before.

If she pointed it toward the light from the window, there was a glint of stone. It wasn't the kind of stone you might find in a jeweler's shop. Neither was it the kind to be found…anywhere. Beneath its fragile, crystalline shell, was something that seemed—impossibly—alive.

Inside the stone, warm whorls of blue fluttered under Jade's touch. *What are you?* she thought. She nearly dropped the locket as it shone brighter and brighter, reaching a crescendo before withering to pale again. Jade shook it. Nothing. She growled, using the soft of her palm to beat it. Again, no result.

An uproar of shuffling feet hurried Jade back to her senses. She looked once more at the endearing picture of her father from so long ago, thriving and youthful, as though he could speak to her out of the photo. She thought that if she could see him, she wouldn't know what to ask first. Her father seemed happy in that photo. How could he have been happy after leaving behind such a magnificent world? Had he done it for her? Now Jade yearned to be back in his arms. She was desperate to know he was safe and healthy. She wanted to know why he'd run from this place, who he was before he was her father. Now, so far from the familiar, sweet smell of his favorite tweed jacket, and the faded wrinkle of a smile running down his cheeks, Jade realized she hardly knew him at all.

Since she'd arrived at Constantine, she'd come no closer to finding him, and was beginning to fear time was running out—if it hadn't already. She looked up in the mirror again, and tried to imagine James's face somewhere in hers, in the set of her jaw, the dark shine of her hair.

"I'll find you," she promised him. "I'll do *anything*." She cursed at her reflection, because it wasn't the face she wanted to see. She wanted to find her father and go back to their ragged house.

Jade wanted her other life back.

CHAPTER 12

Jade stifled the tears threatening to pour down her cheeks, and wiped away the ones that already had. She took a deep breath and clenched the locket in her hand so tightly that she could almost feel the jagged glass cutting into her skin. She grabbed her books and fell out into the empty hall.

Jade hung her head, trying not to meet the seemingly accusatory eyes of the students standing idly in the hall. She was just rounding the corner to get to her class when she walked, humiliatingly, into Matt.

"Sorry," Jade muttered, sliding past him easily. Matt caught up to stop her. He put his hand on her shoulders after slinging his bow and arrows around his back. "You okay? What happened back there? I've been looking all over for you."

Jade shrugged.

Matt pouted. "In a rush?"

Jade nodded. Her head was pounding from the tears, and she was desperate to restrain them.

Matt grinned. "What are you hiding?" he asked, rounding on her so she couldn't pass. He pointed to her clenched fist and unhooked her fingers to reveal the locket. "This yours?" Jade nodded, letting him scan the glass, the picture, and the stone. He arched his brow and fumbled for his bow. "You have one too?" he asked excitedly, flipping it around to show Jade an identical stone in the upper limb of his bow. "It didn't come like that, did it?" he asked, zealously inspecting them. "What you think it means? I bet—" He looked up briefly to see if she was listening and his smile faded. "You've been crying," he said, pulling up her chin gently to examine her face. Jade blinked fiercely, willing herself not to start crying all over again, but something caught in her throat. At last he let go and pulled her into a hug.

"Don't," he whispered. "What's wrong?"

Jade pulled away and snatched back her locket. "I'm wrong, I think." She laughed humorlessly.

Matt heaved a long breath. "Jade, you know what Nathan's like. If I could get my hands on that kid, I swear, I'd...I don't know. Luckily, I think you beat him up well enough for the both of us."

Jade laughed, but still cowered at the thought of what James would have said. She checked Matt's wristwatch.

"Is that the time?" she asked.

He shrugged. "I think it's three minutes early—"

"I've got a class, I'd better go, Matt. Sorry. Bye!" She hurtled through the words. He called something after her, but she was racing away too fast to catch what he'd said.

Jade approached the door to the classroom and opened it nervously. She could hear the teacher's squealing voice inside. "…To take a seat there by the window?" It took a second for Jade to realize whom she was talking to, but the stout old woman pointed to an empty seat next to a familiar face—Aaron. Jade took the seat without word. He seemed frustrated as he moved his books to accommodate her. It crossed her mind that maybe it wasn't coincidence that they hadn't spoken in months… in fact, other than seeing him in passing, she'd hardly spoken to him since her first day at Constantine.

Aaron didn't turn as she dumped her books beside him on the desk. "Excellent. As I was saying, I'll be passing out textbooks with all of this term's assignments so we can study the characteristics of creatures in the Division. This will link well into what you're learning in your magical history class. However, we will be looking at it from a biological point of view."

No one stirred. Aaron was staring absently through the window, where the sun met the horizon. He sighed, shifting in his seat.

"Aaron Henderson?" the teacher asked.

"Yes?"

She narrowed her eyes, regarding him scornfully with her hands on her hips. Aaron sat up and winced in pain.

"Won't you try to focus on what's going on *inside* the class rather than out?" Aaron nodded. "Can you tell the class what you know about the tributary forces and the Trove, please? You mustn't forget the Trove."

Aaron nodded again, his face oddly strained.

"In the Illysium"—he tapped his pen on his note-book, and then leaned back from the table to address her properly—"there are streams of…magic in the ground, similar, I think, to tributaries that lead into rivers. They hold everything together, power homes, charms, pretty much everything we can't do with our hands."

"And the Trove?"

"It's a mythological device," he answered.

"Or at least we believe so," she inserted. "Never dismiss the possibility."

"It's thought to act as a well—a borehole, if you will—to access not only the tributaries directly, but also the main *river* of magic, so to speak. It would unleash enough magic to do…anything."

The teacher regarded him suspiciously. "Yes," she said, her voice drenched with disappointment. "But your previous knowledge is no excuse to dismiss the lesson."

"I understand," he muttered, more out of courtesy than any actual commitment.

"If you'll open your books to the first page," she said, turning her gaze back to the other students, "you can read through the first chapter on this, and check your assignments for tonight, which are due next week. You may begin reading now." The class groaned, and she cleared her throat in disapproval.

A quiet murmur resumed in the room and Jade leaped at the opportunity. "Are you okay?" she asked Aaron.

"Yes. You've asked me this before," he answered, opening the book on their desk.

"Yeah, and you lied to me then too," she said softly, leaning forward to meet his eye.

"Kat, I'm not sure it's any business of yours."

"I wouldn't ask except you look like you've been injured."

Aaron stared up at her to say something, but then returned to the book.

"Aaron, if something's wrong...you should tell someone. Maybe I can help—"

"Katherine, I don't need your help," he answered calmly. The teacher was nearby, eyeing them.

"If you're keeping a dangerous secret—don't you think that's a little irresponsible?"

Aaron shook his head. "That's hypocritical, since *you're* the one who lashed out at the minister's son because you couldn't hold your temper." He paused, looking up to see that the teacher had turned her back. "Besides, you're hiding a secret worse than mine," he reminded her. Jade remembered, and hated being in debt to him. "Just let it go."

Jade clenched her jaw. "Fine," she answered, hardly satisfied.

Thankfully, after that Jade didn't cross Aaron's path for the next few days. However, after Jade's now-infamous encounter with Nathan, no place in the school was safe from her fluttering name. It passed between every student, and if they didn't use her name, it was a shameful equivalent. Meanwhile, the whole business of Constantine being back was almost forgotten in the weeks to come. *Almost.*

After breakfast the next Sunday, Jade was hurrying back to her dorm to finish off a report when a tall, middle-aged man with graying hair and a bulbous belly stopped her in the hall.

"Young woman!" he called, flagging her down with a finger and gesturing for her to stand before him. His voice was demanding and arrogant. "May I speak to you?" he inquired, searching her face.

The halls were empty, and she couldn't help but notice this as he addressed her. She nodded, attempting her best impression of a true Illysian. "Yes, sir."

"I've been told you are among the most talented students here," he said.

Jade swallowed a lump of uneasiness in her throat. It was true, with the exception of charms, which was still the bane of her education. "Thank you," she answered. "Who from?"

"Your headmistress pointed you out to me." Jade nodded. "Where are you from?" he asked, his hands clasped behind his back. Jade could tell by his stance and his conduct where *he* was from—Utopia. He reeked of it. The sudden realization crossed her mind that this must be Nathan's father, the minister of the Oculus.

"Juleria," she answered confidently. She'd read enough about it in books to prepare herself for a time like this, but all the books she'd ever read escaped her.

"Ah," he answered. "Do you miss home?" he asked sympathetically, his pitch artificial.

Jade neither nodded nor shook her head. "I like to learn, and I enjoy not having to work seven days a week," she replied carefully. "Constantine offers both."

The man smacked his lips, casting her an ugly look. Jade thought she heard footsteps down the hall and hoped she was not mistaken.

"The Oculus has taken dramatic measures in the past few years to uphold the highest standard of life for its Julerian citizens, young lady." He tilted his head. "Would you disagree?" There was a tone to his voice that asked Jade instead, *Do you dare to speak ill of the Oculus?*

The silence that subsequently hung between them answered, *Yes, I do.*

"Young girl, what is your name?" he asked now, his hands across his chest.

Jade was about to open her mouth to answer when a loud voice and heavy steps bounded down the hall. "Sir Emerson!" Jade whipped around to see Aaron hurrying to interrupt.

"Sir, have you come to pay your son a visit?" he asked. His sharp features seemed to have melted away. Now he was warm, almost pleasant. Aaron didn't look at her once.

"No, I'm on official business," Emerson answered. His eyes hesitantly turned from Jade to Aaron, who slowly ushered Emerson down the hall.

"And how is Utopia doing? I've heard it's thriving."

"Indeed," he responded.

Jade took the opportunity to bound back to her dorm.

Justine and a few others were lounging in the common room.

"What's the minister doing at Constantine?" Jade asked hysterically.

Several heads turned. Justine stood. "He's here?"

"Yes," Jade answered. Camilla must have been nearby because she and Katy appeared suddenly.

"You mean Grady Emerson…from *Utopia?*" Camilla whispered. All the girls in the common room swarmed around the four of them, bombarding Jade with questions.

"What did he say?"

"What did he want?"

"Can you imagine why he came all this way?"

When Jade, Camilla, and Justine were back in the room later that night, the gravity of the situation dawned upon them.

"Does he know what you did to his son?" Camilla asked.

The question frustrated Jade, because it had been edging at the back of her head since she first saw Emerson in the hall. "I don't think so."

Justine nodded reassuringly. "As long as he doesn't know your name, you should be safe. Otherwise...there's no telling what he might have done. He's the minister. You just can't imagine the kind of power he has. That could've been your life."

Jade knew very well the kind of power that the minister held. If she hadn't read enough about him, then she had heard enough through Matt and Justine to know that he was not one to be crossed. What made the system in the Illysium unique was the efficient brutality with which it was run. The Oculus, as Jade had come to know it, was not a force of police, but a force of terror. Of the thousands of books that had passed through Constantine's library, not one had made record of their murder, their ruthless strategy. It wasn't, Jade knew, that there was no record to make. Rather, in the Illysium, there was only one record—the collective record. A record rewritten by the very body that had marred it. Conveniently for the minister, in years to come, no one, and least of all he, will be accountable for the millions of lives laid waste to by the system he had employed—the system Jade had been spared from.

Jade nodded. *Great*, she thought. *One more thing I owe to Aaron Henderson.*

CHAPTER 13

J ade was grateful when the focus of the school shifted from her to the minister's presence at Constantine. One student heard from another, who'd heard from another, who had overheard another conversation, that Emerson was there to declare Constantine alive or dead.

He was frequently seen marching the halls and disappearing into the South Tower, his head ducked toward Lady Eleanor's as they spoke in hushed tones. He had become a looming presence at the Academy, and those from the Keeping in particular were oddly ill at ease when he passed.

A few days after the minister's arrival, Jade determined to avoid Nathan. With the minister just feet away, she was anxious to steer clear of trouble. Just like everyone else in the school, Jade was treading on thin ice. She caught sight of Matt and Aaron under the arch of the East Tower with Justine and Camilla, and went to join them. She sat where the sun was bright with the oncoming summer.

Aaron's eyes darted toward her when she sat down, and she wondered if he was still upset that she'd questioned him the day before. His response admittedly had not consoled her in the slightest, and with Emerson at the Academy, she only hoped he could keep his secret long enough—whatever it was.

"Jade told us you saw the minister," Justine said through a mouthful of food when Jade sat down. Justine swallowed and wiped a sleeve over her face. "Did you speak to him?"

Aaron nodded. "Just to say hello."

Camilla cleared her throat. "Everyone off the Estate knows Emerson personally. He was particularly fond of Aaron's mother, I remember." Camilla raised a brow at Aaron, but he didn't look at her. Instead, he was staring up at the sun.

"Aaron, you never mentioned you knew the minister so well," Matt started, looking up from his food with a hint of accusation in his tone.

"Does it matter?" Aaron asked. "He loved my mother and hated my father. I think that's the case for most families on the Estate."

"That's disgusting," Justine spat.

Matt nodded and slapped down his sandwich. "It doesn't taste right at all."

Camilla rolled her eyes. "Not the food, Matt, the minister." She turned back to Justine, looking down her nose. "I hardly agree anyway. Emerson's the best thing that ever happened to the Illysium. He's strict, of course, but the Illysium needs that kind of structure. Where would we all be otherwise?"

Aaron took a deep breath and nodded, almost reluctantly. "Camilla's right. It's the system, not the man. Any decent Illysian who goes into the system is spat out just like him."

Jade felt her brow rise, and spoke quietly, wary of the passing students around them. "Emerson is hardly free of blame."

Aaron shrugged. "Fine," he conceded. "But he knows the difference between right and wrong. There are much worse people out there. Anyway, he's done my family a favor."

Matt snorted. "It's hard to imagine Emerson being *capable* of favors."

"How, Aaron?" Justine asked skeptically. "What did he do?"

Aaron's gaze had returned again to the sun, which was quickly disappearing behind lethargic clouds. "He finally talked my mother into signing the divorce papers."

"She carried through with it?" Camilla asked, running her hands through a long braid of icy hair. Aaron nodded, but said nothing more.

Justine shook her head. "Some favor that was," she muttered sarcastically.

"My father was a lying fraud, Justine. He finally got locked up like he should have been all along." Aaron retorted with some impatience.

Justine smacked her lips. "You guys just don't get it. If you'd ever been to the Keeping, just one day, Aaron, you'd realize Emerson's a cruel man, straight to the core. System or no system, he could watch millions die as long as they're out of his precious sight."

"Justine, how dare you!" Camilla exclaimed, leaning forward with alarm.

Matt hurried to calm her. "All we mean, Camilla, is that Emerson has two sides. You just can't see the other because he doesn't want you to."

"Matt, we know Emerson better than both of you combined," Aaron argued. "He's a coward who makes reckless decisions. Whatever harm befalls the Keeping is a preset of the system."

"You're deluding yourself," Justine muttered, partially defeated.

Aaron sighed, his lips pursing toward guilt. "Justine, I know what he's done to you…to the Keeping. All I'm saying is that he's not the mastermind to fear behind it."

Jade considered his point, and while she had always imagined that Emerson was the defiling puppeteer, she recognized the possibility of something much worse. Emerson hadn't taken her father or killed Matt's parents or taken Justine's family. They were all victims of the system.

"I just don't understand," Justine muttered. "When it comes to the Oculus, the system and the man are the same thing."

Jade pressed her lip into a line. "Aaron has a point. From what I've seen of Emerson, the system is far, far worse."

"How?"

"It feels *nothing*," Jade muttered under her breath, as if to say it quietly might make it untrue.

Then, just as Aaron was about to add something, he dropped his train of thought and stood to walk a little distance from them, and dip into a bow for Lady Eleanor. Jade started when she saw the headmistress.

"Henderson, how are you?" Lady Eleanor greeted him, swirling the cape of her robe around her feet.

The arrival of the headmistress had not gone unnoticed by the other students crowded into the courtyard. The noise had fallen almost to silence in wait for her announcement. To their surprise, though, Lady Eleanor had marched past the center of the court, headed distinctly toward the East arch.

"I'm doing well, thank you."

"Excellent. I passed your mother recently, in Utopia. She sends her best wishes." Jade exchanged a glance with Matt, who seemed ready to convulse. The other students in the courtyard listened blankly to the unfolding conversation, and Jade knew that they were all thinking the same thing. *What is she doing here?*

"I'm sure," Aaron answered.

"In any case, I'm looking for a certain Ms. Katherine Orwell."

Jade swallowed hard at the mention of her name. Matt flew a hand to her shoulder as if to stop her, but she was already standing, her legs pushing her up against her will. Aaron still hadn't answered the lingering question by the time Jade showed herself. She bore the silence as best she could and walked dumbfounded to stand beside Aaron before their headmistress. She suspected Lady Eleanor had overseen her attack on Nathan, which could be the only explanation for her request to see Jade.

"There you are," Eleanor said, her tone sharp. Jade nodded, and could see Aaron staring at her through the corner of her eye, with a flicker of confused horror across his face that Jade imagined was mirrored in her own. Eleanor looked between them, and then at the surrounding students. She turned on her heel to walk away, but didn't look over her shoulder as she called out, "Katherine, come with me."

Jade's hand slipped up to caress the locket at her neck, but even its warm surface did nothing to allay her qualms. She followed Lady Eleanor away, not daring to meet a single eye she passed.

Once in the halls, she folded her arms tight across her chest to stop her hands from trembling as she followed Lady Eleanor's billowing folds of cool, silk, black robe. She wished now that she'd never fallen into Nathan's hideous trap. He'd known what she would do. He'd been waiting for it, waiting for the opportune moment to have her thrown from Constantine and stripped of whatever sense of honor it had given her. She gritted her teeth in frustration.

Gulping, Jade followed Lady Eleanor down a spiraling staircase in the East Tower and found herself in a narrow hall with a waning, candlelit chandelier. Beneath the chandelier was a bronze door frame with two brass door knockers. The doors swung back at the sight of Lady Eleanor, and she stormed through to take her seat at a desk inside.

Jade stood waiting in the frame.

"Come in," Lady Eleanor called. "I don't bite," she added when Jade hesitantly walked in after her. "Sit, Katherine." Jade took a seat cautiously. Lady Eleanor's face was grave and unnervingly still as her eyes flittered across a page of typed notes. There was a stack on either side of her, and she seemed to be either very nearly finished, or to have only just begun.

Her reading glasses hung low on her nose, and her black-gloved hand adjusted them gingerly.

"I prefer Jade," Jade said into the silence. Lady Eleanor looked up abruptly. Up close, Jade could see tightness in Lady Eleanor's pale face. Her eyes were watery, her lips dry, and her expression sour.

"Do you?" Lady Eleanor asked. Jade nodded, and they lapsed into another silence.

The room was eerily neat, lined by elaborate paintings of the Illysium, and sharp faces that Jade didn't recognize. The floor was finely polished, and the wooden grain was smooth, dark oak. The walls were painted a deep ruby that made the room feel too small. Behind Lady Eleanor were curtains rolled up so they draped above the plain stone wall beneath them like the inside of a tent. It was a dollhouse that seemed perfectly suited to Lady Eleanor.

"There's a certain type of student we look for at Constantine Academy, Jade," Lady Eleanor began, setting down the paper in the stack beside her. She was nearly finished, Jade decided. Lady Eleanor looked down her long, drooping nose with eyes that seemed to have expressions of their own. "It will hardly come as a surprise to you that I've called you in to address your incident with Nathan Emerson."

Her hands glided swiftly over the desk and she plucked an ink-splattered sheet from under the lamp. When she read it aloud, there was a horrible tone in her voice that reminded Jade of Case Two's trial.

"According to this statement, you and Nathan Emerson participated in a class exercise. After mild foul play on his part, it says you exercised magic far beyond the necessity of the task. Following the professor's order to stop, you proceeded to viciously attack your peer. This resulted in"—she shuffled the paper to see it more clearly—"a fractured rib, two first-degree burns to the chest, a mild concussion, and multiple surface wounds to the knee, head, and shoulders." She tucked the paper into a drawer, and her eyes narrowed to slits.

Jade struggled to keep her brow smooth. Everything inside her was screaming to be released from this chamber of guilt. She imagined her father's face giving way to anger and disappointment, as it had so often done before. She forced away the thought, afraid of the tears ready to spring to her eyes.

"Katherine, are you aware that Sir Emerson is visiting the Academy right now?" Jade nodded. Her voice had vanished in panicked fear. "He asked me to let him see his son yesterday." Lady Eleanor reached for a cup of red tea and put it to her lips. "You're a clever student, Jade. Do help me. How shall I explain these wounds to the minister when he sees them?" She gestured toward the extensive list.

Jade's eyes stung, and she didn't dare open her mouth, in fear that she would only be capable of senseless pleading. Lady Eleanor replaced the cup on the desk and continued.

"Unfortunately, Jade, the minister does not know you. Can you imagine how he may respond when he hears that a girl from the Keeping has made an attempt on his son's life?" She splayed her elbows over the desk and leaned forward. "Do you know what he will do to you?"

Jade's heart leaped fiercely. She imagined Emerson pacing the hall outside, and Justine's voice rang true and clear through her thoughts. *He's a cruel man, straight to the core.* Lady Eleanor seemed to await an answer, but Jade couldn't bring herself to offer one. The comfort that Constantine walls had once brought her now crumbled in the wake of the minister. Nathan had caught her like a spider in a web, and now she was left to answer for her crime.

"Jade. I've put careful thought into your precarious situation, so I haven't yet spoken to the minister." She swirled the head of her spoon around the teacup, pensively. "I think, Jade, that in some respects, you're very much like *me*."

Jade had to purse her lips to stop from dropping her jaw, yet somehow the likeness to Lady Eleanor irked rather than flattered her. "Which is why I'm willing to make something of a concession for you." Jade sat up alertly, desperate not to be sent from the Academy. It was her last chance to find her father. If she failed all else, she could not, and would not, fail him.

"So I can do two things. If I fulfill my duties as headmistress, and expel you from the school, you will be at the mercy of the minister himself, and the safeguards of the Academy will no longer apply to you." Jade gulped at the possibility and waited anxiously to hear her alternative. "Or, you can do a little favor for me, and I can cast a 'forget me' charm on Nathan to make sure your misstep doesn't cost you."

Jade nodded, but uneasiness was creeping into her throat. "What kind of favor?" she asked.

Lady Eleanor tilted her head to the side, and from the shelf behind her, she drew a small book that was lined with emerald leather, worn through at the corners. She flipped it open to a page, and laid it between them so Jade could see the text. "It has come to my attention," she explained, "that you are among the most talented students here. In only a year of training, you have demonstrated a powerful supply of magic." She looked down at Jade's lap and reached for a hand. When Jade didn't move, Lady Eleanor grabbed it with her scratched gloved and forced up the sleeve of Jade's shirt.

"Yes," she remarked hungrily. "This book can teach you to use your magic properly, to control it. If you can learn to complete this charm, Jade, I will spare you from the minister. But you must show this to absolutely no one. That is of vital importance. If you choose to comply, I will give you two weeks to learn the charm."

Jade looked at the text, and could tell by skimming the page that the charm wasn't the ordinary kind she'd seen before in class. It required a level of magic Jade had never seen written in a book before, magic she wasn't sure she could produce.

"And if I can't?" she muttered, picking up the book and leafing through the pages.

Lady Eleanor shook her head. "It is imperative, Jade. For your sake and mine." Something hard stuck in Jade's chest that filled her with fear.

"What is it?" she asked, gesturing to the book.

Lady Eleanor licked her lips, and tapped the plain leather that covered it. "This is a charm book, Jade. There is only one like it in the whole of the Illysium."

Jade looked on the inside of the front cover, signed in Lady Eleanor's unmistakable hand.

"What does the charm do?" she asked, still stricken with panic at the sight of Lady Eleanor's sly smile.

Lady Eleanor stood, her expression as stony as ever. "If you master the charm, and obey my instructions, it will spare you from the minister. For now, that is all you need to know."

***

Matt was waiting for Jade when she reemerged at the top of the stairs in the East Tower. "Hey." He waved, a broad smile breaking through his weary face. "How was it?" He took Jade's heavy books from her arms, and she thanked him, holding tight to the little emerald book so that he couldn't see it as she slipped it into the folds of her jacket.

"It was fine."

Matt frowned. "You wanna talk about it?"

"I don't think so," Jade answered. She could see the disappointment in his brow, but couldn't say anything to ease his nerves. Her own nerves were jittering like hot wires.

Matt narrowed his eyes. When she caught his gaze, he laughed. "Why so down?" he asked, stopping in the hall to face her squarely. "You weren't expelled, right?" Jade nodded. "And you're still alive." Again, Jade nodded, and she felt his words edging a smile onto her face. "And your reputation earned ten points for beating up Nathan."

Jade laughed and Matt seemed glad to have won her over, but he could never know what happened. He could never know what she'd agreed to. A deal with the devil.

If she told anyone what had happened, it would be Matt—or maybe Justine. Camilla wouldn't care, and Aaron would tell her everything she already knew: that it had been reckless, dangerous, and selfish. At least, that's what she imagined Aaron would say. Matt was a good choice. He was quiet enough to let Jade sort through her erratic thoughts in peace, but when she yearned for anything else to think about, it seemed as though he would start talking again, right on cue.

"…I told her not to wait up, though, so it shouldn't be a problem."

"Sorry, who?" Jade asked.

"Justine," Matt answered patiently. "She was waiting for us in the courtyard, but I told her I'd take you to your room."

"Oh," Jade muttered. She couldn't think of a single other word to say.

When they finally reached the North Tower, Matt had fallen strangely silent. He stopped at the dorms and turned on his heel to hand Jade the rest of her books. He folded his arms over his chest. "Jade, tell me. What did she say?"

Jade shook her head. She wanted to tell him so that he might offer her advice out of the netted snare she'd woven for herself, but she knew her choice had been made for her. She would obey lady Eleanor in return for her life at the Academy, a chance to see her father again.

"I wish I could," she mumbled.

Matt clenched his jaw and shoved his hands roughly into his pockets. "Jade, you have to tell somebody. You look…scared."

Jade sighed. "I'm not," she asserted. "And I promised her, Matt."

Matt grabbed her wrist as she turned to leave. She faced him and he let her hand drop. "I just—" Matt flexed his jaw. He had joked with Jade about how he used to stutter, and whenever he was nervous, it would come back with a vengeance. He tried again. "I just want you to trust me."

An earnest smile filled her face as she backed away toward the dorms. "I do."

CHAPTER 14

The mystery of Emerson's presence at Constantine was soon cleared up. Less than a week later, the school gathered in the assembly hall to be addressed.

"*Sit down!*" he roared over the noisy bustling of feet. If Lady Eleanor had silenced the hall many times, the minister muted it. He was heaving. "Not once"—he began, pausing with his hands on his hips—"*never* in my career have I found reason to visit this school." He glared at them. This was a particularly significant announcement, as Jade had recently learned Emerson was almost three centuries old, and had had seven wives and fifteen children.

"Students here know who they are and what purpose they serve. Am I correct in my assumption?" No one responded. "*Am I correct in that assumption?*" he asked again. There were immediate nods in agreement. Emerson pointed to a boy in the audience. "What are you?"

"An Illysian," the boy answered timidly. Jade could barely see his face, but it sounded like Tom.

"I will ask again. *What are you?*" he addressed another student.

"The best of the best," she answered, her voice as quiet as a mouse. "Warriors of the Illysium." What they had all once boasted proudly, Emerson's presence had reduced to a meager squeak.

Emerson nodded. "Warriors of the Illysium," he repeated. He wiped the sweat from his brow, which was knitted angrily. "And what governs the Illysium?" he asked the same girl.

"The Oculus."

"Yes!" Emerson bellowed. "So why, students"—he pressed his lips—"why do you continually question its ability?" His jaw was clenched. "Warriors of the Illysium serve the *Oculus*. Not two weeks ago, I was alerted to a disturbing message written on the wall of the South Tower of this school. Not long after this school began, Constantine was locked away and killed. The Oculus removed her from the Illysium for conducting experiments that we deemed inexcusable. Many on the jury oversaw this themselves. How then could you *doubt* that she remained where the Oculus had caged her, killed her, and buried her?"

He shook his head. "It is out of mere respect that we use her name in this school, but *nothing* and *no one* could bring her back, even with all the magic running through the tributaries of our world.

"I have stated categorically—*categorically,* children—that Constantine was a brave soldier and nothing more. She does not live. She does not breathe. She is gone. This is not her madhouse, this is an institution administered by the Oculus." He paused, short of breath. "From this point forward, you will never dare to question that. Is that understood?"

The students nodded dumbly. He stormed off the platform and left them all stricken with a mixture of angst and kindling excitement.

***

"I don't know," one boy said at dinner. "The whole business seems fabricated to me...red paint? It's a bit overdone." A cluster of students had gathered in the courtyard before the South Tower. They sat now where the paint or ink had once smeared the brick.

"But it makes sense," Justine interrupted.

"Of course it does," Jade said, balancing her tray on her knees. The other students looked surprised to hear her speak, but she went on anyway. "If he was telling the truth—or at the very least *believed* his own words—what need would there have been to investigate in the first place? Obviously the Oculus thought it was a credible threat, right?"

There was nodding in acceptance of this reason. Others, mostly from Recasteria, were eager to counter her. "Probably safety precautions," one girl said.

"Or maybe he was here for something else," the same boy who'd spoken before piped in. "We don't have hard evidence."

"Why do you do that?" Jade asked, addressing the two who had spoken. They looked at each other and back at her.

"Do what?" the boy asked. Jade considered retracting her words, but a voice in her head told her to go on. She spoke warily.

"Why do you all act like the Oculus has never lied? They're no less Illysian than you are, and you would lie, wouldn't you?" No one said anything. "Surely you don't all agree with what they've done." Still silence. "Not *everything*."

Every eye seemed to avoid her gaze, not daring to disagree because it was true, but also not daring to agree for fear of the consequences. Even Justine turned away as if Jade had confessed to murder. Jade flinched when the emerald book on the inside of her jacket nudged her sharply in the ribs. She hadn't opened it once since Lady Eleanor had handed it to her, but she knew she couldn't avoid it forever. If she didn't learn the charm soon, her deal with Eleanor would crumple and with it, her position at the Academy. She resolved not to put it off any longer, still wary that the minister lurked somewhere near, and at a moment's notice could be told of Jade's misconduct.

"All I'm saying," Jade went on, standing, "is that if you have eyes—don't let someone else look over your shoulder." Their incredulous faces stared up at her through the darkness of the oncoming night.

By the time Jade could regret, or even consider, the consequences of her remark, she was back inside, following a gutting urge she felt to find a quiet place in the Academy, where she might confront the mysterious, terrifying charm Lady Eleanor had assigned her.

Jade searched for a quiet room in the East Tower, walking briskly until she ducked into a dark room. With a flick of her wrist, the lights buzzed into life. The room was a decent size, with a few unused oak shelves, and one long desk in the center, fit to hold a dozen people. Jade drew the curtains at the windows and shut the door to be sure she wouldn't be disturbed. In frantic anticipation, Jade spread a collection of used charm books out on the desk and brushed the hair out of her face.

She glanced around once more and then timidly drew the emerald book out of her pocket to rest it up on the table. She found it curious that there was no title either on the spine or the front cover. While at first glance, the book had seemed leather bound, once she inspected it, she saw that in fact the pages were of thick parchment, sewn together with fine string, secured between two coarse sheets of animal skin.

Jade had only seen a book like this once before, at an exhibition her father had taken her to in the Division. The book she'd seen had been encased in glass, roughly sewn up the edges, from the sixteenth century. She was certain now that the emerald charm book was hundreds of years old, and wondered how many hands it had passed through, good and evil, to end up now in her quivering palms.

Gulping, Jade flipped through the pages until she reached the one Eleanor had appointed her. There was no header to begin the page, nor page numbers anywhere to be seen. Terrified, she began to read:

The following should be exercised under the supervision of a coven of class V Illysians, appointed by the highest minister. Follow instructions as written below (see key).

9-8-5-2—2-4-3-4—34-5-75-75-768—9—37-5—12-3—756—9—6-34—193—76-6—86—8—9—395—24—3-6-57-865—6—4-567-734—5-42-14-86-5-406-234-867-2586-.

The key inscribed at the back was unlike any Jade had ever seen before. She was unfamiliar with charms of more than a few digits, and marveled at the complexity of the spell. Jade raked a hand through her hair, her brow creased as she tried to make sense of the numbers and illegible symbols written into the parchment. By the length of the charm alone, she knew the magic required would be exponential, and the key was too complex to be intended for one person. Her teacher had once told her that some charms required a coven of Illysians, complex, interlacing streams of magic. Jade had nothing but the charm, a key, and her own, often unpredictable supply of magic.

She knew of only one other student in the school capable of decoding anything as complex as what she faced now, but Jade couldn't turn to Aaron because she had sworn herself to secrecy. *For your sake and mine*, Lady Eleanor had warned.

Jade set to work, moving between the key and the stream of numbers. As she decoded more and more of the charm, a shrill voice in her head cried out for her to stop. Lady Eleanor was a woman Jade had grown to fear and distrust during the months of her stay at the Academy. She despised Lady Eleanor's control over her, and the confident ease with which she had manipulated Jade.

The bell chimed the passing of first one hour, then two, and Jade couldn't help but feel a dire urgency to uncover the charm that evening. Her head throbbed with a sickly fear of what Eleanor could do to her otherwise. The memory of Lady Eleanor's gloved fingers snatching at Jade's wrist was enough to urge her on. Besides, she had once promised to do anything for her father.

Again the bell chimed, and Jade's pencil still scratched across the page. When she'd finally decoded the string of numbers, she sat back and narrowed her eyes to study the movement of the charm. She let her hands follow the rhythm of the piece up and down through the air until the movement was smooth. Then a familiar mantra chanted through her head. *Think, then do. Think, then do.* Her hands were growing tired and almost clumsy by the time she had mustered any magic. It began as it usually did, in the pit of her stomach, but the rhythm of the charm was faster than she was used to, and she could feel her nerves on edge as her magic spiked.

Her hands glowed mildly, and it was usually a warning bell for her to stop, but nothing had happened. She dared to push further, pressing deeper against the invisible shield that begged her to stop. Still there was nothing. Now her hands burned frighteningly. The cool light that normally radiated through her fingers had spread into her forearms, bathing them in a tub of fire, and a light breeze swirled around the room like a gathering storm, but still Jade pressed on.

She dared to launch herself into the unknown depths of the charm, and she struggled to maintain the impatient rhythm of the movement, always searching for something, a sign, or the flicker of light that might tell her it was working.

Snap.

The sound came from underneath her, and Jade shrieked, but concentrated on funneling her magic into her fingers. She listened again for a similar sound, but there was none, only her quick, frantic breath and the hiss of empty air all around her. She could feel the magic stinging in her veins so sharply, it almost hurt. Yet she knew the charm was still incomplete.

She continued, willing herself not to stop even in her panic and pain. She waited longer and heard another snap as the wooden planks bent back of their own accord, iron nails leaping from their positions in the floor. The floor gave way, and there was a deep rumbling as if from a cave. Jade swallowed hard. She could feel the jarring reverberations through the cool surface of her locket, and she prayed this wasn't the kind of charm she thought it was. They didn't exist…Surely it couldn't be….

A hand came through the floor.

Jade screamed and fell back into the wall, her own hands scraping against the floor as she scrambled away. She clapped a fist over her mouth to smother her own cry: *What have I done?* When she turned again, the gaping hole in the floor was widening, and a pair of beaten claws dug at the wood. As the charm bubbled and seethed in her veins, a wrenching sting tore from her chest as if someone had struck her heart. She collapsed and released the charm. As Jade's hands cooled, and her magic deserted her, the snapping halted, and the hand of the creature that had sneaked through fell limp again. It disappeared.

Jade was shaking and burning when the nails slipped back into position, and the wood restored itself. She didn't dare move, and when all was still, she could hear the voices of laughter draining into the room from the courtyard. She swallowed the lump of horror in her throat and scrambled up. She had never exerted so much magic before, and now her limbs trembled as she fumbled for the emerald book and slammed it shut with a mix of terror and awe. She remembered the upturn of Eleanor's lips when she'd first handed Jade the book, the challenge.

It would be another few days at least before Jade's magic recovered. Still, she couldn't think about that. All she could do was blink hard at the floor where the distorted hand had beckoned her forth, and then, at the sight of her own shadow, propel herself through the door and out into the light.

The next evening Jade surrounded herself somewhat purposefully with company. She hadn't so soon forgotten the horrible, dismembered arm from the night before, and knew that if she were alone, the nightmarish memory would return to her and she'd have no hope of escaping it. So she laughed and grinned and tried to forget, even though she was secretly anxious to confront Lady Eleanor.

"Katy, Isabelle? Run and fetch us some more dinner, please," Camilla ordered from her comfortable position collapsed on the grass in the courtyard. "I'm starving." Isabelle groaned, but both of them stood and went scampering away, gathering their own empty plates as they went.

Justine raised her brow in disapproval and shook her head. "One day they're going to get sick of you, Camilla." Camilla sat up to shrug dead leaves from her hair.

"I'm sorry, did you say something, Justine?" Camilla pursed her lips austerely, in a way that only one from the Estate could. "That reminds me. Earlier, in the courtyard, you shouldn't have brought up Aaron's parents that way. It's a sensitive topic."

Justine furrowed her brow. "Why?"

Camilla leaned towards them to whisper in hushed tones. "The whole Henderson family is a real scandal on the estate. His father was never really around when he was younger. My parents told me it was because he was having an affair with some woman in Utopia. I think his mother knew too. Anyway, his father went to Constantine. He was very clever, but threw it all away after the divorce. The minister had him put up for adultery and treason, or something or another." She looked around to be sure no one was listening.

"Anyway, I should be going." She stood up to dust herself, and her hands swirled through a charm Jade barely recognized. Within moments she'd slipped into a silk, strapless, black dress that didn't reach her knees and applied a fresh coat of makeup. She smacked her lips.

"Only you would teach yourself a charm like that," Justine commented, looking up. "Why bother?"

"Only you would even ask that question." Camilla stood, sliding on an obnoxious pair of red shoes that she'd conjured. "Besides," she added, adjusting her hair, "I have a hot date tonight with Matt."

Jade and Justine exchange a look of surprise.

"You're still together?" Justine asked, shocked.

"Obviously," Camilla said, waving her hand.

"I can't believe you're with him. Do you even know him that well?" Justine asked.

"That's why you date, Justine—so you can get to know people. Besides, it's all for the greater good."

"What's that supposed to mean?" Jade asked doubtfully.

"There's a prefect I like, but the only way to talk to him—"

"Is to use Matt as your puppet?" Justine asked.

Camilla rolled her eyes. "As if he likes me any more than I like him. It's not 'using' if we have a mutual agreement. And you two had better keep that information hushed, because this needs to be convincing." Camilla knotted her whip through the loop at her waist. Somehow it completed the ensemble. Jade wondered if Camilla had planned it that way. "But I guess you two wouldn't know much about love, would you?"

"Dating the first guy you see just so you can kick him around isn't love," Justine said.

"Hmm." Camilla narrowed her eyes, and then her attention faltered. "Well, speak of the devil…" When Jade and Justine followed Camilla's gaze, she was looking toward Matt, his arms piled high with hot plates of food from the dining hall.

"You'll never believe who I ran into, picking up food for your highness," he said sarcastically, spreading the food down on the floor. When he caught sight of Camilla's dress, his eyes widened.

Justine pushed herself up onto one elbow, and while Camilla and Matt were talking, she turned to Jade. "I meant to ask you, did Lady Eleanor bust you for socking Nathan? I was so scared when she took you from the courtyard, and I waited up for you last night to talk, but…"

Jade sighed. "Sorry about that…It's a long story, but no."

Justine considered her answer for a minute, but then shrugged.

"I figured it wasn't too bad, or she wouldn't have let you back out. And what about your weapon? Do you know yet what it does?"

Jade pulled it out of her pocket, and her hand brushed against the skin of the emerald book. She quickly pressed it back into place and took out her matchbox.

"Of course." She pulled out a match and struck it against the side of the silver case. The flame was brighter than normal, but if Jade looked at it long enough, it seemed dimmer as well. She blew it out.

"A bright weapon for a bright girl. Makes sense." Justine smiled.

"No," Jade argued. "A bad weapon for a terrible student—*that* makes sense."

"*Please*, Jade, you're the best in the whole class. I've never seen anyone with *half* the magic you have. Anyway, it's not the weapon that makes the warrior; it's what you do with it."

Jade wanted to say, *but I bet the weapon helps*. Instead, she mumbled something about being thankful for the advice. "How about you? How did you get the flute to work?"

Justine pouted her lips in thought and drew it from her back pocket. "I don't know. Eventually, if you spend enough time with your weapon, usually you can just... feel it. Aaron's lucky, his weapon just comes naturally to him, you know?" She shook her head and at the thought looked up to Matt. "How come Aaron isn't with you?" she asked. When he didn't hear her, she kicked his ankle with her toe and asked again.

A furtive shadow leaped across the wall behind them, and Jade stole a glance around the courtyard. She knew the shape and recognized the striding gait that disappeared into the tower.

"Where did you say he went?" Jade asked.

"Our room. He stayed behind to finish something off. Why?" Matt asked, peeling Camilla's arms from his neck. Jade pushed up from the floor and shrugged on her jacket.

"No reason," she answered.

"Where are you going?" he pouted as she turned to leave.

Jade shrugged. "Nowhere. I'll be right back," she lied, hurrying to follow Aaron's fleeting steps. It was unlike him to lie to Matt, and now Jade was curious to know why.

She slunk into the shadows as she followed, her own steps noiseless against the stone. The walls had been warmly lit in the North Tower, but at night the rest of the towers were plunged into darkness, silent until the sun came to wake them. Aaron was slipping now into the winding staircase that rounded the East Tower, and they were nearing the courtroom. It was too dark there for Jade to see him, but she followed the silver glint of his sword flashing through the dark.

Just as he approached the doors into the courtroom, he stopped and took a sharp turn. Jade almost gasped as he stepped into the pool of moonlight that showered the South Tower. Rather than turning to run, Jade felt an urge to discover where he escaped to at every possible hour—mealtimes, evenings, mornings, holidays. She walked stealthily behind him, covering herself in his shadow.

When he reached the arch that led into a spiral staircase, he hesitated, staring at the barred gate. Then he felt along the ridge of the arch, paused, and moved his arms so as to cast a charm. As if they'd been mere curtains, the bars parted, and he stepped through, letting them slide back into place before he continued into the hall. Jade looked around quickly to see that there was no one to discover her. She imitated the movements of his hands, and there was a shock inside her. Her hands barely glowed, still drained from the night before, but she stepped through anyway.

She ducked under the arch and watched the iron bars slide back into place behind her as they had before. Excellent. Jade listened carefully for his receding steps and found them along one of the halls. Only some were lit by the candlelight of chandeliers. She followed Aaron until he parted with the staircase and bounded down a hall that ended with a plain wooden door. Aaron pressed his shoulder against it, silently turned the knob, and disappeared. When he was out of sight, Jade ran toward it and crouched down. She could see inside through two thick beams, and had to strain to make out what was happening inside.

At first all that could be seen were feathers. Furling, white, magnificent feathers that ended at sharp points. There were claws too, and golden-brown fur, and strong limbs that clutched at the stone floor beneath. Somewhere to the left, Jade could see a long, winding tail that coiled around the creature's firm body. Its forearm alone stretched almost to Aaron's head. The ground shook as the beast stood and rounded on Aaron. A giant clawed appendage groped the air to snatch Aaron off the ground, and Jade almost gasped, but he sidestepped it.

"No," he said firmly, seemingly unstirred. The creature ruffled its wings and let out a sound somewhere between a growl and a squeal, but Aaron didn't move. He simply unsheathed his sword, and like a bull, the creature shot back its wings and pawed the ground anxiously, squawking.

"Be still," Aaron commanded. He placed his sword on the floor, and Jade silently willed him to pick it back up, if not for his safety, then for her own peace of mind. The creature flapped its wings, refusing to be silenced, and rolled back its head. The wall shook when its wings touched it. Without warning, a yellow, scarred beak tore at the air, lunging for Aaron's throat. Jade caught her breath, but in the same second, Aaron jumped out of harm's way. He circled the bird, allowing it to follow him with accusing eyes.

In a flash Aaron grabbed a bag that had been sitting in the corner of the room and moved up the wall, catching his fingers on invisible grooves and climbing high enough that in seconds, he'd flipped onto one of the roof beams. Now the creature squawked madly, beating its wings so hard that it might have made the entire tower collapse. Aaron extended the bag before himself and something dropped out. The beak that had attacked Aaron plucked it out of the air.

"Sit," Aaron commanded. There was a colossal thud and a quick fluttering of wings. More meat dropped out of the air, and then more and more, until the creature was lying on the floor again, apparently having forgiven Aaron. Aaron swung from one beam to another and then glided through the air onto the creature's back. It was no wonder he wasn't in a warcraft class. He was already brilliant. He returned to the floor again to scrutinize the creature, and replaced his sword in his sheath. He dared to stroke the beak, and to Jade's surprise, there was no retaliation.

When the creature had finished licking the bones white, Aaron disappeared from sight. Jade pressed her cheek harder against the door to find a better angle, but still could not see him, although she could hear his footsteps.

The door swung open.

"Katherine?" Jade flushed as she tumbled over. How had he seen her? He clenched his jaw in what looked like anger, but after a moment's consideration, offered her a hand. "I was afraid someone else had been watching." He helped her up and shut the door behind them, then went back to the extraordinary creature. Jade hadn't spoken to him since her meeting with Eleanor, but if he remembered at all, he didn't ask. Jade only hoped that he wouldn't detect the guilt written on her face. "Do you know what she is?" he asked, patting the creature's head.

Jade nodded. "A griffin."

"They're the most loyal creatures in the whole of the Illysium."

"I know," Jade answered defensively. "They have natural compasses that can direct them to people instead of the poles."

Aaron nodded. "They're also extremely protective." Aaron turned to face her, towering. "Why did you follow me?" His expression lay between anger and curiosity, and his manner was somehow as aggressive and calculating as ever.

"I saw you go into the South Tower," she answered.

"You were following me before that." Jade didn't bother denying this. The search in his eyes made clear he was not one to be easily lied to.

"What do you do down here?"

"Answer my question, and then I'll answer yours."

"You were injured the last time I saw you in class. I thought this might be the reason. Was I right?" she asked.

Aaron considered her. "I train her." He looked back at the griffin. "And feed her."

Jade reached out a hand to touch the griffin's smooth feathers that looked soft as plumes of silk.

"No!" Aaron's hand latched around Jade's midair. When she gasped, he quickly loosened his grip. "Like this, or she'll hurt you." He guided her hand toward the griffin's wide pearly cheek, and pressed Jade's hand into the plush feathers. It fluttered its wings, reveling under their gentle touch.

"She's wonderful." If animals with beaks could have smiled, this one certainly did. It tilted its head to one side, and its watery gray eyes twinkled. "What's her name?" Jade asked.

"I don't know," he answered, dropping his hand.

"Why?"

"I can't name her until I'm sure she wants a name."

Jade tilted her head. "How can you be sure she doesn't want to be named now?"

"When she trusts me," Aaron replied, "*then* I can name her." When Jade looked back at him, he was scrutinizing her the same way he'd been examining the griffin. The intensity in his gaze made her want to crawl behind the door again.

"Where did you learn to do that?" she asked, nodding toward the beams he'd balanced on.

"Here. A year ago."

"You've been here two years?" Aaron nodded.

"Almost. I would stay at Constantine forever if she asked me to."

The comment took Jade by surprise. "So, you believe it too?" He furrowed his brow in confusion. "The story about Constantine being back. You think it's true?"

Aaron looked up at the roof. The night was heavy now, and there was cold drifting through the room. The candles were flickering. "Why shouldn't I?"

"You like Emerson, don't you? He said Constantine was nothing more than a martyr."

"I don't like Emerson any more than I like what he does. It's my parents who liked him—my mother anyway. My father didn't care for anything, much less the minister." Jade nodded, remembering their conversation in the courtyard before Lady Eleanor appeared. There was a silence as Jade processed this. Every day she yearned for her father, and here was someone who not only didn't miss his father, but worse, had hardly known one.

"Where are your parents?" he asked.

Jade averted her eyes to the griffin, which had now nestled its enormous head into its paws and closed its eyes at Jade's feet as if to purr its approval.

"I don't know," she answered, scared to say anything more. She dared to look up at him.

His eyes were scanning her face for something. Finally, he said. "I've heard a few of those stories this year." He looked behind him at the door as the clock struck the passing of an hour. "You should leave. If you leave now, no one will ever know you were down here."

"Can't I help train her?"

"Kat, if you're found here, you'll be expelled. Besides, griffins are dangerous. If you don't know what you're doing, you could die." Jade sighed, but he continued. "In any case, I didn't choose to train her, *she* found *me*. She was strutting around the East Tower, and I brought her here until I could send her back home."

"Where is that?"

"The White Caps. Here at least she has food. She'll last another few years here, but then she'll be strong enough to get out on her own."

"The White Caps?" Jade repeated.

"Big mountains north of the Lost Kingdom—where the elves live." He said it so seriously that Jade almost laughed.

"There are elves in the Lost Kingdom, and just north of that, there are griffins living on White Cap Mountain?" she asked with a raised brow.

Aaron shook his head sternly. "The White Caps—plural. The griffin, the Cyclops, and all the other ancient species live there. The Lost Kingdom is for nymphs, elves, and pixies. Species don't usually mix. They stay well away from us."

"Why are you worried about her being reported? Maybe someone else could find a way home for her."

"Kat." Aaron shook his head pitifully. "You're quite ignorant, aren't you?"

"I wouldn't say—"

He went on to explain. "This griffin is legally a *trespasser.* That means that I could be charged with affiliation with trespassers. You don't want to become an accomplice. It would be the end of your education here."

Jade pursed her lips. "Well, you can't exactly stop me."

Aaron looked at her out of the corner of his eye and smirked. "I never said I'd try." He dipped into a bow before she could answer. Then he left her alone with the extravagant creature.

CHAPTER 15

The next morning came much too soon. The sunlight that streamed in from the slit of a window behind Jade struck her eyes.

When she reached the assembly hall, and the last note of the organs faded, a fire caught the corner of Jade's eye. No, not fire, a red mane and an ivory tusk. The face that belonged to these was familiar, but from where? The tusk was slung around her back in a worn leather sheath, and she bore it as proudly as Aaron bore his ruby-embellished sword. Her head of ringed hair was like a rosebud in springtime, and her eyes shone brightly in the light of the hall. As though she had a sixth sense, the woman's fierce, stormy, blue eyes darted away from Lady Eleanor and landed on Jade. Now Jade remembered those eyes from Case Two's trial—her first day of classes at Constantine. She hadn't seen anyone sent to Quarantine since and was grateful.

Jade wanted to turn her gaze back to the stage, but her eyes were locked on that face. At last the woman looked away. Lady Eleanor was saying something about the students' performance thus far in their studies, and how pleased she was with the weapons they had received. At last they were dismissed for their first lesson, and Lady Eleanor bounded down the stage and out the door. Jade could feel people shoving past her, but her eyes were searching aimlessly for Rosebud. When she found her, she was already vanishing through the door.

"Jade, aren't you coming?" Camilla's voice echoed over the noise. Jade nodded absently and turned to her. Camilla had her hand tangled in Matt's hair, and let it drop into his hand when she caught sight of Jade.

"What lesson do I have again?"

"History. You're with us," Matt said hastily, letting go of Camilla and ushering Jade toward the door.

When they entered the classroom, one of the prefects was standing at the front, twisting his weapon absently in his hand. At the sight of the students, he stood lazily and hurried them to take a seat. Matt and Camilla took a seat at the front, and Jade hurried to find a seat as far away from them as she could manage. There weren't many. Finally, she took a place next to a young, plump boy with ginger hair and a scattering of dark freckles across his face.

"Who is that?" Jade asked him, pointing to the prefect.

"I don't know his name...Auden, maybe? I think he's replacing Professor Jackson today."

"Why?"

The boy shrugged. "He'll probably tell us soon." Jade dumped her things on the table.

"What's your name?" she asked, scooting her chair so he had more space.

"Frederick," he said uncomfortably, his face turning pink as though he were holding his breath.

Jade frowned, but then nodded. "I'm Jade."

Soon the prefect was handing out textbooks and took his place again at the front of the class. "Hey, guys," he greeted, earning a slight chuckle throughout the room.

"Get off the stage, Auden!" Matt bellowed, cupping his hands over his mouth. He rattled the arrows in his quiver in disapproval, grinning broadly. From where she sat, Jade could see his face—a huge smile spread across it—and couldn't help but smile herself.

"Shut up, Ferguson," the prefect shouted back, balling up some paper and throwing it at him. Matt ducked, and it hit Camilla squarely in the face. She reacted furiously, and slapped Matt's cheek. Hard. Jade could see her blushing from the back of the room as she looked sheepishly at Auden. This must be the prefect Camilla had been doting over the evening before. Now the room was beyond his control. Even Auden was laughing, and Frederick let out a nervous giggle.

When the laughing died down, the prefect returned to his uninterested expression. He explained to them that Professor Jackson was away on official business and would be returning soon. Then he proceeded to give them a long-winded assignment regarding views on the Division.

"And don't write anything dumb, Matt." The students giggled again. "Because Professor Jackson will be reading it."

At the front of the room, Auden sighed when Camilla raised her hand. He acknowledged her reluctantly. "If it's an opinion paper, how can the textbook help?"

"Why don't you open it and see?" he answered.

Jade thought it was a valid question, but she could see Matt suppress a grin. His expression sobered when Camilla caught sight of him. He rubbed her shoulder reassuringly and dove into the assignment.

Jade regurgitated everything Constantine's library had ever told her about the Division. The Oculus deemed it a "corrupt but necessary part of our stepping-stone to hell." She quoted this in her final sentence and stacked the four sheets of paper aside. According to this book, the Division consisted of non-magical creatures—invisible nymphs and faeries, and humans. These creatures all once lived together, but in battle between the gods, the weakest were punished by the Oculus and sent to live forever below the supreme species of Illysians, who were blessed with the power of magic. The story was a lie, of course, as was much of what the Oculus published, but it would be enough for this assignment, and for now, lie or not, agreeing with the Oculus was the only option.

Just as the bell rang, Professor Jackson came to collect their papers and hurried the prefect away from his post. Jade wanted to stay behind and ask him something, but he was gone as soon as he'd come. He stalked away, his scar burning brighter than ever and a more prominent limp in his leg.

Warcraft passed in the same fashion as ever. However, another prefect told them once more that the teacher was on official business and would be back soon. Jade was dubious and found herself eavesdropping on a hushed conversation between Christine and a few others.

"You're young to be in this class. What did you say your name was again?" one of the girls asked Christine. She introduced herself briefly and asked in return if anyone had had the regular teacher in first period. Everyone returned with the same conclusion that his or her teacher had been missing too.

"Seems like more than a coincidence," Christine whispered, her eyes on the prefect, who surveyed them with suspicion and contempt.

"Well, I think it has something to do with—" Frederick jabbed a finger toward the wall.

"Constantine? Impossible," a stout young boy countered. "What could she have to do with it? The minister just left."

"It could be true. I heard the teachers saying something about it during assembly," Christine insisted.

"God...they ought to tell us and not keep lying." Frederick fidgeted madly with his fingers.

"You want to know the truth?" Nathan asked, shoving himself between them. "I know because my father told me this morning." The eyes in the circle glanced between Jade and Nathan, but when nothing happened, they turned their attention to him again with wide eyes. His face was still scratched, but Jade felt somewhat relieved that he had recovered.

"Tell us!" Frederick begged.

"Please!" Christine added imploringly.

"They're planning punishments," he answered smugly.

"What? Why?" Frederick asked.

Jade had her ears peeled for his response.

"Someone here is from the Division."

CHAPTER 16

J ade stormed down the hall toward her room when they were dismissed. "Pegasus," she growled, using the command to open the door. After throwing her bags onto her bed, she paced the room angrily, rolling the matchbox around in her hands for comfort. Aaron was certainly the only person who knew, that much was certain. Nevertheless, whether because of some kind of unconscious denial or because she truly believed it, she could not, no matter how hard she tried, imagine he had said anything.

Yet he had. How else would they know? She'd finally found a place here. She wanted to curse the time she'd spent talking to him. Yet, stronger than the hatred she felt at her own gullibility was her desperation to find him.

She wrapped her fingers around her locket nervously. She pressed her lips against its cool exterior, and then shoved it back into her shirt, diving for the door and out again into the North Tower.

Among every face in the dining hall, not one belonged to Aaron. "Jade!" She turned on her heel and Matt grabbed her by the arm. "Did you hear?" he asked anxiously, almost excitedly. "Did they tell you about the teachers?"

Jade felt bad lying to Matt, but she didn't have much of a choice. "No, what's going on?" she asked as casually as she could manage. She was only halfheartedly listening when he answered, because most of her attention was preoccupied by her search for Aaron.

"You haven't seen Aaron, have you?" she inquired, letting Matt lead her to the buffet of food. Her heart was beating fast at the prospect of her punishment. Her thoughts pulled her back to her first law lesson—Case Two. Jade didn't even want her mind to venture toward the possibility of her own execution.

"Sure, he was in the dorm a minute ago," Matt answered, filling his plate greedily.

Jade hurried him along the line, taking the bare minimum of food. "Thanks."

"Don't mention it."

"Mention what?" Camilla's shrill voice sounded behind them, and she wrapped her arms around Matt's neck and kissed him.

Jade's eyes landed on Aaron's dark head of hair.

"Nothing, I've gotta go—I'll see you in a second. Here." She handed her plate to Camilla and was threading her way through the crowd before they could stop her. Aaron froze when he saw her headed his way, but then casually resumed conversation with someone.

Jade could hardly see with the number of people shoving her to and fro like a stubborn tide. Aaron stood with a man—his hair was gray and receding.

"Professor Jackson!" Jade called, hurrying to reach him at the front of the hall by the mural. Professor Jackson had taken an end seat, and he and Aaron were hunched over, heads bent in stern conversation.

He glanced up at the sound of his name and flashed a brilliant, though distorted, smile. "Jade Orwell, my star student!" Jade offered a warm smile. "Your recount of Constantine's downfall was superb. A brilliant historian you are, Jade, truly a natural if I ever saw one. I'm just helping Aaron with a question, but I'll be right with you."

Aaron glared at Jade, who returned the expression hastily. She was thinking of what to ask when a realization came to her. *Star student?* Surely Professor Jackson wouldn't have said that if he didn't mean it. And surely he wouldn't have meant it if he knew that she was from the Division, which he so blatantly despised. Yet, he must have known. He wasn't there in the morning because he was being told. That much was clear to Jade. Unless names hadn't been mentioned, unless—

"Mr. Henderson, I hardly know the details, but I realize rumors are circling among you students…"

Aaron returned his attention back to Professor Jackson, who was now addressing them both. "What have you heard? Have they said anything?"

Aaron's expression was dark when he locked eyes with Professor Jackson. Something in Professor Jackson's stern gravity made Jade believe he could be trusted. "Did they find one of them…someone from the Division?" Jade asked.

Professor Jackson arched his brow, and Jade wanted to suck back in her words, which were hanging idly between the three of them. "More than one," he answered in hushed tones.

"Do you know the punishment?" Aaron asked, his face twisted with worry.

"I'll be honest with you, Aaron, when *this* heals." He gestured to the scar running the length of his face, and Jade couldn't help but wonder if Lady Eleanor had scratched him with the same nail that had snatched at her wrist. "What I will tell you, though…" He cast a wary glance down the table where Lady Eleanor was taking a seat. Professor Jackson drummed his fingers along the table. "Some important decisions are being made, and a word of advice"—he beckoned them closer and continued—"keep your heads down if you want to make it through the afternoon."

"Thanks, sir," Jade blurted, watching Lady Eleanor approach.

Professor Jackson didn't have to turn to catch on, and neither did Aaron. "Anytime, Ms. Orwell. I'll see you in tomorrow's lesson." Jade nodded, and just as she and Aaron were about to leave, Lady Eleanor was there.

"Had a good morning?" she asked in her shrill, demanding voice.

They each nodded respectfully.

"Was the professor able to help you?" Again they nodded.

"Yes. As ever, Lady Eleanor, your choice this year in staff was superb," Aaron commented.

Lady Eleanor's eyes lingered on Jade curiously. Jade cowered, and the emerald charm book beat against her chest. "Leave him," she ordered both students. "You're hungry, I'm sure," she added kindly, offering a placid smile.

Jade waited as Aaron bowed deeply and turned on his heel. "What was *that?*" he snapped once they'd passed out of earshot, into the empty hall.

"Excuse me?" Jade returned, taken aback.

"Keep shoving your nose into things, and you'll get us both thrown out!"

She laughed in her anger. "Don't pretend like you have *anything* on the line," she spat, fury turning her cheeks red.

"What?" They were turning into the long, empty hall-way leading into the East Tower now and Aaron stopped.

"You told them about me."

"I did *not*," he replied, a hint of aggravation slipping through his normally impenetrable demeanor.

"Then I don't see why the punishment should concern you at all!"

"Is it so impossible for you to believe that I might just be looking out for you?" he hissed, his jaw clenched and his eyes wide as if to emphasize the absurdity of the notion. The question surprised Jade. She glared at him still, but knew he was telling the truth.

Her face relaxed in defeat. "Aaron, you're the only one who knew. I thought—"

"You were wrong," Aaron interrupted viciously. His brow smoothed again and his tone lowered. "Why would I have done that?"

Jade shrugged. "How else do they know?" Aaron looked past her in thought, and then pulled her into one of the empty classrooms that lined the hall. He flicked on the lights.

"I don't know, Kat." He rubbed a hand over his jaw. "Who else did you tell?" he asked.

"No one," she swore, sliding off her jacket. She realized her mistake too late, and the emerald charm book that housed all her guilt went cascading across the floor to lie face open at Aaron's feet.

Jade almost dove for it, but knew it would arouse too much suspicion, so instead she waited nervously for Aaron to bend and pick it up. Jade held out her hand for it, but at this Aaron hesitated, staring at her outstretched arm, held out a fraction of a second too early to have been unintentional.

"What is this?" he asked, turning the heavy thing over in his hands.

Jade knew she only had a few more seconds to salvage herself. To dismiss the question would only heighten his curiosity, but to answer him directly was impossible. "It's a charm book." Jade shrugged, daring to take a casual step toward him before he could flip through the pages.

"What kind?" He looked at the spine and the cover for a title, as Jade had done at first. Finding none he shuffled through the parchment.

"Aaron, no!" Jade erupted, stretching her hand to seize it from him. Startled, he yanked the book out of her reach and spread it open to the page she'd marked.

"I'm offended," he muttered, licking his finger and flipping the page again.

"*You're* offended? You're the one going through my things!" Jade said, angrily now, wanting him to drop the book and look at her instead. When he fell silent, Jade panicked. "It's not what it looks like—" she started, desperately.

"It looks very important to me." He didn't say a word as his eyes scanned the page and his mocking smile fell. He turned and held open the book to Jade so she could face her shame. "Katherine, do you know what this is?"

Jade couldn't answer. She'd never seen Aaron as grave as he seemed then, his eyes wide with alarm. He looked at her in a way he hadn't before, as if he feared her.

"Kat, this charm is illegal. You could kill yourself trying to do it alone. Why do you have this?" Still Jade couldn't answer. Her worst nightmare was unfolding itself full-fledged before her, and she could do absolutely nothing. She imagined the disgust on his face if she told him, if he ever knew. "Katherine, *answer!*" he boomed.

Jade knew it was only out of fear that he yelled at her, but all the same she was terrified, not of him, but of herself. What had she done? In one stroke Eleanor had tried to murder her and had isolated Jade from the only other person in the Academy smart enough to help her out of the deal.

She burst into tears. How had she been so gullible? She buried her red face in her hands and hated herself for her own stupidity. She didn't look up as she heard Aaron's footsteps pad toward her. She was thankful he didn't say anything as she tried to mop guilty tears from her face. She hoped he wouldn't tell the others. He blew out a breath and looked back down at the charm and the key as Jade had done. She watched, guilty, through a vision of tears.

When he was finished, he grabbed her jacket and slid the book back into the lining, then folded it and extended it to her without a word. Jade struggled to recompose herself. She couldn't shake from her mind the horrid, sharp accusation and horror in Aaron's voice. Worse than being angry, as Jade had imagined he would be, Aaron had looked at her as if she were a stranger, a monster.

He crouched until he was level with her eyes. "Katherine, you must tell me. Who gave you this book?" He spoke clearly and softly as if by way of apology.

Sobbing, Jade answered, "I can't tell you, Aaron. Not you, not anyone."

"Kat, who's doing this to you?"

"I can't. They'll find out!"

"*Who*?" When Jade didn't answer, Aaron brushed his hand through his hair, understanding the gravity of her dilemma. He paced before her in thought, and he must have understood her desperation, because he didn't try to guess the answer, although he probably could have. "Kat, how can I help if you keep guarding secrets?" Jade bit her lip. She barely knew how to help *herself*. "Kat, you have to get out of it. Whatever this is, it has to stop. You're going to get hurt."

"I know," she muttered bitterly, her hand twisting her locket in smooth rhythms. She wished her father were still with her.

"Katherine, you have to get out of it. At least try," Aaron demanded. Jade wiped the tears sloppily from her cheeks. "If something goes wrong, if this person... threatens you again, promise you'll come to me. You know I could help you if you let me."

Jade nodded, a timid relief flooding through her. It was nice, for a change, to feel as though she could finally depend on someone other than herself.

***

The next afternoon Jade plucked Justine out of a hoard of students. "Law, right?" Jade asked. Justine nodded zealously, but Jade dreaded the class. The first one had given her nightmares.

"You okay?" Justine asked as they entered the hall.

Jade pursed her lips. She'd been up crying half the night, and wasn't about to admit it now. She nodded.

"You look…down."

Jade shrugged.

"Christine was saying something about the teachers today…that Nathan told her firsthand."

Jade nodded.

"You believe it?"

Jade nodded solemnly.

"You wanna make a pact?" Justine asked.

"What?" Jade asked.

"Make a deal with me," Justine said as they took a seat on the top balcony, where they could get the best view. Justine clasped one of Jade's hands in hers, and Jade was forced to look her in the eye. Part of her wanted to wrench her hands from Justine's. The last deal she'd made had haunted her ever since, and she wasn't ready to take on another one. "If one of us gets taken in, we get each other out, okay? No matter what."

Jade nodded. "I'd come for you."

Justine smiled. "You'd better, because I wouldn't even let them take you in the first place." She managed a chuckle, but it was dry, and there was a serious underlying fear that Jade could feel mirrored in her own voice. "Anyway, what are warrior friends at the Academy for?" Justine added.

A party of teachers was gathered onstage. Professor Jackson was limping more than ever, and something seemed to have reopened the gash on his cheek. He dabbed it with a bloody cloth and joined the cluster of teachers. Soon students filed in, and Jade thought decidedly this must be it.

Whatever the teachers had spent the morning discussing would unfold here, on stage for all eyes to see. She didn't want to think about the look on Professor Jackson's face when he realized where she came from. Nor did Jade want to imagine the smug expression Nathan would wear as she was sentenced. Strangely, the most pained thought was about Matt when he found that she'd lied to him, that she didn't trust him with her secret.

"Whoa, what has you so stressed?" Matt laughed, pulling Jade's fingers from the seat. She hadn't realized she was digging her nails into the cushion they sat on. She shrugged absently, but felt around for her locket.

At last the hall quieted again, and she turned her attention to Lady Eleanor, who stood in front of a long line of teachers. "Good morning, students," Lady Eleanor began. "Shall we start with the anthem?" No one said a word until the organs started playing and the hall filled with music.

The song soothed Jade's nerves, and the tune carried her into another world. She wondered now, when they dragged her away or cast her into isolation, if Constantine really would be there for her. She'd always, in some respect, seen Constantine as Lady Eleanor's extended staff, but what if Constantine was more than that? Surely Constantine was on Jade's side. Didn't Professor Jackson say she liked the Division? Jade could hardly focus on that, but found it comforting at least to imagine she could rest her weighty worries in Constantine's protective walls.

Rosebud, as Jade had now decidedly named the redhead, slipped through the door, and Jade couldn't help but stare. The woman kept her eyes locked on Lady Eleanor, and her dark, stormy blue eyes seemed to turn icy cold with rage.

"Students," Lady Eleanor began again. "You may be thinking that the fashion in which we gather you all here today is curious. I would not be surprised if you found it questionable even, but then, we are dealing with questionable circumstances, are we not?" She surveyed the room with dark, beady eyes, one of her black-gloved hands pushing back her wiry hair.

"Given these curious circumstances, we ask that each student return to his or her room and rest until we come to examine you." She slid another spidery hand down her sides to flatten out the black gown she wore. "Any student found outside his or her room will be punished as we see fit." She offered a caustic smile. "Disobedience here is the *utmost* offense, and we do not tolerate it lightly." She twisted into the air and was gone before Jade could take her gaze from Rosebud's ivory tusk.

Justine clutched Jade's hand as they walked out of the room, holding tight enough for her nails to leave small, red marks. She didn't loosen her grip until they'd safely reached their room and were inside. Camilla had already arrived and was adjusting her hair in the mirror.

"Good day, wasn't it?" she asked sarcastically, smacking her lips.

"Brilliant," Jade answered.

"Did you know Matt has a severe allergy to my perfume?" Camilla asked randomly, picking up the bottle and staring at the back of it.

Jade couldn't help but laugh. She could always leave it to Matt to do something funny, even under the direst circumstances. "Since when?" she asked, leaning back on her pillows.

"Every time I come near him, he starts sneezing and tells me I have to go away immediately." It seemed to dawn on her how bizarre this behavior was, but Justine and Jade did nothing but exchange a dubious glance.

"I think Matt's just trying to be funny," Jade said in her most soothing voice. Camilla stuck her jaw out in defiance.

"Well, that's what I get for dating anyone off the *Estate,* isn't it? No manners, no sense of courtesy, rude, impolite…" Her words were muffled as she jumped into her bed and pulled the sheets up high over her head.

No matter how tired Jade was, she couldn't bring herself to sleep. Her mind was racing with anticipation. Lady Eleanor was bound to discover where she had come from. Had this anything to do with her deal? Had Jade unknowingly agreed to murder? All these questions cut through Jade's futile attempts at slumber, so she gave up and lay with her eyes open, staring at the crimson velvet tapestry above her.

She tried to think like Lady Eleanor, imagine her plans behind this escapade. What exactly had she said about their ill-constructed deal? She had merely handed Jade a dangerous book, and sworn her to secrecy and obedience. Jade thought of what Aaron had said and couldn't help but despair. Was there a way out? She couldn't bear the thought of serving Lady Eleanor anymore, or withstand the guilt of executing her darkest work. Of course, maybe she *could* be strong enough if it kept her nearer her father. For James, Jade was willing to sacrifice everything, because she knew somehow that he *was* alive, waiting for her, trusting her to find him. Her warm, pulsing locket told her so.

Even so, Lady Eleanor was no doubt as hate-filled toward the Division as any other Illysian. Their deal would be void, scratched out like a pencil with an eraser. There was no deal in all the worlds strong enough to break the divides that separated the Illysium from the Division, and Lady Eleanor would make no excuses for Jade. Deal or no deal, if Lady Eleanor found her out, Jade would be cast from the world without a second thought.

"I think it's me." Justine's voice startled Jade. It was right beside her, but small and scared. "I'm the one from the Division they must have found."

Jade was shaking her head vigorously. "You've never even been to the Division." Jade pulled her onto the bed and sat her up, whispering so Camilla couldn't hear. "It won't be you. It's impossible—"

"Constantine did it!" Justine hissed, her eyes wide with terror as they rolled over the walls of the room, expecting a fierce retaliation for having told the secret.

"What did she do to you?"

Justine shrugged. "I don't know, but when I came through the portal, she did something…changed me! Every now and again, I feel it, like my magic is draining away from me…here." She traced the same vein Matt had traced along Jade's arm her first night at the Academy. "They're going to take me."

"I wouldn't let that happen. Not in a heartbeat. You're right here with me, aren't you? Safe and sound, just like always, and I won't leave you until you say so. Okay?"

Justine nodded frantically, and her breath was quick. Worry creased Jade's brow, because she'd never seen Justine so scared. They jolted up when they heard a halting screech of brakes and clinking glass coming from down the hall.

A harsh hand rapped on the door.

CHAPTER 17

The needle was long and fat. Aaron tried not to look as it penetrated the flesh of his arm. It went deeper and deeper until he thought he felt it reach his bone. He scrunched up his face tight to hold back the scream of agony forming in his throat.

"Hold still, back straight, big breath," the nurse cooed, pulling back the syringe so that she could draw enough blood. *Hold still, back straight, big breath*, Aaron recited until he was almost numb from the pain. He looked enviously at Matt, who'd had the fortune of being sedated after pretending to hyperventilate. The nurse removed the needle. "Shirt, please," she said, gesturing for him to remove it. He obeyed, casting it onto the crimson sheet of his bed. They executed the same practice on all four limbs, his abdomen, and his back.

I'm not going have any blood left when this is over, he thought bitterly. He knew it had to be done, though, and he recognized the procedure from years ago.

He'd spent enough time in the district office with his mother to know that it was used to track traces of the Division in the blood. Aaron wondered how accurate their equipment was, fearful of being wrongly accused. When the nurse was finally done, she squirted the blood into separate vials and took diligent notes on each. She collected his blood in a tray.

"Wait here," she said stiffly, backing out of the room with his blood.

Matt was slowly coming back to life, having been sprawled clumsily across his bed. He sat up dizzily, massaging his arm. "Where did they go?" he asked groggily, his voice hoarse.

Aaron wasn't listening to him as he continued on about the absurdity of their assumptions. "As if they think *we* would be from the Division. My parents would laugh if they ever knew—"

"Stay here," Aaron ordered, standing up suddenly. He pulled his shirt back over his head and reached for the door.

"Where are you going?"

"To figure out Stage Two."

Matt raised a brow. "Stage Two?" He followed Aaron to the door, grabbing his own shirt and weapon on the way.

Aaron pushed a hand against Matt's chest before Matt could step outside. "No. You need to be here when they come back."

"To say what? My roommate lost his mind temporarily and went off to *figure out Stage Two*?"

"Sure, but leave out the latter half." Before Matt could stop him, he was racing away down the stairs and slipping silently through the door. He left his shoes inside and ran barefoot along the halls, listening intently for something—voices, footsteps, the click of heels.

When his father had come back from his mysterious getaway to White Caps Mountains, they had taken him, but what happened after the blood draw? Aaron had to stop and lean against the wall to think straight.

His limbs were weak, and he had become short of breath faster than he was used to. He wracked his brain for that memory—stumbling down the white walls with his mother's pale hand holding his firmly as they waited with his father. It had been the usual distress and panicked worry that seemed to follow his father everywhere.

"Don't move, Aaron," his father had said in an authoritative tone. "I'll be right back." When he wasn't right back, Aaron had slipped away from his distracted mother and followed his father down the hallway. He clenched his jaw, trying to remember.

He'd thrust aside the memories of his parents, and aside from what information they forced into his brain, he ignored the comings and goings of their affairs. Then it came to him—the gruff doctor with auburn hair and his father shaking in a seat. The room was different from all the other rooms. On the plaque it had letters, not numbers, but Aaron couldn't read at the time. Aside from that there was a padlock on the front. *Interrogation*, Aaron thought. His father had passed interrogation before they brought him on to Stage Three, but then there were the cords and the straps binding him to the chair and a machine that monitored his racing pulse…

Aaron didn't like the memory and hastily returned it to the furthest corners of his mind. *If I were Lady Eleanor, where would I interrogate?* Then it struck him, and as he was moving to emerge from the shadows, he heard a sound. It was only a slight shuffling, but it was enough to make him freeze. Only a few feet away, someone was padding down the hall. There was a slight whimpering as she caught her breath and sighted Aaron in his small crevice. He recognized the slight frame and braided hair, but couldn't place a name to her face.

The little girl put a finger to her lips, gesturing for him to be quiet.

"Christine, don't be afraid, we only want to help you," a voice cooed from farther down the hall. Aaron shook his head warningly. He didn't know her well, but he was sure if they wanted to do anything, it wasn't to help her. "*Don't,*" he mouthed, sensing her temptation to dash from the confines of the pillar. She creased her brow and then, as if she were about to fall asleep, she closed her eyes and tipped forward, stepping timidly into sight.

She barely had time to gasp before something struck her squarely in the chest.

"Tie her up, we don't have much time." Aaron recognized one of the nurse's voices, and he felt a taste for revenge brewing inside him. Christine lay limp on the stones, and several pairs of rough hands tied rope around her wrists and ankles. Aaron clenched his jaw and followed them stealthily, leaping from shadow to shadow until they'd reached a familiar part of the South Tower.

They passed the hall leading toward his griffin, which he willed to remain quiet. Aaron's suspicions were confirmed the minute he stepped foot into the hall. He waited for them to unlock the secured door and wedged his foot inside just before it closed. He slipped through, ducking below the ledge of a one-way mirror into the interrogation room.

A group of Ocumen walked into the whitewashed room, drowned in sharp, fluorescent light. The room Aaron stood in was dark and damp. He hoped desperately that no Ocumen would return. There were only four walls and the secure door that led into the open hallway. He'd have to work fast. The nurses were clustered around the new suspect, and they brusquely rushed to latch her onto that machine—that terrible machine that dug those terrible memories from inside him.

As Aaron remembered, they started off with the simple questions to test the behavior of her pulse. For every truth, her pulse rate was fast and steady. Any deviation from that would result in punishment. Three of the white-coated women stood before her, questioning. Along the back of the interrogation room stood a squad of Ocumen. That was different.

They were heavily armed with ammunition, and one had been called to stand beside the nurses. "Your name?"

"C-Christine," she answered, trembling with fear. A thin sheen of sweat built on her delicate face, and the nurses paused, examining the machine.

"Age?"

"Eleven—no, twelve. I just turned twelve." Her breath was quick as she stared apprehensively into the nurse's unyielding gaze.

"When was your birthday?"

"Two months ago," she answered, taking deep breaths in and out to calm herself.

"How did you celebrate it?" the nurse asked, her voice caustic.

"The same as always, we—" Her voice caught in her throat at the memory. "We invited my family to dinner at the house."

"The house you lived in, presumably?"

Christine nodded, lifting her chin to see what the nurses were writing on their boards.

"Were you close with the family?"

Christine nodded vigorously. "My parents love me. They know where I am, they'll know—" The nurses all glanced up to face her, and Aaron wanted to slap a hand over her mouth and drag her out, but if they thought she'd called for help, punishment would only be worse. "They'll know if you hurt me!" She was screaming now out of desperation, and her pulse was beating wildly, the buzzing of the machine skyrocketing.

"Do we have reason to hurt you?" the same serene voice asked politely, standing now. Christine's jaw dropped as she realized what she'd done. Aaron backed away from the window and looked around the small dark closet he stood in. There must be some way for him to help.

A bloodcurdling scream reached his ears before he had a chance to do anything. He darted back to the window to find Christine in a worse state than before. The Ocuman drew back his hand again and slapped her.

"Thank you," the nurse said calmly, pulling out a handkerchief to pat away the sweat on her own forehead. "We only want the truth, Christine."

"I told you! I'm telling you—I don't know. I'm an Illysian just like you. I have parents, and you can ask them." The nurse stood, shaking her head. She turned to address the others, and Aaron realized he'd been holding his breath. There was dim light coming into his enclosure from the interrogation room, scattered onto the walls. Next to the secure door a white sheet had been crudely pinned up. When Aaron inspected it, he caught sight of his name.

Aaron Henderson (Stage One)

There were three columns. The first was labeled Stage One, the second Stage Two, and the third Stage Three. Stage Three was undoubtedly the ensuing punishments. Adjacent to most names, including his, a green stamp had been printed in the first column—"Validated." He scanned the enormous list, and his eyes landed on Christine's name. In the first stage, "Denied" was printed in thick red ink that soaked through to the wall. The stamps were placed neatly beside the list on top of the ink beds that belonged to them. He let his gaze wander the list for names he recognized. Matthew Ferguson: "Validated." He heaved a sigh of relief, and heard footsteps nearing the door.

He knew it was Lady Eleanor by the squeak of her leather gloves and the shrill voice demanding the door to open. Aaron's heart was racing. Maybe if he hadn't just had several vials of blood drawn, he might be able to keep his thoughts in line, and his head wouldn't be spinning at the thought of her discovering him. There was another name, though, just one last name he had to find.

He couldn't see properly in the dark, and Lady Eleanor's footsteps seemed to be pounding against the inside of his skull.

He dragged a finger along the paper. *There!* he thought with zeal. Jade's first stage was stamped "Denied," in the same red ink beside Christine's name. He ran a hand through his hair to push it back and fumbled for the stamp. He lifted the ink bed. "Open." Lady Eleanor's voice came from outside the door. Aaron froze. Even his heart seemed to stop beating. Nothing happened. He knew he only had about eight seconds. Lady Eleanor knocked harshly on the metallic door. Aaron's senses finally caught up with him, and he unlatched the box for the ink bed. *Five seconds left.* He grabbed the stamp by the thick wooden handle and rammed it into the green ink bed, his eyes darting between the number on the wall and the sheet. He thrust the inked stamp into the second column beside the name and stepped back to ensure it was right.

Katherine Orwell—"Denied"/"Validated"

Aaron quickly moved his hands to replace the stamp and the ink bed, hoping above all hopes that it would work. Two seconds. Lady Eleanor was fumbling with keys now, muttering something incoherent. Aaron scrutinized the area for something to hide behind. *One second.* He unsheathed his sword and moved over a square panel in the roof. He grabbed onto the ledge and hauled himself up with silent steps, replacing the panel beneath him just as the door swung open.

Aaron pressed his ear against the panel. He heard Lady Eleanor open another door into the interrogation room, just as another wretched cry erupted from Christine's throat.

"What are you doing?" Lady Eleanor's voice roared, her heels clicking ferociously against the ground. "How dare you!" There was another shuffling of feet.

"You asked us to interrogate," the nurse said, fear ringing through her tone.

"I don't recall asking you to smear her face with blood at *this* stage!" She growled something angrily. "You're hopeless, all of you worthless, writhing villains. Clean her face."

There was a whimper, but something stifled it. "And then?"

"What's the verdict?" Lady Eleanor sighed.

"Denied," the nurse said calmly.

"No, please, please!" Christine's cries were muffled by something, as though she were speaking through a carpet.

"Send her on to Stage Three. From now on we need to be a little more *discreet* with our practices, boys and girls," Lady Eleanor added reproachfully. With that there was another click of heels, and she was gone again.

Aaron could hear a thud and then a scraping sound as someone dragged Christine out of the chair. It was the nurses who would come out first. He found himself devising a plan to take out the nurses, slip past the Ocumen, and grab Christine before they could take her to Stage Three. When he heard the nurse's steps, he moved to slip open the panel of the roof that he stood on, but it wouldn't budge. "Constantine!" he hissed into the darkness, sure that she was stopping him.

Aaron's fingers were cutting into the wooden splinters now, but it was magic that glued the panel to its place, and no strength could remove whatever charm she'd placed on it. When Constantine finally did render the panel to his grip, he dropped down to find the same Ocumen occupying the interrogation room, but it was otherwise empty.

Christine was nowhere to be found.

CHAPTER 18

"Pegasus!" Justine said excitedly, bursting through the door. Jade looked up from her bed and ran to Justine, wrapping her arms tightly around her. "I'm alive!" She laughed exuberantly, sprawling herself across the familiar mattress at the end of the room.

"I was up waiting all night. What did they do?" Jade asked, sitting cross-legged on her bed so she could face Justine.

Justine shrugged. "The line was long, but once I got in there, they just asked some questions, wrote some stuff down, and sent me right on my way." She was quick to fill in the details. Jade's stomach was growling after having skipped her last meal to speak to Professor Jackson. Besides that, the blood drawing hadn't helped.

"They didn't interrogate *us* at all," Camilla said, holding a pair of earrings to the side of her head and inspecting them in the mirror.

"Good for you." Justine said sarcastically.

Camilla turned, digging her heels into the carpet. "Well, don't you have a mouth!" She cocked her head to the side.

"Just wait 'til I get started," Justine replied, but she was smiling and threw her arms up in exasperation, falling once again into her mountain of plush bedding.

"Try not to kill each other while I'm gone." Jade grinned and opened the door to leave.

"I couldn't kill her if I tried. That poison yesterday *obviously* didn't work." Camilla smiled at Justine sheepishly from behind her hand mirror. "I should come with you, Jade. I told Matt to meet me in the breakfast hall anyway."

On their way out the door, Jade heard Justine shout, "Careful, Cami, don't want to upset his allergy."

Camilla rolled her eyes, but couldn't suppress a smile herself.

When they reached the dining hall, they hurried to find some food, and Jade quickly piled everything in sight onto her plate.

"Leave some for the rest of us," Matt joked behind her, passing Jade in the queue.

"Matt!" Camilla's voice came to them from a distance. Jade muttered something about joining them in a minute, but secretly wanted to run back to the room and eat there. As she approached the table, she could see Matt sneezing again, hard enough to shove back his own chair.

"Don't even try it—I know all about your little trick," Camilla was saying, wiping something from his face.

"Who says it's a trick?" he asked, throwing an arm around her chair. Camilla looked over at Jade as she sat down across from them.

"Ah." He grinned, and Jade let a smile touch the edge of her lips. "Neither of you has seen Tom, have you?" he asked, absently searching the crowd. Jade and Camilla shook their heads.

"Well, this must be a first," Camilla said, watching Aaron take a seat. "Aaron Henderson coming to eat with us *commoners* for breakfast." She looked to Matt, who'd swung forward now in his seat.

Aaron raised a brow. "I eat with you all the time."

"Not for breakfast," she argued.

Aaron barely saw her. He sat down with his eyes on the door, where Mr. Reynolds stood. His eyes flittered toward Jade, and she knew he was wondering if she'd solved her dilemma or not.

"That's because he usually wakes up about five minutes before assembly," Matt explained, biting greedily into his toast. "Anyway, I'm surprised you aren't tired now, Aaron, given that you didn't come back to the room until after I'd gone to sleep."

"You *left* your room?" Camilla dropped her jaw, but closed it abruptly. "I didn't think you had it in you to disobey our headmistress."

Aaron let a devious smile play on his lips. "Desperate circumstances…"

"Did you find anything?" Jade asked. Aaron looked warily at Camilla, who raised a brow expectantly.

"Aaron—I hardly ever tell secrets," Camilla snapped, tilting her head.

"I don't recall it being that way on the Estate," Aaron commented. The edge in his tone was almost unnoticeable.

After a moment of silence, Aaron turned in response to Jade's question. He didn't know where to start, but decided that warning Christine not to step into the hallway was as good a place as any. He tried to skip over the more gruesome details, but even that could never make the story sound right, sound pleasant. When the bell announced it was time for assembly, he had finished a haunting account of Christine's imprisonment. No one stirred.

"What will they do to her?" Camilla asked, lines of worry forming in her smooth brow.

Aaron pushed his plate away. "Just be grateful it wasn't you," he said, standing.

Jade thanked him quietly for stamping her name, but Matt erupted.

"Just be grateful it wasn't us?" he repeated, fuming. "Be glad it was Christine instead, right?" Aaron didn't flinch as Matt's breath quickened.

"There was nothing to be done," Camilla said in Aaron's defense, pulling Matt back into his seat.

"Is that a joke?" he asked, looking from face to face.

"He's right, we have to do something." All eyes turned when Jade said this. Camilla looked alarmed. "Now that we know. Otherwise we're—otherwise we're just like them." It was, of course, tempting to pretend Aaron hadn't seen it at all, and that the story had been just that—a story. But Jade would never be able to.

Matt slumped back in his seat, remorsefully. "We've got to help her."

"Thank you, Sherlock," Camilla said, her voice dripping with sarcasm. "Unfortunately, we won't have time tonight. I have essays due of all sorts. Anyway, I doubt Lady Eleanor is going to do any serious harm. For heaven's sake, she's a headmistress, not a serial killer. Tomorrow we'll meet in front of the West Tower around dusk. Until then"—she raised her brow reproachfully—"not one word," she said, narrowing her eyes toward Aaron. She beckoned Matt to follow her, and the table quickly dispersed as they allowed themselves to be herded to lessons in the East Tower.

***

"Here, let me show you. The view is amazing," Justine was saying, grabbing Jade's arm that night after dinner. Jade was stuffed full of spiced chicken, and she begged Justine to slow down. The halls were cold and damp, and Jade could feel goose bumps all along her spine.

"Hey." The voice was familiar, and the face that emerged around the corner was too, but Jade couldn't place it.

"Hi, Greg," Justine said, slowing only minutely to face the boy.

He paused after he'd passed them and then called back, "You…you haven't seen Frederick, have you?"

Jade hadn't seen Frederick in at least two days. They both shook their heads, and then waited for him to leave somewhat dejectedly before hurrying up the stairs again.

"Justine, where are you taking me?"

Justine giggled excitedly and dragged Jade along a narrow little hall that extended off the highest level of the North Tower, up steep, dilapidated steps. "Be patient, I promise we're almost there."

Jade groaned, fumbling with the books she'd salvaged from the library.

They emerged at last onto a platform. There was a door with silvery light seeping in through the hinges. "What is this?" Jade asked dubiously, clutching Justine's back.

"Close your eyes," Justine ordered. She pushed Jade carefully through the door, and when it opened again, Jade was standing on top of the world. The hike up the steps had brought them to what looked like inches from the Illysian stars. Constantine Academy sprawled out beneath them in a vast, magnificent array of bronze-tipped spires and fiery crimson curtains peeking through the windows. The walls were refulgent in the darkness, and the whole of the Illysium seemed to look up at Jade like an ocean at high tide. Jade stood there, trying to absorb the vastness, the immensity of a world she might have fallen in love with. When she turned back, Justine was lying on the roof shingles, with her hands crossed behind her head.

Jade sat to join her. "When did you find this?" she asked.

Justine answered somewhat solemnly, "Yesterday, after the interrogation." Jade settled onto the cool shingles beside Justine. "You know something?" Justine said, her voice reduced to a whisper.

"Hmm?"

"Frederick will be the fourth one."

"What?"

"I've been counting since I left the interrogation room. Frederick will be the fourth to go missing."

Justine's voice was breaking, and even in the darkness, Jade could see tears.

"Frederick is probably in his room waiting for Greg or whomever to come back—"

"No!" Justine yelled, almost angrily. Her voice was sharp, acerbic. "No, he was *taken*, I know it," she whispered. "I'm so sure, it...it scares me. It's like they're disappearing left and right. Frederick...Frederick passed the interrogation too. I was next to him. *Next* to him," she cried, her lips trembling.

"No," Jade whispered. She turned over and sat up to grab Justine in her arms. "Trust me, Justine, you're safe. I'll look after you," she cooed, rocking Justine as her father had often done to her. She could feel hot tears on her shoulder, and all the fear returned to her—her muscles tense, her heart pounding resistance. Camilla's words passed through her: *she's a headmistress, not a serial killer*. But Camilla had never seen Lady Eleanor the way Jade had that afternoon in her office. She wished she could expose Lady Eleanor the way Case Two had been. She would sit at the front of the court and point an angry finger at Lady Eleanor. *A sentence to Quarantine for fraud and attempted murder!*

"Shhh." Jade hushed Justine's tears as they sat looking over the precipice of what felt like the edge of the world. "I promise, you'll be safe. I promise." It felt like there wasn't anything else to say.

***

When the music from the organs died and the anthem had been sung, Lady Eleanor spoke of her appreciation for their good behavior last night, and explained vaguely what the test was for. She didn't mention one word about the Division. Just as she finished her last sentence, Camilla shifted in her seat, and her whip loosened from its secure hold on her belt, and dropped to the floor. Jade bent to pick it up and was about to hand it to Camilla when she stopped dead.

Jade tried inconspicuously to untangle it. She fumbled with it anxiously in her hands. The leather was coarse and strong, but it was the hilt that had caught her attention. On its hilt was a single ornament in the dark graphite—the blue stone. Exactly as hers had done the first time she touched it, Camilla's stone warmed to Jade's touch, glowing a fluorescent blue. Tiny lights like miniature fireflies clanged inside it wildly. It reached a crescendo, and just as before, it flickered and died.

Camilla was gaping. Jade jabbed a finger into Matt's shoulder. *Look!* she mouthed, handing him the whip by the hilt. She remembered he'd seen the same thing on his bow.

His eyebrows arched, and he nodded, gesturing for her to turn back to Lady Eleanor while he inspected it. Jade was itching for the assembly to be over long before it finally ended. She scrambled to catch up with Matt after he'd returned the whip to an anxious Camilla.

"What do you think?" she panted, finally falling into step with him.

Matt shook his head in thought. "I'm thinking it's not a coincidence."

***

"What do you think, Jade?" Mr. Reynolds had his eyes on her.

Jade's mind was blank. "Sorry?" she asked dumbly, tucking her long black hair behind her ears.

"What do you know about black spanners?"

At the front of the class, Camilla's hand shot up, and Nathan cast Jade a smug expression, turning in his chair to catch her response.

She wracked her brain for something remotely intelligent to say. "They're Divisional creatures that... evolved from demons in the Underworld," she added, looking pointedly at Nathan. He turned back to the instructor and folded his arms across his chest.

"Can anyone elaborate?"

Camilla was still flailing her hand in the air. Mr. Reynolds had no choice but to choose her with a sigh.

"The black spanner is impure and is the most dangerous creature in the Division, because it is damned to live forever with demon blood in its veins, and only a sliver more magic than mortals. They're normally bred in captivity for use as guards, because no one can kill them. Also, they are naturally brilliant fighters. In addition, it's little known that Gammadorn was the first to create one, and most of his army was composed of them during the war against Constantine."

Mr. Reynolds shook his head and paced the room. "Correct on all but one account." Camilla showed every sign of interrupting, so he continued hastily. "Black spanners can be killed very easily. The only problem is that nobody wants to. The murderer of a black spanner is damned to live as one himself—that is, of course, if he makes it through the mutation.

"The full mutation won't come for a few weeks or even months after he has committed the crime, but when it does come, it can be fatal. The aftereffects can include minimal scarring, permanent loss of memory, or death. Very few black spanners make it through unharmed. Does anyone here know why you are damned if you kill one?"

Camilla's hand shot up again, and Mr. Reynolds looked away from her. He looked instead toward a timid-looking girl whose face flushed when she was chosen. "Well…they, um, are mutations of angels with black wings. And if you kill an angel, no matter what kind, or for what purpose, it's a sin?" Her answer sounded more like a question.

Mr. Reynolds sighed. "For that convoluted answer, I'll assign you all two essays and reading to complete for next week." The class groaned, and Jade knew she wouldn't have time to complete it. Nevertheless, she wrote down the homework for Justine, in hopes they might work on it together.

When the noon bell dismissed them, Jade was exhausted and tried to will herself to stay awake for the remainder of her lessons. When she approached the courtyard, she found herself in search of Justine's black locks and dark skin. Justine had told her this morning that she was going to one of Professor Jackson's "extravagant lectures." Still, given their conversation the night before, it had her on edge. Instead of Justine, Jade was met with a rowdy cluster of students crowding the yard. They chanted in unison, their eyes glued to the stone wall between the North and East Towers.

Jade stood on her toes to find Justine in the audience, but she was nowhere to be seen. Jade was just turning to go when the audience began counting down. Intrigued, she turned to thread her way through the crowd and see what they were looking at. Auden was sitting cross-legged on the grass before the wall. He flickered in and out of visibility with a ball held out at arm's length. His eyes bulged, and his face scrunched up in discomfort as he disappeared again for a substantial time. The throng of students counted down from ten.

"What's he doing?" Jade asked incredulously, not really expecting an answer from anyone around her. They were much too engrossed in the spectacle to have even heard her—all except one.

"Well, well, if it isn't my dear friend Jade." Nathan's nasal voice sounded at her ear. He rolled his eyes. "He's using his weapon. What does it *look* like?"

"It looks like you're being a—" The uproar of the crowd drowned out the word she'd chosen, but she was certain he'd heard it, because he strutted away muttering something unintelligible. Jade turned back to Auden, who was breathing heavily, and stuck a lazy hand out to Matt for some water. Matt hooted something encouraging that made the audience laugh. He waved heartily when he spotted Jade, but hastily returned his attention to the ravenous audience. Jade finally succumbed to her curiosity and took a seat around the edge of the court. She dug into her food eagerly, but paused periodically to watch the performance.

"An astonishing three minutes! Ladies and gentlemen, give him a round of applause!" Matt said zealously, putting on his best game-show-host voice. The audience erupted into another cacophonous cheer. Matt cleared his throat.

"Would a third contestant like to step up to the stage and claim his place?" There was an explosion of hands in the air, and Matt turned to Auden for him to choose.

Auden held his finger in the air dramatically and then pointed it at Matt, with a devilish smile playing on his lips. "Payback is sweet!" he yelled, raising his arms as if to relish in the approving jeer.

Matt laughed, but didn't reject the invitation. He stepped into the small space of grass that had been cleared for him and slung his quiver around his back, adjusting the leather strap around his torso to tighten it. He pulled an arrow from it with ease. Even the most untrained eye could see that his weapon truly had become an extended limb. He drew back the arrow, holding his arm high, and paused to aim perfectly. The audience was silent, and he smiled, his eyes twinkling with excitement.

Matt loved the way his heart pounded whenever he used his arrows. He was awed by the ease of the slender instrument, and the beautiful whistling as the arrow flew past his ear. He didn't know what he would do, until his eyes landed on just the face he'd been looking for. Perched between two pillars along the edge of the courtyard, Jade was sitting with her head down, contemplating. How could her focus be so steadfast toward everything except him?

***

The arrow sprang so fast that when Jade saw its trajectory aimed for her face, she could do nothing but freeze. She held a rigid breath, and heard several gasps of amazement. The arrow flew into a crack half an inch above her head, and Matt drew back three more, aiming each one so they jammed themselves into the cracks of the stone just above her.

When she opened her eyes again, Matt was flashing a brilliant smile. *Pay attention,* he mouthed with a wink. Jade chuckled, but he was already out of sight, immersed in the crowd. Jade laughed and pulled the arrows from within the cracks in the stones. She dropped the four of them into her bag. Knowing Matt, he'd forget to pick them up.

She looked up to see if she could find him in the throng of students, but he was buried. With this thought, she looked up at the grandfather clock on the North Tower. It chimed three times. She slipped into a jog up to the dorm room, her thoughts racing in time with her steps, hoping to find Justine there. She only had a few minutes until lessons resumed, and Jade couldn't place the unsettling nerve creeping up her back. She needed to see Justine. Some unfamiliar compulsion drove her to seek her out before the next period.

"Pegasus," Jade muttered hastily, having climbed the stairs and reached her dorm. The door struggled open, but closed again as though forced back. She said it again with more conviction and clarity. This time, there was no response, and the door stood resolute, unwavering and still.

"Jade?" Justine's voice came through the wooden grain.

Jade felt a flood of relief. "Justine! Thank God. I was just looking for you. I hadn't seen you. I thought you'd be in the lecture hall—"

"Listen, I can't talk right now. I'm not feeling well."

Jade could feel a panicked protest building inside her throat. "Are you okay? Do you need the nurse or—"

"I'm okay, I already went to the nurse, I just need some time to…get better."

Jade felt her face go hot with worry. "You don't think this has anything to do with"—she waited for some students to pass—"you know, the blood drawing, do you?"

"Don't worry. Seriously, I think it'll pass. I just… Don't come in, please. Just catch up the notes in class for me, will you? I need time alone."

Jade fought the urge to knock down the door. Justine had been complaining about a fever the night before, but Jade was starting to wonder if it was something more serious.

"Justine, let me take your temperature at least—"

"Jade, I'm sorry, it's not that…I just don't want to see anyone. I promise I'm fine, just catch up the notes, will you?"

"Justine!" Jade begged, her yell muffled slightly by the carpet. "Justine, open the door!" She glanced around quickly for a clock. There was none, but she could feel the minutes ticking away. She should've been in class. "Justine!" she hissed again. She clenched and un-clenched her fists, wrapping her hands around the cool metal matchbox in her pocket. She fumed for a minute or two. Hopes of conversing with Justine again had van-ished altogether.

She sighed in defeat, but she heard something. She pressed her ear against the door. There she heard a sin-gle, unmistakable note, and nothing more.

CHAPTER 19

Dinner had ended, and Matt was itching to find Jade. He scoured the hall for her, but no matter where he looked, his eyes never landed on her face. He was walking at Auden's side, and decided that even if he did see her, any attempt to speak to her would be futile. He dropped his eyes, feeling as though he was blatantly forgetting something. It was at this thought that he turned to Auden.

"You haven't seen Tom, have you?" Matt asked, realizing Auden was still midsentence. Auden had a way of speaking that made him seem like a video on replay as opposed to a human being. He was ruthless in his unswerving self-praise. Matt couldn't fathom Camilla's obsession with him. At the moment Auden was in the process of describing to Matt his latest noteworthy achievement.

Auden looked annoyed, but shook his head. "Have you seen Frederick? I looked for him all day. The kid told me he'd do my essay for tomorrow," he muttered as they turned into the dorm.

Matt only knew the name because Jade had sat next to him during first period a few days ago. He thought maybe they knew each other, or that she'd desperately wanted to sit next to him that morning, the way Camilla chased after Auden. That didn't make sense, though. Frederick was good company enough, but he was short and somehow gangly. His hair was greasy and fell to his shoulders in a tangled mess. After pondering this, Matt came to the conclusion that she had been avoiding *him,* but why? Was she angry or jealous? He hoped it was the latter.

Matt ducked beneath the door frame after Auden. The living quarters were busier tonight than usual. He left Auden with a group of prefects, and sauntered away to a quieter place in the room. The smell of a kindling fire, old leather, and sweet pastries filled his nostrils. He sat down on a seat that faced the fire and cupped his chin in his hand, biting into a jelly doughnut.

He was forgetting something.

Matt tried to rewind to earlier that day, before last period, before lunch, before assembly. Stop. The day before, he'd been sitting with Jade, Aaron, and Camilla—the memory came back to him faster than he'd have liked. Aaron's unsettling recount of Christine's capture made him flex his fists. He clenched his jaw, and his eyes darted toward the watch on his wrist. Matt sprang up. *West Tower at dusk.*

He hastily began threading his way through the crowd. Just as he made his way toward the door, a voice erupted behind him.

"Hey, Matt!" Matt not only recognized the voice, but also the face too. He couldn't put a name to it, though, and only vaguely remembered the boy from a class he took. Did they sit together in history? He racked his brain for the boy's name.

"Hey!" he answered, wanting more than anything to escape into the cool, fresh air in the courtyard. "What's up?" He turned on his heel now and rested a hand on the knob of the door that opened out into the halls.

"Some impressive stuff back there today. You've been practicing with your weapon, huh?"

Matt furrowed his brow, but then he remembered his supercilious performance. He could practically see Jade rolling her eyes. Matt laughed, brandishing his bow.

"Thanks, Greg." The name came to him, along with everything else he knew about Greg—not much. Greg was a burly, sixteen-year-old sportsman. He'd grown up with Matt in the Keeping and had helped construct the newer buildings for the Oculus since he'd turned twelve. Matt wasn't surprised, since most parents in the Keeping wanted their children to join the construction business— it was the safest. Matt, on the other hand, was given the short straw. The year he'd signed up for construction, only one space was left, and he'd signed his cousin up for it instead of himself.

"You haven't seen Tom, have you?" Matt asked.

"No, have you seen Frederick?" Matt shook his head. "Sorry. Auden was looking for him too. I'll see you later."

Greg made his way toward a cluster of equally bois-terous friends, and Matt took the opportunity to duck out of the room.

Matt shook the memory from his mind and took care to walk among the shadows, because as much as he hadn't minded Greg's interruption, he didn't want to elicit any further conversation from anyone. Besides, there was a quick-paced excitement kindling inside his chest, and he was disquieted by the possibility they would plan something without him. Matt was convinced that whatever discussion awaited him in the courtyard would bring him a few steps closer to finding out what had really happened to his parents.

"Matt!" There seemed to be no end to the interrup-tions. He almost groaned in frustration, but restrained himself. As the slender figure approached him, Matt couldn't hear footsteps. She was silent among the dark-est shadows, as if she did this as a hobby.

Only one thing gave her away. A long strand of cas-cading black hair caught itself in the moonlight, and he felt himself grin. "Jade, aren't you coming to the court-yard?"

Jade shook her head anxiously and grabbed his wrist. The look in her eyes reminded him of the first time he'd seen her, when he walked through the door into Constantine.

A fierceness behind her gentle composure silenced Matt as she led him back to the dorms. She was unusual-ly quiet as they scurried through the halls, her head dart-ing left and right for any sign of movement. She stopped just short of the door leading into her common room and turned.

She gulped hard and said, "Something awful happened. I've been looking around for her all day, and I came up at lunch to check, and she said something about not feeling well, and so now I checked again, because I thought—"

Matt put a firm hand on her shoulder. "Jade." She shut her mouth abruptly, a crease of worry forming in her brow. "One word at a time." He was annoyed to find himself saying that, because it was what his father, or more accurately, his speech therapist, used to say every time he started talking. The advice was useless in any case, because the words came out in one blur, no matter what. He refocused his thoughts on Jade.

"Remember what you were saying about wanting me to trust you?" He nodded. She put a finger to her lips, gesturing for him to be quiet, and they slipped into the common room. The girls' common room was much lighter than his, and it smelled sweet, but not like pastries—like something else. With so many people in the room, he knew some of them must have noticed him and Jade running up the stairs to the dorms. He wondered what they were thinking, but Jade didn't seem to pay any attention to them as she climbed the winding stairs, clutching his wrist.

They surfaced into a wide hallway that branched off into various dorms. Jade stopped at the fourth door down, and muttered something under her breath.

It was Justine's careful drawl that answered from inside the room. "Listen, I can't talk right now. I'm not feeling well." Matt searched Jade's face for some kind of surprise or worry, but it was stone hard. "I'm okay, I already went to the nurse. I just need some time to…get better."

Jade still didn't speak, even to ask if Justine was okay. Matt searched her face for something, anything, but it was clear she wasn't going to do anything at all. Matt turned to the door.

"Justine…Are you okay? Do you need us to—" Jade gently tugged on his arm and when he looked down at her, she was facing the door and shaking her head.

Matt furrowed his brow, confused. "Don't worry," Justine's voice resumed. "Seriously, I think it'll pass. I just…Don't come in, please."

"Listen," Jade whispered, over Justine.

"I need time alone…Jade, I'm sorry, it's not that…I just don't want to see anyone. I promise I'm fine. Just catch up the notes, will you?"

"So, wait," Matt said. "That's it?"

Jade jammed a shoulder into the door. The knob turned reluctantly in her grip, and at last the door swung open.

Justine was hiding. That's what Matt thought at first, but there was nowhere to hide. So she was gone.

"She left?" Jade nodded, fumbling through massive crimson sheets, and checking under the bed.

There were three beds in there and a painstakingly familiar scent. He turned in horror to see a bottle of Camilla's lavender perfume. He despised the smell. Matt casually stepped away from the drawer and sat himself down on a bed, thinking it must be Jade's, because her sweatshirt was dangling from one of the posts on the headboard.

"A long, long time ago," Jade sighed, moving on to search the next bed.

"Sorry?" Matt asked, distracted.

"She left a long, *long* time ago."

"But we were just talking to her." Jade shook her head.

Matt stood, confused. How could she say they hadn't been talking to her? There was no charm to replicate voices, and if they weren't talking to her, then whom were they talking to?

Jade exploded from behind the bed. "Got it." She sat Matt back down, racing to dust off the tape recorder. She pressed Play, and they listened carefully.

"Listen, I can't talk right now. I'm not feeling well… I'm okay. I already went to the nurse. I just need some time to…get better."

Matt pressed Stop.

She met his eyes, which were wide with understanding. "They took her, Matt." The words came out in a squeak—a slight, weak murmur that cast down her face. "I shouldn't have left her this morning. She was safe, and now—they were just *waiting* for me to leave, I'm sure of it." She could feel her voice shaking. She was furious, angry at her own carelessness, her own stupidity.

"This *isn't* your fault." Matt adjusted himself so he sat adjacent to her on the bed. "How could you have known—"

"She warned me!" He eyes were blinking fast to hold back angry, burning tears. "I promised her." She stood, pacing, then clenched her fists and slammed them into the vanity so that the mirror on the wall shook. "I *promised*."

"What do you mean, she was taken?"

"Just like they took Christine!" She spoke angrily, and Matt took a deep breath. Horrible images of Christine returned to his mind. Jade raked a hand through her long hair. "What am I supposed to do?" She paused to catch her breath and moved to sit on the bed opposite him. "I don't know what to do."

A thought stunned Matt into sobriety. "Tom," he muttered.

***

Before long, they were hurrying back down to the courtyard with plans to relay their findings to the others.

They were rounding the entrance to the North Tower when Matt stopped dead in his tracks. His face paled. Jade almost didn't want to follow his gaze. She could hear the grappling movement before she saw it. A string of figures moved in solemn unison along the darkest shadows in the courtyard. Jade's breath caught in her throat, constricting her airway.

The halls were silent and dark now. Most had returned to their dorms or to the common rooms. Matt and Jade stood as the only witnesses.

Justine stood there, with her chin up, though her eyes were glazed over. Ocumen in straight, gray uniforms flanked the students on either side. Justine looked up, and for one hundredth of a second, her eyes met Jade's. Jade dashed forward, only to be pulled back by a harsh hand clasped around her arm. She shrieked, and another hand clapped over her mouth, stifling her breath. *Justine!* Her mind called out. *Justine, Justine!* But her lips couldn't move under that rough hand. Now her eyes stung with tears, real, fast tears.

"Trying to get yourself *killed?*" Aaron's rumbling voice growled into her ear.

Jade saw Justine through watery eyes, though their eyes didn't meet again. It would have taken Jade a mere two seconds to wrestle out of Aaron's grip. He was strong, but he wouldn't be expecting it. Besides, she was a fast runner, and maybe even faster than he was. They stood there for a minute at least, and he kept his grip on her, undoubtedly because he saw these thoughts playing across her face. Not only did he hold her there in anticipation of a fleeing escape, but he also made her watch helplessly as Justine and the others dragged themselves to a long winding staircase down into the South Tower.

Aaron let her go only when he saw Justine disappear, and the wooden door into the tower slammed shut. Jade clenched her jaw and glared at Aaron as though he'd tried to murder her, but he returned an apathetic, unforgiving stare. As Jade drew back a fist, the fleeting words of her father seemed to formulate and then dissolve in her head. She aimed at Aaron's face with all the momentum she could muster. When he stopped her hand midair, it only made her angrier. She did it again, and his other fist came up to stop her. She aimed one at his gut, but his palm caught her before she could hurt him. Soon she was pounding futilely at his chest, angered almost to the point of tears.

"Jade, what are you doing?"

She and Aaron turned, and in that second, Jade caught him square on the chin with her right fist. He turned back on her furiously, his eyes dark, and Jade dared him to hit her. She looked back at Camilla, jerked her arm from Aaron's hand, and shoved past him.

"Nothing," Jade muttered lividly.

"Then come on!" Camilla led them to a small class-room in the West Tower, two doors down from where their warcraft class was held. Jade sat down on a chair with her arms crossed fiercely over her chest. Matt took a seat on her desk, his face creased with worry. "We'll get them out, Jade. That's why we're here," he reminded her.

"Fine, I'll start," Camilla insisted after a moment's silence. Evidently she hadn't seen what had happened in the yard. "We know it has to do with the test, right? And Nathan told Isabelle in her Myths and Legends class they were testing for people from the Division—"

"We know, Camilla, but that doesn't explain any-thing," Matt interrupted, leaning forward. "Not one of those people came from the Division." He counted them off on his fingers. "Justine was from the Keeping—"

"Justine?" Camilla exclaimed. "What has she got to do with it?" They all stared back at her, and realization dawned on her face. She shook her head violently. "No. Impossible, I just saw her this morning before I left for breakfast."

"She was taken," Jade muttered.

"No!" Camilla erupted. "How? How can you be sure?"

"*I just saw her!*" Jade yelled furiously, her eyes dart-ing toward Aaron. She was glad to see him rubbing his red chin.

Matt hurried to continue. "And that one kid, Fred-erick, was from your neck of the woods, right, Aaron?"

Aaron nodded curtly. "A few miles west."

Camilla seemed to remember this vaguely, and nodded. "Then there's Katy, and she was from my neighborhood." She sighed heavily, rubbing a weary hand across her forehead. "You're right. None of them were from the Division. What did they do?" She bit her lip, scanning the room.

Only Matt seemed partially interested in the conversation. It took Jade by surprise when Aaron addressed her.

"Kat, I'm not sorry."

Jade looked up. "I can tell."

"What's wrong?" Aaron demanded.

Jade furrowed her brow. A rock would perceive human emotion better than he seemed to. "I was this close to her, Aaron. *This* close," she emphasized, gesturing with her forefinger and her thumb. "I could have done something—"

"I had to make the call," he said.

"Next time, Aaron, *I'll* make the call!" She realized when she stopped talking that she'd raised her voice, and Matt and Camilla were poised as if they expected her to attack him. "And Camilla, they didn't do anything to themselves. They're victims." Camilla looked taken aback, but paid prompt attention. "Justine told me the night before that she thought it was her. I said it couldn't be, but then, remember when you first came to Constantine?"

"Of course," Camilla said with a wave of her hand.

"Justine thought Constantine had done it to her, because she felt different when she came through. But *how* could Constantine have done that? She'd have had to change the door, and everyone has a different door. It would take too long."

"So...?"

Jade rolled up her sleeve, tracing a lengthy scar that was mostly healed but still barely visible.

"The entrance exam. Anyone who exposed any blood would have been vulnerable to venom, right?" They nodded. "Constantine customized the exam based on weaknesses. She must have used specific demons to infect random students with Divisional blood. That's why they tested positive."

"But why?" Camilla asked hysterically.

"I don't know!" Jade hissed back in frustration. "Whatever it is must have happened between the time they came here, and now. If it *was* her, and she *is* back, she did it through the demons, not the door." They looked at her as though she'd introduced a cure for death.

"That makes sense," Matt murmured.

"But Sir Emerson—The minister said explicitly that—" Camilla spluttered.

Jade sighed. "Camilla, stop listening to the minister when there's evidence right in front of you. Constantine must be back, and worse, so are her experiments." The bell chimed eleven strokes, and Jade stood from her seat. "Justine and Katy and Tom and Frederick…What if they're just the beginning?"

CHAPTER 20

The organs died along with the last note of the anthem. Aaron hadn't spoken to Jade in the past two days, and since then, she'd gone to visit the griffin twice. Jade had been tormented all through the night by a beaten face that looked much like Justine's. The more she thought about it, the more she began to determine Aaron might have been right in his decision to hold her back. He'd saved her from doing something spontaneous and thoughtless, and maybe even fatal. But she'd never tell him that.

"Good morning, students." Lady Eleanor clasped her black, gloved hands under her drooping nose. "You may have noticed, as we reach the last quarter of the school year, that a few students have gone missing." She smiled complacently and began pacing the stage. "We know that among such a brilliant, sophisticated, intuitive group of students like yourselves, conclusions have been reached." She narrowed her pellet-like eyes and seemed to meet every face in the room. "The fact is, some students have been taken."

Jade cast her eyes sideways and caught Camilla looking back at her with arched brows—not that they'd been taken, but that Lady Eleanor would admit it. If she'd been planning to tell them all along, why transfer them to the South Tower in the dead of night?

"But not where you think." Lady Eleanor held up a finger in contradiction. "Does everyone here understand what Constantine is?" She waited for general agreement. "Constantine is an elite group of prime Illysian children with qualities that most fail to acquire even in later years.

"Among you are the leaders of the next generation, the most highly trained soldiers in the world. When you graduate, you are expected to be four times the warrior you were when you passed your first entrance exam. You are expected to be perfect. And you will be." She paused. "After having taken blood samples of the students here, we came to the realization that some had contracted a disease during their entrance exam. The demons sent for them were infected. Unfortunately, by the time we realized this, it was too late. The infection was irreversible." She seemed to genuinely lament this.

"Yesterday, after lengthy discussions with the head of the Oculus, my colleagues, and the students, we decided their infection would not only hinder *them*, but also your education. Our only choice was to send them to other Illysian schools in the area that they could easily adapt to, without the unwanted strain our rigorous course would force upon them. We thought it best to alert you of this decision afterward, not because we're cruel, but rather because we know the strong bonds you share with your friends, and we are aware of how close you've become. We couldn't possibly have forced you through such a *painful* farewell." Lady Eleanor exhaled despairingly.

"I leave you, on that note, to return to classes, and to reflect on your blessings of good health." She twisted into the air and was gone.

"It's just so awful." Camilla sighed, shaking her head with regret.

"You didn't honestly believe her, did you?" Jade asked Camilla, raising her eyebrows. "I'd go down there myself before taking her word for it."

"Camilla, how gullible are you?" Matt added as they turned into the courtyard to cross into the West Tower.

"Not at all," Camilla snapped, readjusting her books in her arms. "And I'm not saying she was telling the truth, but...maybe she didn't know."

"You're kidding yourself," Matt returned blatantly. "Whatever she's done to them has nothing to do with transferring them to other schools."

"If she hasn't transferred them, why would she keep them? What will she *do?*"

Matt sighed, setting his books down on a desk next to Jade.

As Matt opened his book, Jade felt a sharp pang of guilt in her chest. She remembered vividly Lady Eleanor's fingers passing the book into her arms. She had the most curious feeling that her deal with Lady Eleanor had something to do with what was being planned…and she'd done nothing to stop it. Jade wanted nothing to do with it.

"You okay?" Matt asked, waving a hand in front of Jade's face. She nodded absently, but he looked hardly satisfied. "You know, I can tell when you're lying."

Jade shrugged. "I'm just thinking of my talk with Lady Eleanor."

"Don't," Matt ordered as if he could control her thoughts. "Really, just forget about it. It's over, right?"

Jade nodded, but in reality her conversation would never be over. Her promise would continue to unfold until Lady Eleanor had used her, exhausted her to death. She still couldn't fathom the intent of Lady Eleanor's charm. She remembered the dismembered arm and her own shaking limbs, but the question still remained: what had she done? Jade was only sure that she'd brought another being into the room. Had that being come from another time? Had the being been real? Was the being summoned or projected as if onto a screen? One thing was for certain. Lady Eleanor had powerful plans, and Jade didn't want to be a part of them.

About the only thing to lift Jade's spirits was the next warcraft class. After lunch she and Camilla went to class together, where Mr. Reynolds had set up another training set. Nearly every lesson recently had pertained to physical training. Here at least was something Jade could excel at. Since she'd mastered her first flip, the others had come easily. In this room she'd learned to climb ropes in seconds and fly through the air in ways she'd never imagined.

Sometimes, when she would visit the griffin in the South Tower, she would remember marveling at Aaron as he climbed to the ceiling. She wondered now if she could climb it even faster. Even so, it was hard to do much of anything with Justine's constant, heavy absence blocking Jade's thoughts. It felt worse even than when James had gone. Justine had been safe—she'd been safe in Jade's embrace just days ago, and now the empty bed, the empty room, the silence that followed in Justine's wake was unbearable.

When the lesson was over, she walked back to the dorm with Matt and then hurried to her room. "Pegasus," she blurted. She barged through the open door and found Camilla changing.

"Are you going to dinner?" Camilla asked when Jade set her books down.

"Of course. Why?"

"You want to sit with me?" she asked.

Jade nodded. With Katie and Justine gone, neither of them had anyone else. They walked down through the common room out into the foyer.

"Jade, Camilla!" someone called from behind them. They turned to find Matt and Aaron walking toward the dining hall. Aaron nodded to them both, looking somewhat disinterested as they passed under the arch. Matt marched ahead to save seats, elbowing people out of his way. The best seat was always near the back toward the kitchen. It also happened to be farthest away from the dais, where Jade noticed that Mr. Reynolds had taken Lady Eleanor's seat.

"That's new," Aaron muttered, leaning into Jade's shoulder, and gesturing toward Mr. Reynolds. Jade stared at him, surprised. Their last conversation hadn't ended well, and Aaron was one to hold grudges. "Katherine... did you—" He pulled her aside so they wouldn't be overheard. "I'm sorry about Justine, but did you sort out... Are you done with that book?"

Jade sighed. The charm book was still in the lining of her jacket, untouched. "Apology accepted. And trust me, I'm trying." She offered a nod of reassurance as they moved toward the seats Matt had found. For some reason Aaron's long-awaited apology wasn't nearly as gratifying as Jade had hoped—maybe because she knew he didn't owe her one.

She sat next to Camilla and within a few minutes, dinner was served in steaming heaps on silver platters. This was a normal dinner at Constantine, but every time she wondered at the beauty of such a rich feast. She'd never eaten this way, and she wondered if her father could have cooked this well if he'd had the money.

She looked up again at the dais and waited for Lady Eleanor to enter through the double doors with her sweeping cape. When Mr. Reynolds stood in her place, the whole hall quieted.

Mr. Reynolds adjusted his tie haughtily and curled his hands around the podium. "Students, as you're already aware, your headmistress will be leaving soon. She's been called away to court—" He paused as a quiet whisper rumbled through the hall. The Oculus rarely met as a group in Chief Court. "So," he recommended quickly, "I will be taking over for Lady Eleanor tomorrow morning and for the succeeding week."

He surveyed his skeptical audience. "As you were," he ordered, sitting again in his new seat.

Jade let her eyes linger on Mr. Reynolds. He seemed far too comfortable in that seat. Sometimes the way he spoke with the headmistress, it made Jade wonder if he was in love with her or terrified of her. She sympathized with him and somehow understood his unseemly desire to please her at any cost. At that thought Jade's stomach started churning, and her appetite disappeared. She understood, because she too was terrified of Lady Eleanor.

Lady Eleanor had a somewhat scornful and gentle way of speech that made her seem not altogether motherly and also frighteningly violent. Jade remembered the iron grasp on her wrist when she was sitting in Lady Eleanor's office. She'd thought her bones would crush, and ever since then she'd felt the same tight leash around her hand. It guided her away from conversations that might reveal Lady Eleanor's cruelty, conversations that might save the school from her plans, conversations that might have saved Justine.

"Katherine?"

Jade jerked her head up and saw Aaron staring at her. There was a wrinkle in his smooth brow that looked like concern. The way he stared at her, she wondered sometimes if he could see all her thoughts written across her forehead in black ink.

"Yes?" she managed, silently begging him not to question her in front of the others.

"Could you pass the salt?"

Jade swallowed her last bite in a hurry and felt it catch in her throat. The salt wasn't anywhere near her. She tossed it to him anyway before standing abruptly.

"I need to go," she managed in a flurry of sudden panic. She wanted to end the torture of Lady Eleanor's looming shadow over her shoulder, and an idea had just struck her. It was mad, but she had to try. She had promised.

"Excuse me?" Camilla said, making as if to follow.

"No." Jade blurted too quickly. "I mean, sit. Stay here. I'll—can you meet me in the library? There's something I should—" Jade almost tripped over the chair as she backed away. "We need to talk."

"Wait." Matt grabbed the tail of her shirt and stood. "Is there something wrong?"

Jade shook her head. "Will you go to the library?" He nodded and reluctantly let go. Jade went racing away and thought she saw several heads turn in her direction. She ran out through the double doors before anyone could stop her. She was running just fast enough for her feet to start hurting.

When she reached the brass knockers, she was panting, hoping Lady Eleanor hadn't left yet, hoping against all odds she would still be there.

The clock struck ten, so she still had two hours before the lights in the halls turned black. She stood anxiously before the towering doors of Lady Eleanor's office. Here was her last chance to undo the harm she might have already irreparably caused. She heaved a sigh and pulled on the brass knocker, waiting for her pulse to slow

"Come in, Jade," Lady Eleanor called from inside. Jade couldn't guess what prompted her to assume it was Jade behind the door, but she accepted the invitation and stepped through. "I expected you sooner." Lady Eleanor smiled placidly, capping her pen, and hurrying to put away the paper she was writing on. She was facing away from Jade at another desk and scooped up the papers.

There was an unsettling screech and the tinkling noise of glass as she slid a white cart out of her way. The sound stirred something in Jade's memory that she couldn't quite place. It was strange for Lady Eleanor's office to be so cluttered, and Jade found herself wondering what in the cart was worth the disturbance. "You've attempted the charm now, have you?"

Jade nodded, taking a seat before Lady Eleanor with a grave face and focusing her attention.

Lady Eleanor chortled. "But you haven't succeeded yet?"

Jade nodded again. "It requires a lot of magic. Practice." She needed to be careful with her words. She still wasn't certain that her scheme would work, but had to hope it would at least intimidate Lady Eleanor into releasing their promise.

"I'm certain, Jade, that with time you will master it." She caressed a ceramic mug before her and licked her cracked lips until she was satisfied. "What is it you came here for? To ask a question?"

Jade bit her lip. She didn't know how to start. Manipulation did not come nearly as easily to her as it did to Lady Eleanor. Still, she was Constantine-trained; espionage was what she lived for. "Do you have another copy of the charm book? I don't want to write in the original. Just to make notes and things."

"I'm afraid no other copy exists, Jade. In fact, mine is the only one in the whole of the Illysium."

Jade nodded, remembering Eleanor's signature on the inside cover. "I know what kind of charm it is. The one you assigned me." At this, Lady Eleanor set down her tea and stirred it.

"Do you?"

Jade nodded. "It took time. I thought it was an illuding charm, or a constructive charm." She waited to see the flickers of expression pass through Eleanor's face that told her whether or not to go on. "But it's not either of those, is it?" She paused. "It's a summoning charm." Lady Eleanor looked up at her now. "That's why it's illegal. Worthy of Quarantine. Nothing comes in or out of the Illysium without the minister's approval."

At this thought, Jade suddenly remembered where she'd heard the screech before, and why it had triggered something in her memory. It was the blood drawing. She'd held Justine's cold hand tight in her own when one of the nurses had knocked on the door and Jade had first heard that whine of rusted wheels. If Jade was still, she could smell the tangy odor—it was fresh.

Thoughts came together in her mind like thread work and she jutted her jaw forward, her new fury making her bold. "You lied to me."

Lady Eleanor's face turned to stone, and Jade liked the fact that Lady Eleanor had been taken by surprise. "You are mistaken."

"What are you really going to do with those students? Surely it wouldn't reflect well on the school to have them dispersed around the Illysium for the whole world to peer at."

Lady Eleanor smiled. "Don't question me." Her smile vanished. "You're excused. We won't speak of this again."

Jade stood and let the chair screech across the floor as she backed away. With calm steps Jade walked from the room to the double doors, but she stopped. "You're right. I'm not working for you anymore."

Lady Eleanor fumed. "So be it! I will report you to the minister." She stood as if to do so straight away, but Jade stopped her.

"Wait, there's more. You can tell him if you want. Then I will wait for him in my dorm with an illegal charm book signed in your hand, and will give him all the evidence he needs to put you in Quarantine for the rest of your life." Jade's breath was quick. She was half relieved, and half terrified, that Lady Eleanor would strike her on the spot. Jade went to the door.

She left just as Lady Eleanor smashed her ceramic mug to pieces.

CHAPTER 21

The lights were beginning to dim in the halls, and the night air was seeping through the cracks in Constantine's walls as Jade traipsed down the corridor and through the courtyard. She heard the grass crunch beneath her feet and hoped she would still find the others waiting for her in the library. She'd never walked around Constantine Academy alone at night, but it somehow comforted Jade. The Academy had become her home, and finally, Jade thought, she could be certain it would always be that way.

When Jade reached the East Tower, she slunk through court and then down a narrow set of marble stairs chipped and worn with age. The library was far down, and somewhere near where she imagined the South Tower to be if she could walk through the back wall. The doors were as extravagant as those leading into the assembly hall. Inside was dimly lit, with only small chandeliers lit by candlelight, and during the day with whatever streaks of daylight shone through the slit windows.

A plethora of hallways was crammed with shelves upon shelves of books. The books were leather bound, and they looked ancient, if not decayed. When she'd first seen all the books, she thought some of them must have been empty cardboard frames made just to fill the shelves. But rather than cardboard, each shelf stored millions of pages of the Illysium's haunting past and, according to the Oculus, its radiant future.

Jade fought the urge to call to the others. Between each shelf was a long corridor that led to a cluster of oak writing desks and pen supplies. She traced her fingers along the dusty, leather-bound books, slipping into halls that wound around one another like a maze. The spiral never seemed to end, and even though she knew where she was going, the light was so dim that she couldn't go too far without having to stop and double-check her surroundings. The carpet was musty, and dust seemed to steam from the wool. At last she caught sight of Camilla's back and hurried toward it.

"There you are, Jade," Camilla said reproachfully, her eyes searching Jade feverishly for an answer. "What happened?"

"They're still here," Jade breathed. "The students."

"How can you be sure?" Aaron asked into the silence.

"I went into her office. Lady Eleanor's."

Aaron raised his brow and opened his mouth to say something, but then thought better of it. "And?"

"I saw the blood. The vials."

"Was it fresh?" Aaron asked.

Jade nodded. "I think so."

"How do you know it was theirs?" asked Matt.

"He's right. Where did you see it?" Camilla added. She drew up her long blonde hair into a tight bun, and it made the lines of her face fiercer.

"In her office. She didn't mean for me to see them."

"Kat, why were you in her office?" Aaron demanded. There was a sharp edge to his voice.

"I needed to speak to her," she answered nonchalantly. The comment didn't go unnoticed, and realization illuminated Aaron's face. He cocked his head to the side in suppressed disbelief.

"What is she using it for?" Matt cut in.

Jade looked past him into the depths of the library. She knew the idea was preposterous, but the quaking little girl inside her could imagine Lady Eleanor walking up behind with a dagger, ready to spill their blood for conspiring against her. Matt's question hung in the air.

It wasn't enough blood to have drained the prisoners of life, and that it was kept fresh meant she would draw more soon, that for now, they were still alive. Jade racked her brain for a reason, but none came. Lady Eleanor's mind was a void. Through all the picking Lady Eleanor seemed to have done through Jade's mind, Jade had gleaned nothing in return.

"I don't know," she answered dejectedly. "But we can't wait to find out. We need to find them before it's too late."

"And do what?" Camilla hissed. "Walk them out the front gate? Sneak a hundred sick people past the dining hall?"

"Camilla, they aren't *sick,* they're our classmates," Matt reminded her.

"They're *infected,*" she growled back. "And we hardly know what with. I'd get Justine, but otherwise, I'm not risking my life for Constantine's mad experiment."

"We aren't asking you to," Aaron muttered impatiently. "The most brilliant strategists in the Illysium teach at the Academy, and you think we intend to risk our lives?" Aaron spoke firmly and with conviction. "We're not throwing dice. There are four of us, and we've been at Constantine almost a year. That's more training than most men see in the military."

Camilla's face contorted with indecision. She looked between the other three, appraising them, considering the team, their strengths, their weaknesses. She stared indecisively.

"Fine," she said at last with notable resignation. "But if we do this, we have to do it well." The others nodded. "No mistakes," she added sternly.

"Lady Eleanor will be gone one week," Jade started, already moving to plan their next steps. "That means we have a week to go down there and get them out."

"Not all at once," Aaron interjected. "There are hundreds of stories in the South Tower. It stretches for miles down. We need to find out what they're doing down there."

"And what for," Matt added, raking a hand through his golden-brown hair. He blew out a long breath, and Jade offered him a look of reassurance, even though the possibilities of failure were playing out hideously in her mind.

"How do we know it won't be too late?" Camilla asked. "Just because Lady Eleanor's away doesn't mean Mr. Reynolds couldn't do something, or any of the teachers, for that matter."

"She wouldn't leave something like that in someone else's hands," Matt said. "When she's back, she'll do it herself, whatever *it* is."

"Still, we need to think practically, carefully. Mr. Reynolds won't make a single slip, especially not with the headmistress gone." Camilla frowned at the wooden table like it had presented an impossible enigma.

Jade didn't look up at the others, trying not to remember what they were doing, that they were planning what could easily be their deaths. She'd done it countless times in battle strategy, but it had never been real. There would never be consequences, until now.

"We have to start as soon as possible," Jade urged. She was just as reluctant as the others, but she knew it had to be said. "The greatest advantage we have is the element of surprise. But no one goes down alone. Ever."

"How do we get into the South Tower in the first place? The main entrance has so many charms on it, you can barely see through it," Camilla reminded them.

Jade and Aaron exchanged a quick glance. "There's a side entrance," he explained. "It's locked, but there's an easy charm, if you know it."

"Do you?" Camilla asked.

"Yes."

Matt nodded. "And then we need to separate—"

Aaron cut through Matt's words. "Absolutely not."

"How else will we cover enough ground?" Camilla agreed. "We'll separate and share what we find. We can't do it any other way."

Aaron leaned forward, struggling to level his voice. In the orange light, the shadows under his eyes darkened. "Camilla, there could be hundreds of guards waiting for us to do something reckless like that." He sat back again.

"This is not hypothetical, and if you make a bad choice, you will have all four of us killed."

The conversation went back and forth that way all evening. Even when the lights were out and the whole world was asleep, they sat awake in the dead hours, going back and forth until they had it just right. They planned it right down to the minute. When they sneaked furtively back up into their rooms, they had agreed irrefutably on one thing—stick to the plan above all else. *Without a plan,* Professor Jackson once said, *we can't think ahead. When we fail to think ahead, we die.*

When Jade slipped under her covers, she wriggled her toes and fingers to rid herself of the shivering nervous feeling that came with thoughts of tomorrow. Fortunately, in her exhaustion, she fell asleep immediately. In her dream she was walking up the road to her house in the Division. It was a gravel road, and she somehow knew that her father was inside and that something wasn't quite right. She opened the door and heard Justine's voice, but it sounded far away.

James's mouth was moving, but there was no sound. He sat across from Justine in the living room, and Jade could see his face, but the details weren't there, like a blur of a memory. She was shocked to see Justine's golden-brown skin. Even from the back, Jade recognized her. She tapped Justine's shoulder, but when the head turned, it wasn't Justine's face at all, but Lady Eleanor's. She was laughing.

***

The next afternoon, when Jade's silver plate of food was half empty, she caught a glimpse of her haggard reflection. Her black waves of hair were strewn about her head, falling into her face. She raked her hair back with a hand and gulped down a swig of water.

"Are you saving this seat?" Matt's voice pulled Jade from her reverie, and she shook her head, moving her tray aside so he could join her. Her thoughts, however, were preoccupied with Nathan, who'd just come in through the double doors, brandishing his weapon—a copper-plated shield with his family emblem pressed into it. It was the face behind Nathan, however, that caught Jade's ambling attention. Jade recognized the blazing red hair before she saw the ivory tusk. *Rosebud*, Jade thought, her eyes widening.

"How did you sleep last night?" Matt asked, his eyes tracing the lines of her face.

Jade shrugged, her attention drifting toward where Rosebud stood, poised. "Well enough. You?"

"Do you think we can do it tonight? Just the four of us?"

Jade reluctantly tore her eyes from the double-door entrance and squeezed Matt's hand. He looked at her, surprised.

"Who is that?" Jade blurted, hardly helping to assuage Matt's concern. She couldn't resist. The woman was staring right at her now, practically beckoning her. Jade stood, pulling Matt with her.

"Wait? Who?" Jade locked her eyes on those stormy blue ones that called to her, but then Rosebud turned, quite deliberately on her heel, and walked briskly through the double doors. Jade had always been captivated by Rosebud, but now more than ever. Jade wondered how old she was. Her pearly smooth skin, her small face, round nose, and red cheeks all seemed too young to be an adult and too fierce to belong to a teenager. Only students had weapons at the Academy, and hers looked powerful. Maybe she knew something the rest of them were still trying to figure out.

Jade tugged Matt out of his seat and remained in tight pursuit of the red mane of hair. She tried unsuccessfully to maintain some sense of equanimity as she chased through the halls of Constantine Academy.

"Jade, where are you going?" Matt was panting to catch up with her. His footsteps were loud against the stone.

Jade murmured an incoherent response, but when they reached a shallow hall in the east corridor, Jade halted, and Matt stopped behind her. Rosebud had taken them right into the yawning mouth of Lady Eleanor's office.

"Jade, we shouldn't be here." Matt was backing away. Lady Eleanor wouldn't be gone until that night. His fear of this place exceeded even his fears of the South Tower. Jade stared at him and back at Rosebud. He didn't understand.

Did Matt not see Rosebud slipping into the office with an alluring glance toward them? She'd rushed in, shutting the door silently behind her, and then simply deserted them. Was she waiting inside? Was it a trap, or was she testing them? Everything in Jade's mind was screaming for her to turn back around, and acquiesce to the subtle tug of Matt's hand around her wrist.

Rosebud was dangerous. She seemed powerful and hostile in the set of her firm jaw and offsetting mane of red hair. Jade stared into Matt's golden-brown eyes, and he nodded toward the stairs behind them.

Jade went running in the other direction.

She reached the door and pushed it open easily, expecting to find Rosebud on the other side. Instead, there was silence. She was surprised to hear Matt pounding down the hall after her, but relieved as well. There was something astray about Lady Eleanor's customarily ordered office. Papers were strewn on the desk, and mounds of empty ink pots lined the floor carelessly.

Matt narrowed his eyes, drawing out a bow and arrow as they treaded into the room in silence. This is what Rosebud had wanted Jade to do. She wanted her to see this, but why? Jade reached out to touch one of the papers, and Matt blocked her hand.

"Don't touch anything, they're probably charmed," he warned, retracting his hand. Jade did the same, but continued to scan paper after paper on the desk.

Jade shoved her hand into the pocket of her jacket, twirling the silver matchbox around in her palm. She hooked and unhooked the latch as her panic sent her almost into hysteria. She didn't know what held her to the spot, but there was something in the room that was eerie, a silent presence that pressed in on her. She hoped it was Rosebud.

Among the crumpled mass of documents in the far corner of the room was a freshly printed stack of white paper titled "Operation MAD." The paper looked fairly ordinary, but Jade read along the fine print, scanning the text until she found two signatures: Lady Eleanor's signature, and *Peter Reynolds O.* slashed across a dotted line in blue ink.

"Mr. Reynolds," Matt mumbled over Jade's shoulder. She recognized the harsh shape of the writing and the rushed stroke of the letters from somewhere, and could have sworn by her life she'd seen the signature before. She couldn't place it, but an idea in the back of her mind was trying to edge its way through everything else that fogged her memory.

She could feel Matt's hand wind around hers, and she only then realized hers was shaking as she read over the printed writing. Matt read too, and Jade used most of her energy to stop from lighting a steel-tipped match and leaving the stack to burn. "Mass Annihilation of the Division" was written in dark ink and scattered maliciously over the white paper. There was an unending list of names that preceded the obscure procedures involved, and though Jade couldn't find Justine's name, she knew it was there. She felt a burning, crushing desire to avenge the victims that Lady Eleanor had imprisoned. Just as she reached to sift through the rest of the stack, Lady Eleanor's voice sounded behind them.

Matt drew his bow over his shoulder and aimed at the door instinctively, but it remained closed. He grabbed Jade by her hood and thrust her into a mahogany wardrobe in the far left of the room. It was small and musty inside, but Matt managed to fit in just as the double doors opened.

"Do it!" Lady Eleanor was demanding as she came through the door. Jade could feel her heart pounding against her chest, and had to hold her breath to stop the door of the wardrobe swinging wide open. Matt pressed a finger to his lips for her to be quiet, and bent down to look through a small keyhole near the knob.

"Your Lady, this kind of thing takes so much time," Mr. Reynolds's voice squeaked. He was mostly out of sight, but Matt could see Lady Eleanor tracing her long, leathery gloves over the list of names and rolling back her eyes as though she were breathing in some pungent floral essence. "I cannot have them in the South Tower forever. Deal with it."

Mr. Reynolds sighed. "When would you like it done by?"

Lady Eleanor smiled placidly and stroked a gloved finger over his cheek. "I'll be leaving soon. When I return, you should have done the job."

Mr. Reynolds gulped. "I just—" At his interruption, Lady Eleanor's face darkened. "I'm not sure Quarantine's the right place for them," he finished.

In a flash Lady Eleanor ripped the black glove from her hand and brought her nails down on Mr. Reynolds's face with vengeance. She replaced the glove with a practiced hand, before Matt could even return his eyes to see what had caused the damage. A swelling, red wound on Mr. Reynolds's face was leaking cherry-red drops of blood. His hands flew to soothe it.

Matt stifled a gasp, and drew back from the keyhole, whispering to Jade in such quiet tones that he was surprised she heard him.

"And what do you think now?" Lady Eleanor asked, retiring to her desk. Mr. Reynolds whimpered compliance. "Good, now take me down there—I'll tell them the good news."

Matt's face scrunched up in fury at the thought of Tom stranded in the South Tower, sentenced to Quarantine for a crime he never committed. The thought brought back painful memories of Ocumen dragging his parents away. He replaced the bow just over his shoulder, pulled back the arrow, and aimed through the keyhole. He wouldn't miss.

Jade placed a light finger on the tip of the arrow, and when he turned to her, she was shaking her head sullenly. *Stick to the plan*, she mouthed.

Lady Eleanor and Mr. Reynolds left the room abruptly, leaving Matt and Jade to tumble out of the wardrobe and run with trembling limbs into the court of law. They arrived in time for the anthem. When all the students had taken a seat, and Jade had lost Matt in the crowd, she spotted Rosebud standing with her ivory tusk at the entrance doors, her icy-blue, questioning eyes locked with Jade's.

Jade felt her own head nod almost imperceptibly, and then Rosebud vanished through the doors.

CHAPTER 22

Law passed uneventfully. With Lady Eleanor having finally left, they all sat in the court waiting for an hour to pass. Jade's mind was still entrenched with Lady Eleanor's decision. She was glad not to have to watch Lady Eleanor sentence anyone to the South Tower. She was disgusted by the hypocrisy of it all. Lady Eleanor sent others to their deaths for subversion, while behind her own double doors, she flouted the laws of the very system she worked for. Worse still, Jade had made herself a part of it.

It still struck Jade as strange that in spite of the thousands of prisoners shackled to the walls of the South Tower, it was the most silent cavern in all of Constantine Academy.

The South Tower was settled deep into the wet marshlands that Constantine was built on. The prisoners were no doubt kept deep beneath the Illysium, but the thought that none of them ever cried out in the night, or shrieked from the agony of absolute confinement, perplexed Jade.

She and Matt hadn't told the others yet about Mr. Reynolds's order to have the students moved soon. There was no point. Changing the plan an hour before it was executed would only worsen matters. In any case, they had expected it.

Jade was thinking only of Lady Eleanor's words as she clambered through the door out of the girls' common room that night, Camilla close behind. Matt and Aaron were waiting for them in the East Tower by the assembly hall. They were silent at first, maybe because their nerves were rattling like shackles against an empty cage. It was just like that at Constantine lately. Jade always had her nerves on edge for something. Aaron drew his sword and signaled for the others to draw their weapons. Jade didn't bother with hers. It was useless anyway.

Aaron led them around the southern entrance, down a narrower hall, and to the familiar little gate that led into the Tower. It was black inside. Jade surveyed the scene behind them with quick eyes. Blue moonlight drowned the hall, and the stars seemed to bow their twinkling heads at her through the gray clouds. *Hurry*, they said, but Jade was wishing she could run.

She felt a warm hand on her waist, and Aaron pulled her through the gate to where Matt and Camilla stood anxiously waiting. This was where the plan began. Aaron was strong with his weapon, so he was in front. Camilla could practically see through the dark, so at the first sign of movement, she would warn the others—she was at the back. Jade and Matt flanked Aaron and Camilla on either side: Jade for speed, and Matt for lethal accuracy with his bow and arrows.

Matt's footsteps seemed loud in the quiet—he'd never mastered the silent step. Jade knew he couldn't help it, but was irritated all the same. When they reached the narrow hall that housed the griffin, Jade wondered if it could hear them creeping past. It had been weeks since she'd seen it, and now more than ever, she would have liked the comfort of its strong, pearly wings and iron claws. She was surprised they hadn't seen any guards yet. She was grateful for that and yet all the more apprehensive. If Lady Eleanor hadn't left any Ocumen, perhaps there was something far worse waiting for them.

As they walked, they could hear an almost imperceptible whine accompanied by a gust of dark wind coming from one side of the hall. It sounded like a door swinging open on unused hinges. Jade's footsteps froze and she groped for the tail of Aaron's shirt. He was frozen too.

"Katherine, what is it?" he whispered, his own panic evident.

"Men," Camilla breathed back.

"Big? Short?" Aaron hissed.

"Two, both tall, very heavy." She listened for the pace of the stride, the weight as their feet hit the floor.

Matt drew his arrows as they all began to hear the steps loud and clear. Torchlight rounded the corner.

Jade shook her head violently. She mouthed, "We need to follow them." When she turned, the others must have seen, because they had already disappeared into the shadows. It took Jade a second to do the same. The ceiling was made of thatched wood, easy to grip, and with the uneven walls, she reached it without too much difficulty. She sneaked into the shelter between two beams just as the light passed under her. She could see Aaron gripping the beam parallel to her own.

That was one thing Constantine Academy had taught her well—hiding. The four of them waited a dreadful few seconds after the sound of the steps had disappeared before stepping back into the hall.

The men were easy enough to follow. They must have been wearing boots and uniforms, because after each step, there was a shuffling of starched fabric.

The noise led them up a set of stairs toward a lit hallway. Jade might have thought they were back in the North Tower by the dorms, except for the silence.

This staircase wasn't like the others. It was very wide. At the top was a wooden door. Aaron gestured for them to fall back. They did, and they watched and waited for the door to close.

"What do you think is in there?" Camilla asked as they stared up at the door from farther down the grimy, yellow steps. "Is that where the prisoners are?" She hadn't really addressed anyone in particular, so no one in particular answered.

A bloodcurdling wail erupted from behind the door and seemed to ripple down the walls and all over them.

Jade stifled a gasp and felt Camilla clutch her wrist tightly. It had been so unexpected, so sharp, so quick. They might have imagined it, except for the ringing echo in their ears. Jade felt her head spinning. The sound froze her thought.

The sound repeated itself not once, not twice, but three times, and each time it pulled them further into panic. Who was screaming? The endless imaginings of what could be happening behind that inch of wood taunted them.

Jade's heart was thrashing around in her chest as though it might leap out and run for the North Tower. Hundreds of students slept there in safe ignorance. She had done that too, unaware that a few feet below, a hideous nightmare was unfolding itself into reality. She clutched her locket.

They had reached the back wall, and another wail rang out. Camilla tugged on Jade and Matt, her eyes begging to leave. Jade bit her lip, but her curiosity won over her rationality. Matt was already inching up the steps when Jade came to. Aaron lingered behind, torn.

Jade mustered every ounce of courage she could manage and swung the door open. Behind it was an extremely narrow, hand-dug tunnel that led to a window of dim light. From the deep shadows of the crawlspace, they could see into the room. She gestured to the others to follow. They did so with hesitation. Jade could see little through the opening in the wall, but what she could see and hear was enough to make her shudder. Jade saw someone in a straight, gray uniform with a giant metal rod. There must have been another Ocuman in there, because a body came flying at the wall, tied up by shackles, unable to brace its fall. Red tubes of blood ran from the strangled arms into a guttering machine that creaked distinctly. Jade knew the sound.

"Where did you come from?" With terror, Jade realized she recognized the long, beaten, pale face. Matt's face darkened with rage.

Aaron gripped his shoulder. "Don't," he urged.

It was Tom. "Where did you come from?" the Ocuman asked again, fury amplifying his voice.

Tom had tears running down his red, battered face. "The Keeping. I told you, I'm from the Illysium."

The Ocuman brandished his iron rod and threatened to bring it down on Tom's face. Tom cowered back, bracing his knees against his chest.

"What is that?" Jade asked, her face constricted with horror.

"A pillager," Matt whispered.

"What does it do?"

He pursed his lips, clenching a hand around his bow. "Strips the magic from your veins," he whispered back.

"The damage," Camilla explained, "can range between a headache to…death. It depends on the size," she whispered, rubbing her own arms and looking back at the door.

"Who let you in?" the other Ocuman bellowed, crouching before Tom. Camilla had been right; both Ocumen were tall, and you could see heavy muscle even under the uniforms. Jade took inventory. The four of them could easily take on one, but two, so well trained, so big…that was a different fight.

"The school, I swear. Let me go!"

Jade's breath was quickening, and she wanted to tear through the Ocumen and pluck Tom from under their harsh glares. She still had memories of his bright face at dinner, hanging onto Matt's left shoulder, a smile full of teeth. But nothing about this scene was bright or full. Camilla's hand gripped the whip coiled around her belt.

"Are you helping in any way, shape, or form to vanquish Lady Eleanor's power here, in collaboration with Constantine and/or any fellow students?"

Tom shook his head, his cheeks dewy with sweat. The Ocuman seemed as though he was about to spring another question, but he fell silent and disappeared from view.

"If you don't tell us, one of your *sick* friends will." There was a clicking of a latch, metal scraping against the floor, and then the pillager was in view again, pointing toward Tom. "I'll ask you one more time, *what* are you?"

"I don't know!" he cried, real tears now falling through his red cheeks. "I grew up in the Keeping. I passed the test, and I came here because…" His hoarse and ragged voice trailed off, unable to keep shouting. *We thought it was safe.* Jade finished his sentence for him. Constantine was supposed to be the safe house, the refuge for the millions of ignorant hopefuls who thought a better life could be found here.

The Ocuman knelt down on his knee and drew the pillager up to his shoulder like a hunter's gun.

"Please, don't. Please." Tom could have been whispering to no one, for all the Ocumen seemed to notice.

Except he wasn't whispering to no one. Before Aaron could stop him, Matt shot an arrow through the Ocuman's head as the pillager fired. It went straight through the helmet. Thick, red blood dropped onto the floor. The Ocuman was stunned. He fell with perpetually wide eyes.

Aaron didn't even have time to reprimand Matt for jeopardizing them. All four of them leaped into the light. Around the corner they found four more Ocumen. Aaron cursed and Camilla sprang into action. Her whip lashed down on one before Jade could even take her eyes off Tom. Aaron was the same with his sword, but the pillager was hard as stone, and the Ocuman grabbed it from the floor and used it to block Aaron's slicing blade.

The other two rounded on her and Matt. The Ocuman was a foot taller than Jade, but he was gangly and somehow off balance. He wasn't carrying a weapon, which put the fight on even grounds. When she was barely close enough, she tumbled into the air and did a backhanded rift. She landed behind him, but he was hardly disoriented.

Somehow it felt as though all her education and training had been preparing her for this moment. He was fast, not easily ruffled, and clearly experienced, but he wasn't Constantine-trained, and Jade was. She forced all her strength into every strike to his chest. It was flip after flip, kicking, casting, but it was no good. He was back on his feet every time.

Jade tried to gather every memory she could of battle strategy: when to strike, when to wait, to feign weakness, and for forth. It was all no good. She stopped striking. He'd caught her twice on the back of her head. If anything she was only making him angrier, stronger. Mid-strike, she caught his hand in hers, and she and could feel the magic in her inching to the surface. It was orange, and her fingers her glowing. He growled and tried to wriggle free, but she had him cornered.

The force of her cast hit the Ocuman ruthlessly. His eyes opened wide with terror, and his body jolted forward. He spluttered something incoherent. He fell limp, and his body sat there on the floor. The red-orange glow that had been in Jade's fingers was in him now, fading from his chest.

That was the first time Jade ever killed anyone.

When she turned, the other Ocumen were on the floor, dead or dying.

Aaron rounded on Matt. "What were you *thinking*?"

"You would have just stood there and let them kill him right in front of us!"

Better one life than five. Aaron's eyes simmered. Matt looked at Tom, bound at the feet and wrists. He was shaking and pale, and he wasn't moving except for rasping, shallow breaths. "We need to get him out of here."

"No," Camilla started, more gently than Jade had ever heard her speak. "If we take him, Mr. Reynolds will know for sure we've been down here."

Jade looked to Tom, whose chest had stopped heaving. "Guys," Jade muttered from the floor. She pressed her forefinger and middle finger to Tom's neck. "He's—"

"No!" Matt shoved her hand away and pressed his own two fingers against Tom's neck. Then he turned Tom's head roughly and tried the other side. "No, no, I—"

"Matt, he's gone," Jade said.

"We have to stick to the plan," Aaron reminded them. "We got what we came for. If we do anything more, Mr. Reynolds will know we were down here. We should leave."

"Forget the plan!" Matt yelled. "The plan was blown to bits the minute we came in here!" His voice softened. "We *can't* leave."

Jade helped Matt up. She could feel him shaking.

"We have to go, Matt. We could still help the others."

After a few moments, Matt released his grip on Jade's hand and stepped back, wiping his face with his hand. He nodded stoically, his eyes fixed on Tom's empty face. He blinked hard, his lips tight.

"Why would she do this? This must have been Constantine. Lady Eleanor would never—" Camilla stuttered through an impossible explanation.

"Constantine started this with the demons in the entrance exam, but it's Lady Eleanor who wants to see it through the end."

"But why? It doesn't explain the vials of blood; it doesn't explain anything."

Jade looked down at Tom and back at Camilla. "If she's ordering them to be interrogated, she can't be working with Constantine. Aaron said when they interrogated Christine, they didn't know where she'd come from. For now at least, Lady Eleanor is as blind-sided as we are. Maybe she doesn't need their blood, she just needs them to be weak so they'll tell her what they know."

"If you're right, then why would Constantine train them only to infect them again and have them pulled?" Matt asked.

Jade shook her head in defeat. "That's the question."

Camilla raised her brow and watched as Matt unbound the iron shackles around Tom's hands and feet. Aaron carefully unfastened the IV from Tom's pale skin. Matt exchanged an apologetic expression with Aaron, because they all understood why Tom was being untied. The untied body of a Constantine-trained student could be the only plausible reason for the death of four Ocumen in one room. It was also the only thing that could save the crime from being traced.

Jade tugged at Matt's sleeve as the others were leaving. "We'll be back tomorrow." She smiled mildly. The anticipation was a mix of dread and determination.

***

It was strange how normal the day after seemed. Nobody knew what they had seen in the night or what they'd done. Jade was endlessly counting down the hours until they could return to the South Tower, but the clocks seemed to tick through eternity. Last night they had been lucky, but tonight they were doing something very different—tonight they were freeing prisoners from the South Tower. All she could do was hope they were half the warriors Constantine Academy had trained them to be.

Trying to pull her mind from such nightmares, Jade went down to the library to finish homework that, in light of recent events, seemed pointless. When she first stepped in, it took a moment for her eyes to adjust to the dim light. The librarian, Ms. Tutts, waved to her and beckoned her toward a colossal desk. Jade came forward hesitantly, pausing a few steps away.

"Can I help you, dear?"

Jade nodded. "Do you know where I can find anything on black spanners or...blood type?"

The librarian laughed, shifting herself out of the seat with a struggled maneuver. "Is Professor Jackson assigning you homework again?"

Jade nodded. It was late and she wasn't in the mood for small talk. Besides, her hour was nearing. She quickly thanked Ms. Tutts, who led her with quick steps into another long, winding corridor.

"Black spanners are the worst creatures out there, you know. They're like infections, and they're even more dangerous because they're the only type of creature that can pass right from the Underworld into the Illysium without leaving a trace." She shook her head. "And don't even get me started on their blood. Every drop is like poison," she said with a shiver. "Or at least, that's what I've heard." She traced the books with a finger and gestured to a shelf. "These ought to help you more, though…Jade, right?"

Jade nodded, surprised Ms. Tutts knew her name. "You know, Jade, I hear you sing the anthem sometimes, and your voice is just what the Academy's orchestra *needs*. Perhaps you'll consider joining us after school one day?" she asked with a smile.

"Justine was really the musical one," Jade answered apologetically. She wondered if Ms. Tutts was only asking to ease the wound of having lost the choir's best participant.

"Right…well." Ms. Tutts let her gaze linger on Jade's face. "The offer stands, all the same."

"Thanks," Jade said.

Ms. Tutts looked down at her watch. "My shift ended a few minutes ago. Can I trust you to go as soon as you're done? I'll leave on the lights for you, darling."

Jade almost shook her head, and asked for company, but instead forced a smile. "Thanks."

Ms. Tutts nodded and shuffled away with loud, hurried footsteps. Once alone, Jade raced to pull out a book labeled *Sterling Blood and the Other Kind*. She tucked it under her arm. She traced the leather spines that lined the shelf, reading the titles as they slipped under her finger. She had only a few minutes to spare before the others would be waiting for her, so she picked up another book and leafed through the pages. She was just about to return it to the shelf when a light pair of steps sounded behind her. Jade turned.

"Ms. Tutts?"

"Jade," someone whispered. It wasn't Ms. Tutts. Jade whipped her head around just as she neared the entrance, but saw nothing save an identical bookshelf behind her. She cursed herself for having come down alone, and silently replaced the books on the shelf.

"Jade." It was the same voice, coming from an aisle next to her. She pressed an ear to the bookshelf, hardly daring to breath through the silence. "Come."

Jade spun at the sound, her heart trembling so fiercely that she could imagine it drumming through the walls. She hated being seen, and worse still by something she couldn't see herself. The voice was distinctly female, but that hardly quelled Jade's unease. She certainly knew of one woman she wouldn't want to meet at the bottom of that tower—at midnight.

The steps sounded again through a gap between the books a few feet away from Jade. She curled her fingers around the shelf and crouched to peer through, trying not to imagine the unknown eyes that could be staring back at her. Jade pressed the silver box in her back pocket, staring dumbly through to the next aisle.

"Run." The plea came through two red lips that appeared between the gap. Jade leaped back.

"Christine?" she exclaimed, relieved and stunned.

"*Run.*"

"Where did you come from? Are you—are you okay?"

"Cell eighty-three. I—I saw your last name a few doors down."

"My dad?" Jade asked anxiously.

"I don't know. Maybe—" There was a breathless pause, and two wandering eyes fell between the gap, piercing Jade. "*Run!*" she shrieked.

"Why?"

"You have to leave. They—" A thick, guttural sound cut through Christine's words.

"What did they do to you?" Jade asked, terrified by the sudden, strange darkness in Christine's face.

"I don't remember. I don't remember anything, I—" Then there were hard, thudding steps against the floor as Christine staggered along the carpet and fell back, grappling at her own face, which disappeared out of sight under a pile of books falling from the shelf. Christine screamed with such animus that Jade clutched the shelf to see farther into the aisle. The clock chimed, and though Jade knew the others would be waiting for her, she couldn't possibly leave Christine in such a state.

Battling between choices, Jade finally dashed around the corner and started unscrambling the fallen books in the next aisle. She dug through the rubble until she revealed bare carpet underneath. Christine was gone.

***

Aaron stood with his back to the room, brushing dark hair out of his eyes.

"She'll be here soon—she has to be," Matt said. The girls' common room was empty, and midnight was approaching steadily. Matt had said this now three times, including his most recent declaration. Aaron paced the back wall, weighing his sword between skillful hands.

"Matthew, shut up. You're not helping," Camilla snapped, wringing her hands around the whip.

"Don't act like you care about anyone anyway, Camilla. If it were up to you, you'd just leave people in the South Tower to die—"

"What did you just say?" Camilla asked, rounding on him. "This is what I get for giving anyone from the Keeping a chance...and a farmer at that!" Camilla scoffed, clenching her fists. "You should be grateful I even *talk* to someone like you."

"*So* grateful," Matt mocked, sprawling out on the couch again.

"Matt! You are so immature. Not to mention stubborn and rude—I guess I was right, wasn't I? Civility is a *class* thing."

Matt gritted his teeth. "You're despicable," he said.

"And you're the last person in the world I'd ever be with by choice." Camilla groaned. "We're *over*." Matt repressed a sigh of relief, but felt a weary chuckle bubbling through his lips. "I'm going to do something useful and find Jade," she announced, muttering something else about the Keeping.

"We're coming with you," Aaron said, sheathing his sword. "She should have been here by now." He gestured for Matt to follow them through the door. "Has anyone seen her today?" Aaron asked. They both shook their heads. Aaron growled and walked with long strides along the halls leading to the East Tower. "She wouldn't miss this. Something must have gone wrong."

"Maybe she went down by herself," Camilla started, her own voice trailing off as they considered the consequences.

Aaron halted. "She wouldn't."

Matt paused. "Jade's not exactly one to *follow* rules."

Aaron glanced left and right toward the last two Towers they hadn't searched. "She may be stubborn, but she isn't stupid. Come on. There's only one place she could be."

***

Jade stopped at the narrow space between the book-shelves she'd been staring through. Something was horribly wrong.

"Christine?" she called, standing up to walk the pace of the aisle. It was seventy steps. Christine's legs could never have carried her that far in the few seconds they'd had. Besides, the other side of the aisle was a dead end. It was as if she'd…disappeared.

Jade furrowed her brow, looking again between the two ends of the aisle, but she couldn't explain it. If not for the pile of books at her feet, she might have thought she'd imagined the whole thing. What had happened to Christine in cell eighty-three?

Thud.

Jade willed herself not to turn at the sound, but her ears were ringing with the echo and it came again. *Thud*, like a hammer dropping on the muffled carpet. *Thud*.

Thud. Faster and faster until it was nearing, and Jade had no choice but to turn.

"Demon," she gasped, dread filling her stomach.

Jade stopped dead. She recognized nothing but the unmistakably familiar eyes that flashed from beneath thick black fur. Jade gulped down the bead of fear in her throat.

Christine's face split into a snarl, and the human eyes disappeared, giving way to something Jade had never seen before—the eyes of a beast. Christine bared her teeth, a deep growl ripping from somewhere far in the back of her throat. Jade struck one of her steel-tipped matches, and held it between her face and Christine's as the lights began to dim. From her side of the flame, Jade could only see darkness, aside from the light that seeped in from the entrance. If she could just slip past Christine and shut the door, she'd be able to escape.

The long, dark, mangled muzzle appeared in the orb of light cast by Jade's flame. Christine advanced, her teeth morphing into fangs and her mouth watering. This was why Christine couldn't remember—she'd changed. These were the horrifying effects of a madwoman's experiment. Now Jade understood some of the fear with which Camilla had often spoken of Constantine's freedom. She backed away so she was just in sight of the entrance, but it was too late.

Christine had her claws outstretched, and she lunged at Jade, her eyes flashing with unfathomable rage. Jade let out a bloodcurdling scream she didn't recognize as her own. She saw the flame on the match grow brighter and stronger with her fear and brandished the glowing fire at Christine. Her body, even under the fur, was thin, and to Jade's advantage, weak—for a wolf. Christine scratched at her reddening neck and flung back her head. Jade knew she hadn't practiced enough to use her weapon, but it seemed to be buying her some time, because like most animals, wolves apparently didn't take well to fire—and Jade did.

The time it bought wasn't enough. The flame grew bright and fierce, but just as quickly it flickered and died, along with Jade's chances of escape. Christine grabbed Jade in a fierce grip, and clenched two hands around her throat. Jade tried to cast a charm, but Christine was barking in her ear.

Something like a demonic smile played on the corner of Christine's lips before Jade felt her arms go limp, and the sting of several deep claws ripping at her skin.

Jade's eyes rolled back in her head as she let out an earsplitting shriek of agony. She was plunged into darkness, and she squeezed her eyes shut to brace herself for the slaughtering pain. She could feel herself drifting in and out of consciousness.

She opened her eyes in time to see three figures silhouetted in the double-door entrance. Her thoughts were staggered and disjointed, but she tried to keep her eyes open. She felt something strong pull Christine from her body, and then arms were around her, more than one pair. She recognized Aaron's voice ordering Matt and Camilla to get Christine out—how did he always know?

Two arms scooped Jade up, and the ceiling rushed past her in pools of light. Then her meager vision flickered and died.

CHAPTER 23

Aaron held Jade close to his pounding chest as he darted through the halls. He didn't know where to go, but getting her out of the library was a good start. Aaron didn't stop running until he was in reach of the arching entrance to the South Tower, where he knew no one would find them. When he looked down at Jade, she was pale and her eyes were closed. Her arm was bleeding profusely where Christine had attacked her, and she wasn't moving. Aaron pressed his lips together in frustration. He laid her down gently, and swept her black hair from her sticky face.

He took his shirt off anxiously, ripping the bottom half of it into a long strip. He fumbled for Jade's fragile arm, and wrapped the cloth around it as gently, but as quickly as he could. She was still unresponsive, but her pulse was strong and her face red with heat. Aaron tied a rough knot over the wound and sat her up against the wall.

"Kat," he said, tapping a hand against her cheek. "Katherine." Her eyes began to flutter open, and she let her head fall back against the cool stone. She rubbed her forehead and tightened her face in pain. "Put your arm down, Kat. You're injured."

When she looked up at him, her dark-blue eyes seemed glazed over, her brow furrowed with confusion.

"You…you took me?" she asked, trying desperately to remember how and why she'd come there. "But Christine—she changed. You have to stop her. Get her out of here."

Aaron crouched lower and pressed a hand over Jade's mouth. "We're working on it. Matt and Camilla will send Christine to safety once she changes back. In the meantime we need to get you to a nurse."

Jade narrowed her eyes, and they fell on the southern entrance. "Aaron, I know. I know where they are. We can get them!"

"No, Kat," he said with finality, trying to make her see sense. "We can do it tomorrow, or Sunday—you won't be able to fight with these injuries."

Jade's eyes widened. "No, no, it can't wait this time. They—they're taking them to Quarantine soon!" she squealed, scrambling to her feet.

"Kat, they could *all* be werewolves. How do we know they aren't morphing as we speak? Katherine, you *must* listen to me."

Jade bit her lip, but at the memory of Justine's furrowed, anxious brow and Jade's sworn promise, she shook the consideration from her mind. "I'm not a coward, Aaron."

"I know that. You don't need to prove anything. They could be dangerous—"

"There's only one way to find out." Jade dashed around him and ran through the gate.

Aaron swore. Reluctantly he chased her into the South Tower. Aaron let her take the lead hesitantly. She turned when they were well in front of the arches.

"You remember the layout here, right?" she asked. Aaron sighed and nodded, clenching his teeth. "They're in cell eighty-three. Can you take us there?"

Aaron sidestepped her. "Just stay close behind me." They moved in silence along the halls, and Aaron had to turn every few minutes to make sure she was still behind him.

They passed the griffin and the interrogation room, and dove down a long, spiraling staircase into what seemed like an abyss. Jade vaguely remembered the path, but in her panic the night before, she had forgotten her way and was glad now to have Aaron as a guide. Long, dimly lit halls branched off the stairs at intervals of five steps. They seemed to go on forever. There was a stench as well, like rotting flesh, and Jade couldn't tell where it was coming from—until she looked up.

She'd thought it was a massive, unlit chandelier at first, or a strangely embellished dome with tresses of fabric billowing from a breeze she couldn't feel. It was neither. Hanging like upside-down chess pieces were corpses, swinging by long ropes from the underside of the staircase that extended toward the ceiling. Jade almost gagged.

"What is this place?" she asked. She could smell nothing but salty blood and the thick, unbearable scent of filth and pulped limbs. There was no breeze, only a musty, hanging curtain of stagnant air that choked Jade. She could hear the light padding of their steps along the stones, and their quick breath as they descended farther and farther into darkness.

Aaron held a strip of fabric from the remains of his shirt in one hand, and his other fist grasped the ruby hilt of his sword. Jade felt her locket burning more than ever as they dove farther and farther, leaving Matt and Camilla behind with Christine. Jade's senses stood on edge. Every fluttered beat of her heart magnified, yet there was silence all around them.

"I can't hear them," Jade whispered.

Aaron slowed down as they reached one of the halls and turned his head into the candlelight.

"You're not supposed to. I've heard there's a silent charm. There's one on every cell. You can't imagine what we would hear otherwise." Jade could imagine very well what they would hear. It would be chaos, the cacophony of shackles banging against the walls, choked screams of agony, cries for help, wailing noises that pierced the night.

They were nearing the cell now, eighteen floors down, and passing the eightieth cell. Cell Eighty-three was torn through the bars, ripped apart, but empty, and Eighty-four had the heaviest padlock of all. The bars were thick iron, galvanized so they reflected the light perfectly—as if to compensate for the hideous scene behind them. Jade recognized some of the faces, clogged with dirt, dewy with sweat and grime. She remembered Tom the night before as he lay dead at her feet. Jade felt her heart race at the memory and flung herself at the gate to reach out to the prisoners, the students who had been branded Divisional. Justine was the first to run up to the bars and press a hand into Jade's. Her mouth was moving, but no sound came out. It looked like she was gasping for air.

Aaron quickly unsheathed his sword, and used the tip to pick the lock.

"You came, you came!" Justine said breathlessly, falling into Jade's arms and throwing her arms around her neck once the bars dissolved. "I knew you would...I knew." Justine gulped. Her voice was rough and hoarse, as though she hadn't spoken in years. Jade hardly recognized her beneath the bruises coating her dark skin and the grime smeared over her cheeks. A hoard of around thirty prisoners filed out of the cell, stumbling over themselves, dizzy with exhaustion.

"Justine, you have to *listen*," Aaron interrupted. He didn't sheath his sword and instead he held it at his side.

Justine looked down at his weapon and suddenly understood. "You saw Christine."

Aaron looked to Jade, who paused, then nodded. Justine hung her head ashamedly and then spoke quietly. Her voice was quiet and uneven, flitting like a hummingbird.

"It's happening to the rest of us...some are already showing signs. We could change into...*anything.* I mean to say...they were *right* to lock us up." She looked up from the floor now, but Jade was grabbing her shoulders.

"Listen, what happened to Christine will *not* happen to you—"

"She was in the cell next door to us. I heard her get through, but she came out changed already. She probably doesn't even remember it. I was so terrified—" She

303

choked on the word. "If she'd been found by anyone else, that would have been her life."

The other students began to drift away aimlessly down the hall, as if the days spent in the South Tower had scrambled their sharp minds. Aaron stepped in before they could reach the end of the hall and addressed Justine sharply. "You're not safe here anymore. You have to take the rest of them out to a province. Understand?"

"What about Christine?"

"She'll be sent to the same place when she changes back."

Justine's fragile expression hardened again into focus. "Which province?"

"Cross Utopia. If you keep traveling west, you'll run into the Lost Kingdom. Travel in small groups, and meet"—He pulled a pen from his pocket and wrote down a hurried address on Justine's arm—"here. When you get there, tell the woman inside I sent you."

"What is she?"

Aaron pursed his lips. "Elfin. Tell her she's to take you to the Division, okay?" Justine nodded remorsefully. She knew what this meant. "It's the only place you'll be safe—all of you," he added apologetically.

A tear slid down Justine's cheek, but she nodded with silvery eyes.

Jade pulled her into her arms and whispered, "It's not so bad there, Justine. You'll be safe" As the words left her lips, her arms tightened their hold on Justine's thin frame.

Justine nodded, her tears thick and heavy. "I don't want to go," she whimpered, her voice so weak that Jade had to squeeze her eyes hard to stop her own tears.

"You *have* to." Over Justine's shoulder, Jade could see Aaron ordering the other disoriented prisoners away down the hall. "I'll see you around?" Jade offered.

Justine nodded gravely, and looked sideways at Aaron. The other prisoners seemed perplexed, walking in circles and fidgeting anxiously.

Jade stood back from Justine, raised her voice slightly, and said as clearly as she could, "Follow Justine." Jade had to nudge Justine to set her into motion, but then Justine was running down the hall and up the spiral staircase they'd come from, her eyes still glistening.

Jade steadied her bottom lip. This was what she wanted, right? She hadn't expected them to stay at Constantine. She didn't want Justine shackled forever. She wanted her free, but in the South Tower, *free* and *gone forever* were one and the same.

Jade hadn't forgotten what Christine had said about her father.

"A few doors down," she whispered. She took three long strides and found herself in front of a wide-open, octagonal clearing with one iron door and torches lit around the edges. Jade heard Aaron padding toward her.

"Kat—please let me find you a nurse." Jade looked down at her arm. The cotton was almost soaked through with blood, and she could feel a stabbing pain at her bone. There was none of the customary snap Aaron normally spoke to her with, and she thought he really was worried.

Jade shook her head. "Just one more thing." She pointed a long slender finger toward the iron door, rusting around the bolts, with dark red patches splattered over parts of it. If you looked closely, though, close enough that your eyes strained and watered, you'd see it.

A list.

Scratched into the door with an unsteady hand, or maybe a claw, were at least ten names, one below the other. James Orwell was on it.

Jade reached out a hand to trace the list with her bloodied finger.

Aaron held his sword in front of his bare chest and flared his nostrils. He reached his hand out for the knob and retracted it just as quickly. There was a crunch of gravel behind them, and a gush of wind—no, there couldn't be wind miles below the surface of the Illysium. These were wings.

Jade knew they were enormous before she turned around, but she could never have anticipated what they belonged to. It was a man dressed in dark clothing—a straitjacket of sorts that draped around him wrongly. Scars covered his body, down his face, along the veins of his arms. It looked as though someone had disassembled him and tried to put him back together again. His pale skin was stretched thin over his bones like gossamer. His flesh spread finely over his cheekbones, and his nose came to a sharp, inhuman point.

His wings were unearthly. They were dark, like black currant seeds, and extended so far that they brushed the walls. His eyes shone brightly. *Like an angel*, Jade thought. If he'd been any bigger, any taller, more flesh and less bone, he might almost have been beautiful. This was a black spanner.

The feathers of his wings suddenly flipped, and Jade could see splintered points glowing harshly against the gentle light of the torches. The firelight—Jade didn't think once before leaping for the torch. She knew exactly why a black spanner had been sent to guard the door, but she was willing to sacrifice her blood if it meant rescuing her father. Suddenly the spanner batted its wings, and the wind thrust Jade into the torch. She braced herself for the heat as she watched her hand hit the flame, but all she felt was warmth.

Through some mad instinct, she didn't wait for Aaron to slice through the air with his sword. She scooped the flame from the torch, and though it was hot in her hand, she let the adrenaline inside her fuel it. The spanner backed away, beating its wings menacingly. Jade let the fire grow stronger, stretching it out with her mind just as she'd done with countless charms before. When she looked down, her hands were as red as the flame burning inside them, and she strained to stop the fire from dying. Frustrated, the spanner lunged at her, with its black wings extended angrily behind him.

Jade dodged it easily, sliding beneath its legs, though she scorched her wrists. Aaron was keeping the creature as occupied as possible, wielding his sword with an easy hand. The spanner was agile, though, and hostile. Jade let the fire grow just a little more—a few more seconds, and it would be enough. The fire licked up her arms, burning her face and her limbs. Her magic offered little protection. The spanner lashed at Aaron's throat, grabbing him with a spidery hand. Aaron gagged, and the muscles in his chest, running up into his neck, tensed like wires. He clawed at the creature's grimy fists.

Jade couldn't watch. She spun the fire she'd garnered and aimed it squarely at the creature's back with all her might. The spanner stumbled, staggered, but then turned around hungrily. The fire that engulfed him illuminated his black wings, and he bared his yellow teeth like a cat in the night.

Having been shoved backward, Jade had to crawl on the floor to escape his next blow. His fist landed on the floor, leaving cracks in the cement where her face should have been. She didn't recall *super strength* from what she'd read. The creature roared, forcing Jade to hurtle to her feet. He reached out two bloodstained hands and lunged at Jade with a clamoring howl that knocked her off her feet again. Jade was cornered between the wall and the spanner. Her eyes darted for the torch, but it was too far away. Somehow Matt's words shot into her head. *It just has to know what you want it to do.* Jade could feel tears stinging at the back of her eyes. A year of training at Constantine would all amount to her lifeless body on the floor of Constantine's South Tower, inches away from her father.

With trembling fingers, she fumbled, petrified, for the silver matchbox as the spanner lifted up to lunge at her. Jade cried out as a pale hand grabbed her. She thrust the silver box in front of her and begged that Matt was right, that this would save her. She felt a jarring sting in her palm. The metal sliced against her skin, and when she opened her eyes, she wasn't holding the box, but a mighty, gleaming rod, a staff that extended almost the length of her body. She used it to swing hard at the spanner's head, knocking its skull against the wall with a clang. The spanner's eyes suddenly ignited with a dark shadow. The creature pounced on her, pressing a knee into her chest.

Jade could feel the bandage at her arm tearing, or maybe it was the gash opening even farther. She couldn't tell. She rolled over to protect her vulnerable heart, and the demon let out a yowling shriek. The spanner grabbed her roughly by her locks of black hair and pulled her head back, leaving the slight breeze of his flapping wings to waft against her neck.

She used her free hand to reposition the staff, now alight with the magic flooding through her—she was left with no other choice but to kill him, even if the consequences were dire. She just had to turn and strike once. With the iron staff radiant with white-hot magic, Jade whipped her head around, and sucked in a deep breath as she drew it back.

Aaron saw her and beat her to it. His sword cut through the monster's heart, and the spanner went limp to the floor. *Thump.*

For a moment he looked at Jade, his face impassable, unyielding. His green eyes simmered. The moment seemed to last an age, and the fire that had jumped excitedly around Jade's staff now leaped and extinguished onto the stone. The staff rattled to the floor again as a small matchbox.

Aaron struck the black spanner once more for good measure. Twice in one night, he'd spared her from the clutches of death. Twice in one night. She realized she could never repay him. They stared at each other for a split second of agony, relief, pain, and fear. He wiped his sword clean on the spanner's wings and sheathed it.

The spanner's wings vanished. Only in death did he look almost human. Aaron stripped him of his black shirt and pulled it over his own head instead. They both turned back to the iron door. Jade ran up to it and tried the knob. It was locked.

"Dad!" she called again and again. The door shook, but there was no sound. She moved her arms quickly to cast a charm that might remove the silence, but it was too strong. "I can't hear you! *Dad!*" Aaron grabbed her wrist and pointed to the floor. At her feet lay a card, gold and lined with red felt. She gasped and stooped to pick it up.

She flipped the card over with quick hands and saw a familiar symbol. It was the same card he'd shown her before she'd left for Constantine. Something inside her ignited, and the images made sense to her dull eyes. It meant, *Move on. Leave me. Go.* Jade banged on the door. She'd thought her eyes had been drained of all the tears in the world, but she was wrong. Her head pounded.

"Dad!" she screamed. "Dad, I won't leave. I—" Jade couldn't help her acute awareness of Aaron's presence, but she spoke anyway. "I understand what you were saying, about being too strong, about controlling it. I get it now. I'm sorry." She slapped the tears from her cheeks. "Dad, I'm so sorry! I tried to find you." Her voice caught in her throat, and she choked on the tears that ran down her ruddy face. Her hair stuck to her neck, still hot from the fire that had singed it. She beat the door as if it were choosing to stand between her and her father.

"Dad, I'm *so* sorry…" she cried.

It had been a year of waiting. She had passed a year of blood, sweat, tears, lies, and desperation for this moment. She could not fail him. This was her last chance to be with him forever, to hug him, sit in his lap, return to her old life and leave behind the hell she'd found in the Illysium. She looked back at Aaron desperately, but he was looking up at the ceiling. There were cracks.

"Aaron, help!" she shrieked, running into the door in a last-ditch attempt to knock it down. "Dad, I'm coming—"

"Kat, we have to go." He looked fearfully toward the now-undulating ceiling. It looked like the whole tower was about to collapse. "Katherine, we are under *miles* of concrete. Your father will be fine. His cell won't collapse. It's strong—"

"Aaron, please *help!*" Jade yelled again. She knew he was right, but all the same, she had waited *a year*. Her father had waited a year for her to come, and she could not, would not, leave him. How many more years would she wait for this moment again? Two? Ten? She would spend a lifetime waiting for another chance.

How could he deny her? Just to see her father once, hear his voice, feel his beating heart against her ear through a muffled leather jacket that smelled of coffee and mint. She slammed an aching fist on the door, pleading with it to fall.

"Aaron, help me!" Her head was light now. She struck the door until her limbs ached and the wound in her arm protested in agony. Another card slipped under the door. Jade flipped it over.

This card was of a man on his knees beneath an eye disguised as the sun on the horizon.

"Katherine, the tower is *falling!* It must be another security measure!" Aaron yelled. The stone was collapsing. Why didn't he leave her there? He had saved her twice. He could leave her there to be buried beneath the tower forever. Even steven. He stood now in the door frame of the octagonal enclosure, watching in horror as Jade stared dumbstruck at the card in her hand.

She tried to decipher it to understand. The man—a beggar. The golden horizon—a future. The eye—seeing. As the symbols pieced themselves together, she understood.

It said, *I beg you to leave, and I promise we will see each other again in the golden future.*

What happened next was something Jade would never understand, and would regret until her dying breath. As the stone caved in, she allowed herself to be swept off her feet and back up through the crumbling tower. Together, she and Aaron left behind what Jade later knew to be *thousands* of prisoners awaiting freedom. They left every single one of them shackled to Constantine's walls. Only James and whoever shared his iron cell would survive. It was this single thought, this minute comfort, that stopped her from thrashing in Aaron's grip. She watched as though from a distance the silent, mass burial of every hopeless, dying soul Constantine had ever accepted into the dungeons of her madhouse.

CHAPTER 24

A few hours later, the night was gone, and morning had swept away the dark. Camilla held Jade's arm tight enough to cut off whatever circulation she had left. They had fled the scene to shed the evidence, and now all the students stood in a kind of bewildered stupor to stare dismally at what was left of the South Tower.

Aaron had left Jade in Camilla's care, and told Matt and Camilla in hushed tones that the students were safe. Matt watched Jade all the while. Her face was empty, like someone had taken the life from her and poured it out onto the rubble. When he walked her back to the dorm, her step was lifeless, her voice sapped. He pulled her into a hug. Matt gave Camilla leave to go change, and he cupped Jade's face in his hands, hiding it from the eyes of the other students passing.

"Your dad is fine, Jade," he said slowly and clearly, as if to break through the mist over Jade's eyes. "He's alive and safe. His cell was charmed." Jade nodded, but her eyes were still glazed. She would be stuck in that moment forever—screaming in the South Tower, and watching as the door slipped away from her and Aaron dragged her to safety. She had lost the cards in their escape. She could never retrieve them.

Matt paused, trying to understand what had happened in the South Tower that Jade hadn't said. He'd never seen her so upset, and he licked his lips restlessly, afraid she would never forget, never be the same. Nervously, almost impulsively, he had wrapped his arms around her and pressed his lips against her cool forehead. She looked up at him, and a smile broke at her lips, although her eyes were still caked with tears.

Now he, Jade, and Camilla were sitting in the grand hall of the East Tower. Lady Eleanor had left for Chief Court, and Mr. Reynolds seemed to be taking a vengeful control. His face was still brutally scarred from Lady Eleanor's nails digging into his cheek, but otherwise, he wore a customary expression of contempt.

Mr. Reynolds signaled to the orchestra to commence the anthem. The organs started up on the most elegant note. Ms. Tutts orchestrated them with a practiced hand, and suddenly the whole hall was alight with the hum of Constantine's anthem.

Constantine, I cry for you, tell me where to go.
I depend on you alone, to shine a ray of hope.

In times through which I falter and if ever I despair,
No matter what confronts me, I know that you are
there.

I surrender my allegiance to the vision that you
sought,
And give my heart to serve those for whom you
fought.
As you served courageously those you left behind,
I offer you now and forever my humble peace of mind.

Your walls share haunted stories and secrets yet un-
known,
But your school will be my guide my eternal, tender
home.
We come to you together, with our minds and hearts
unopened,
We know that you will guide us; it is us that you have
chosen.

Constantine, I cry for you, tell me where to go.
I depend on you alone, to shine a ray of hope.
In times through which I falter and if ever I despair,
I see clearly what confronts me, and I know that you
are here.

When they turned to their seats, and the organs ceased
to carry their last note, Mr. Reynolds eyed the audience
with a furious glare.

"Students and teachers, an unfortunate thing has happened in the night." Camilla's grip on Jade's arm tightened, and she could remember Justine doing the same

just weeks ago. "In the course of a few hours, someone in this very room has done a *murderous* thing. We collapsed the South Tower in the hopes that we would stop the criminals inside."

The audience seemed to be holding a collective breath for his next words.

"Someone in this room has freed thirty-four criminals from the South Tower and attempted to free treasonous villains. They have also set free a trespasser from the White Caps."

The griffin, Jade thought. The audience erupted into a quick murmur.

Mr. Reynolds stuck his jaw forward and pressed his lips tightly together. "If you have any information regarding this felonious act, step forward now."

No one moved.

Jade was too exhausted to be afraid. She'd expected consequences of this nature, maybe worse, but she couldn't wrap her head around the fact that she had lost so much in one night. She clenched her jaw just to keep her eyes open. The wound in her arm was drying now, maybe even healing, but she'd only barely managed to hide the rest of her wounds.

"No one? Fine." He paced to the other side of the stage. "Parlous punishment will ensue for the culprits. Among the punishments, a two-*hundred*-year sentence to Quarantine." Mr. Reynolds paused. "Though they'll be lucky to make it past a year. Follow me into the courtroom. If no one will come forth, interrogation is our only choice. Sir Emerson will be handling the court today. This matter is out of our hands."

Matt's face was stony as they trooped into the court with the rest of the school. They were lined up and sorted into the seats in a single line, to be called up one by one until each and every student had gone through.

"It's weird," she whispered so only Matt and Jade could hear. "After all this, I'm still glad we did it." Matt and Jade nodded in agreement, but even that couldn't soothe the unsettling in her stomach.

"Don't worry. We'll figure something out," Jade whispered in response. Unfortunately, by the time Matt had been called to the stand and only half the hall was left, they hadn't figured out anything. Rosebud was standing at the door with her head hung, sharpening her ivory tusk with a steady hand. Her red hair was disheveled, but her eyes were stormier than ever.

"What's the plan?" Matt asked in hushed tones as they joined the queue.

"Deny everything," Jade said, feigning a smile.

Matt nodded, searching her face. "Sounds good," he said at last. One of the younger students was on the stand now, and it gave Matt, Jade, and Camilla a few minutes to observe the proceedings properly. Matt had shoved his hands into his pockets, and even though he tried not to show it, he looked nervous.

Grady Emerson was a large man, slightly round about his waist, with gray stubble on his face and watery gray eyes. He held half-moon reading glasses. He looked remarkably like Nathan, and the resemblance only served to make Jade angrier. Nathan was sitting at his side, having been excused from the interrogative proceedings.

"Young boy," the minister said loudly. "To the best of your knowledge, have you, in the past twelve hours, illegally freed a prisoner from the South Tower of Constantine with the sole purpose of committing a felonious act?" The boy was quivering, his hands gripping the podium for dear life. He shook his head. Sir Emerson narrowed his eyes and turned to the Ocuman beside him, who was holding a telling compass—or at least that's what Justine had called it. Before Jade could relapse into a painful reverie, Matt was called to the stand.

"Matthew Ferguson, to the best of your knowledge, have you, in the past twelve hours, illegally freed a prisoner from the South Tower of Constantine with the sole purpose of committing a felonious act?"

Matt clenched his jaw. He wasn't looking at the minister, but at the Ocuman beside him with the telling compass. He turned back with fiery eyes. It was the minister who had ordered the murder of his parents—Matt was certain of it. He'd sent two men into the Keeping to deliver the message that his parents had been taken in by the Oculus so they could be safe. Except they weren't safe, they were dead. Matt flexed his hands and opened his mouth to speak.

"No, sir." Sir Emerson turned to the Ocuman beside him, who looked down at his compass and read it easily. He looked back up at Matt with a raised brow and whispered something into the minister's ear. Matt's palms were hot in his pockets, and he could feel the heat spreading to his head.

"Camilla Holt, please step up to the stands."

Matt felt relief and confusion flood through him, and was escorted out of the court. The same fate lay in wait for Camilla, and she sprang from the stand quickly so no one could rebuke the verdict. They weren't lying. Rather, Emerson was asking the wrong question. They hadn't technically freed *anyone* from the South Tower, but rather, from the East.

Jade was glad at least that neither Matt nor Camilla would have to watch her being dragged away by the rough, spidery hands of Ocumen. She spotted Aaron close behind her in the line, and hesitantly took the stand when she was called. She didn't feel nervous anymore. She was defeated. After training for months to save her father, it would all end with a life's sentence to Quarantine and a dull beating in her sore heart. She eyed the Ocumen to decide how many she'd be able to take on with Aaron's help.

"Katherine Orwell."

Jade snapped her head up at the name. "I prefer Jade," she said clearly, resting her hands on the podium. The minister raised a brow but proceeded calmly. Nathan seemed content to sit in that position forever, towering just above her with a smirk creeping over his face. His thin lips curled into an ugly smile.

"Jade, to the best of your knowledge, have you, in the past twelve hours, illegally freed a prisoner from the South Tower of Constantine with the sole purpose of committing a felonious act?" Jade looked to Rosebud, who had returned her ivory tusk to the leather binding, and was now standing against the double doors. Jade thought she saw a hint of regret in those harsh blue eyes, but maybe it was a trick of the light. If she expected Rosebud to run to her rescue, she was extravagantly disappointed.

Then again, what reason was there to think Rosebud liked her at all? They'd never exchanged a single word. In fact, the most contact they'd had was Jade chasing her into the East Tower, where Rosebud had hastily abandoned her and Matt. She let out a low whistle and turned to see Aaron in the audience. His face was like ceramic.

He was unreadable. Jade knew court would recess for lunch, but Aaron would be called up soon after, and time might not favor him. Above him a loud clock chimed at the strike of every hour—half a minute until noon. If Jade could just fill up the time with something, anything...

"Ms. Orwell, you must answer my question by law. Failure to answer will result in immediate charges." She turned back to the minister. She could practically hear the seconds ticking by—twenty more, and they seemed to go on forever. She looked again at Rosebud, who was pursing her lips as though she'd caught on to Jade's plan.

Jade cleared her throat. Ten seconds. Nathan was leaning over his high podium to catch a good look at her with those devilish eyes. His father leaned forward too, and the rest of the hall was silent. Three seconds. She shook her head clearly, and just as the bell rang with finality and clarity through the domed hall, Jade whispered, "Guilty."

When the Ocuman looked down at his telling compass, he seemed content, because indeed she had told the truth. They simply hadn't *heard* it. Jade was dismissed with a flip of the minister's impatient hand, along with the rest of the student body that remained. There. No problem, no life-threatening sentence, but Jade was still hysterical. She ran to scour the hall for Aaron, who seemed to be making a speedy escape toward the doors Rosebud had been standing in front of. She had gone with the sweeping crowd. He rushed through the students, and slipped away from the mainstream just as they reached the North Tower.

He was heading to his room, and Jade followed him, walking briskly to catch up.

"Kat, go eat," he said when he'd reached the door and had a hand on the knob.

"We need to talk," she said, standing a good distance from him.

"I'm afraid I can't," he snarled, turning now. His eyes were brighter than ever beneath his mane of ebony hair.

"It's important." She waited for a group of girls to pass before she continued. "Five minutes."

Aaron looked between her and the door, as though deciding whether or not to dismiss her. He sighed. "Not here." Aaron opened the door and beckoned her inside.

***

Aaron's room was on fire from the light of the Illysian sun. There were only two beds: one was neatly made, and the other, presumably Matt's, was scattered with notebooks and twisted sheets. Beside Aaron's bed was a long shelf of books arranged in alphabetical order and placed adjacent to a reading lamp. On his desk was a picture of a young woman whose green eyes and dark hair resembled Aaron's. Jade thought it must be an older sister. He turned down the picture as soon as they walked in.

The walls were mostly blank, aside from a bulletin board and several pictures of people at Constantine that Matt had stuck up on his side of the room. There was a mantelpiece too, which remained bare except for a few pencils and an empty vase.

Aaron was sitting with his legs swung over the windowsill, facing the afternoon sun. A light breeze drifted into the room.

"You've come to tell me not to go back," he said.

Jade leaned back against his bedpost and nodded. She could only see half of his face from where she stood.

He didn't bother to take in her response. He examined the sky with concern. "I don't see why."

"You'll be dead by morning if you go back!" Jade erupted.

Aaron laughed sardonically, appearing to muse over the exact weight of his sword as he held it between his hands and scrutinized it.

"Don't you see? I could travel to the end of the Illysium, but I could never live past a year or two anyway."

Jade thought back to what Mr. Reynolds had said about spanners. She lowered her voice. "If you're really convinced you're going to…die, at least have the decency not to let the Oculus do it."

"Christ, Kat, if you think dying alone on my estate would be any better than dying in Quarantine, you're wrong," he barked, still fixing his eyes on the sun. "There's no one in the Illysium who would dare to help anyway."

Jade was furious now. Why didn't he understand? Why was he willing to throw himself away—throw everything away, including his own pride? The realization came to her faster than she'd have liked.

Class was everything in the Illysium, and if Aaron became a black spanner, he'd lose any right he'd ever had to being someone from the Illysium. He would be an outcast like all the other vermin in the Division—at least that's how he probably saw it. The look on his face said as much.

"If you get yourself sent to Quarantine—" She shook her head. Her mouth was moving, but she couldn't find the right words. He looked sideways at her, though his lips were still pressed into a scowl. "At least give yourself a chance. If not for yourself, then for everyone else who cares."

Aaron chuckled bitterly. "Name *one*."

The demand took Jade by surprise. She could feel an answer stuck in her throat, but it wouldn't come out. *She* cared, didn't she? Suddenly Jade wasn't sure what kind of caring either of them meant.

"I care," she answered. "Matt cares. Your parents care."

"There's a long list of things my parents care about, Katherine, and trust me when I say I'm not on it." He leaped up from the sill so he was standing. One step, and he could jump onto the forest floor that led into the city skyline of Utopia. Jade wanted him free from Constantine so badly that she had to stop from pushing him right over the edge. Forcing him away was painful, but necessary, if she wanted him alive…even if it was only for a few months.

The bell rang to signal the return to the courtroom. Someone would come looking for him soon. "Aaron, please, you *have* to go now." She was practically begging. She willed him to run away, to free himself from Constantine's walls.

Aaron nodded, but turned his back to the flaming sun and sheathed his sword. He was looking at Jade with a mixed expression of longing and regret.

"Would you come with me?" he asked.

Jade felt her eyes widen. Asking Aaron to run away had seemed so easy, but now it seemed impossible to ask of anyone.

"Come with me, Katherine." The question hung between them like a shroud.

His face began to fall. Jade had the right words playing on the edge of her tongue, waiting to be let out. She opened her mouth to speak, but it was as if she'd run out of words and didn't have anything left to say. Her mind was frozen. How could he ask her to give it up? Constantine was her only hope at saving her father, who was still buried beneath the South Tower, still counting on her to save him. How could Aaron ask her to leave the only home she had?

Aaron quickly averted his eyes toward the sun. He didn't look back at Jade, fearing that it might reduce him to begging.

"If it makes a difference"—he began, raking a hand through his hair and down to the nape of his neck—"I would have come...for you." Jade stared back at him. *The same way you kept my secret and grabbed Christine and killed the spanner, and saved my life at your expense—without hesitation*, she thought. For a split second, Aaron was gliding in the air, and then was skidding away.

Jade gasped and ran to the window, shock burning like fire in the back of her throat. She slammed into the windowsill, crushing her abdomen, and scrambled up so she could look down at him maneuvering through the brush. She felt her face scrunch up, and she yelled after him to come back to her, though her stomach was in knots. Jade looked once at the room, held her breath for a split second, and then—

She jumped.

END OF BOOK 1